The Wonder of You

Willow Green is a pseudonym for Bethany Rutter, a writer, event chair and personal trainer. She lives in London.

The Wonder of You

WILLOW GREEN

ZAFFRE

First published in the UK in 2026 by
ZAFFRE
An imprint of Bonnier Books UK
5th Floor, HYLO, 105 Bunhill Row,
London, EC1Y 8LZ

A CIP catalogue record for this book is
available from the British Library.

ISBN: 978-1-78512-477-8

Also available as an ebook and an audiobook

1 3 5 7 9 10 8 6 4 2

Typeset by IDSUK (Data Connection) Ltd
Printed and bound by CPI Group (UK) Ltd, Croydon CR0 4YY

The authorised representative in the EEA is Bonnier Books
UK (Ireland) Limited.
Registered office address: Block B, The Crescent Building,
Northwood, Santry,
Dublin 9, D09 C6X8, Ireland
compliance@bonnierbooks.ie
www.bonnierbooks.co.uk

THEN

Wonderwick Woods Films to Begin Production in the UK Next Year, With Open Casting Call

Jess Keatley for *The Stage*, April 2018

Legacy Studios has announced production of a Wonderwick Woods film series will begin in the summer at a major UK studio.

The movies, starting with first book *The Legend of Wonderwick Woods*, will be filmed at Smithdown Studios in Essex, rescuing the studios from threat of closure. Author Sylvara Runequill likewise stipulated a British cast for the project. It's believed there has also been support from the British Film Council who are confident the franchise will revitalise the British film industry.

Legacy Pictures, known for top-grossing films such as *Draculator* and *Annihilation Now*, would 'stay true to the beloved books'.

Children aged twelve to seventeen are being called to audition for the first movie as part of an open casting call, and the Legacy team are expecting to receive thousands of casting tapes per day. Casting director Kelly Wicks said she is 'ready to watch as many as it takes to find the perfect match for Linderley and Rowan', the lead roles in the beloved series.

Sylvara Runequill added: 'As an author it's a huge honour to have my books take on this new life beyond the page, and I've waited a long time to find the right partners for a film. I know Legacy are going to do a phenomenal job and I can't wait to meet my Linderley and Rowan!'

Casting of Wonderwick Series Sparks Controversy

Carmen Harris for LondonNewsOnline

Despite author Sylvara Runequill's initial insistence that the main cast of the much-anticipated Wonderwick Woods film series be British, young American actor Josh Sacco has been announced as the male lead, Rowan Clearwater.

The fourteen-year-old son of Hollywood producer power couple Rick and Amberlyn Sacco has previously starred in *Space Wars 3* and the long-running TV sitcom *At Home With the Joneses*.

But not everyone is happy with his casting, as Sylvara Runequill has reportedly 'expressed concerns' over choosing an American for one of the two biggest roles. Although not specified in the contract, she was under the impression there was an 'understanding' that the part would go to a young British actor.

Much more in line with her vision is the casting of unknown Brit and non-professional actress Emily Montgomery as Linderley Jones. A self-described Wonderwick 'super-fan', thirteen-year-old Emily wowed the Wonderwick casting team with her 'assured but sensitive' audition tapes, and her 'responsiveness to direction' when auditions progressed.

Lisa Halley, Legacy Pictures' Senior Vice President of Worldwide Theatrical Production, said: 'In the cases of Emily and Josh, we hunted high and low for the perfect Linderley and Rowan and are delighted with the casting we've come to. Both actors were our first choice for the roles, and now we've cast them we can't imagine anyone else leading this iconic series.' She did not comment on the apparent controversy of Josh Sacco's casting.

NOW

Chapter One

Post by @CelebRaterAdmin: **WOMAN CRUSH WEDNESDAY: EMILY MONTGOMERY**

Inspired by her appearance on the frow of every major show at last month's LFW, this week's topic of discussion for WCW is Emily Montgomery. Cast your votes, ladies (?) and gentlemen . . .

@PatHunter1979 *She's got that perfect girl next door look . . . definitely a 7.*

@Couch_Potato_King 5

@girl_enjoyer98765 *now she's legal gonna say a 9.*

@ParticularWorm *Nice symmetrical features . . . small nose . . . straight hair . . . body kinda meh. Shame about the big eyebrows.*

@Drone_Philosophy *Don't get the hype tbqh. She's no Darcy Jackson.*

@MovieFan69 *Everyone says she's plain but i think there's something about her.*

@hardtrade *Does anyone else think she seems kind of stuck up???? Would be a 9 if she wasn't so uptight but personality knocks her down to a solid 6.*

@BeanieWeenies *Ovverated. Total plane Jane.*

@WonderWickedlyTalentedAdeleDazeem *Her casting ruined Wonderwick. Linderley should NOT have been played by a Brit. But looks? I'll give her a 7.*

@WhatUpNerds *different coloured eye thing is freaky.*

@Dandelion_Express *Pretty for sure but something kind of unsexy about her especially if you compare her to Darcy Jackson (sidebar: when the FCK are they going to announce Darcy as Loreia Buckthorn for the next film). Frigid vibes maybe?*

@Joe14573 *Feminine face good harmony, ears too big.*

@CarnivoreDude *Ideal skull shape, excellent breeding stock.*

EARS? TOO? BIG? My left hand instinctively flew to my ear as my right swiped the webpage closed. My ears felt a perfectly normal size to me . . . but I would say that, wouldn't I? I was used to them. Maybe Threadsy user @Joe14573 was right? Maybe they were too big? Is that what people were thinking when they were watching the Wonderwick Woods films? That Emily Montgomery (now 'legal', potentially 'ovverated', in possession of symmetrical features) had freakishly large ears? And that was without getting into the comparison with Darcy Jackson. The less said about *that* the better.

'Nearly there!' Mum chirped as we finally turned off Euston Road. I'd been so deep in my scroll hole I'd almost forgotten I wasn't alone.

'Oh! I was miles away,' I said, throwing my phone into my bag and snapping it shut with the familiar satisfying magnetic click. I usually gave away the fancy handbags I got sent to various friends, family and colleagues but this one I kept. The leather felt reassuringly soft but sturdy under my fingers. 'Mum, you know you don't have to come to these things anymore, right?' I asked, gently. Once upon a time she was my chaperone, and now I was old enough to be able to conduct my business on my own, or with the help of one of my team, but it was like she hadn't realised that the chaperone days were over. It's not that I didn't appreciate it, but part of me wondered if she was still going to be coming to kick-off meetings with me when I'm forty.

'Well, you need someone looking out for you, don't you,' she said, resolutely, flicking her hair back off her shoulders.

'That's what people like Glen and Chloe are for,' I said with a smile. 'You know, if there was something else you wanted to do today? Something more fun than going to a meeting?'

'I wouldn't miss it. Now remember, Emsie, you're not going to mention that film you've been threatening to do during the next Wonderwick hiatus, are you?'

I let out a sigh, almost against my own will. 'Mum, "that film" is really important to me, and more to the point, I'm going to commit to it soon.'

'But you haven't yet?' She remained optimistic.

'No, we're still working it out.' I didn't want to give her false hope, but I wasn't going to lie to her either.

'I know there's not much I can do to stop you, but it's about the money. If they know you're agreeing to do these silly little independent films for no money that doesn't exactly give you and Glen great bargaining power for the rest of the franchise, does it?'

'But that leaves me with nowhere to go! If I'm only allowed to do films that pay me as much as Wonderwick, I'm going to have zero choice in what the rest of my career looks like!'

'You're up to your eyeballs in offers! And Lord knows I hope you always will be, but in case you're not, you have to be making smart choices while you are in demand. I simply do not understand why it has to be *this* one.'

'I keep telling you, Mum,' I said gently, reaching across the middle seat to squeeze her hand. 'It's because I really want to work with Edgar Malek. I'm shocked that a director like that is interested in me after doing nothing but Wonderwick for so long.'

'And what is wrong with Wonderwick, exactly?'

'Nothing.' I shook my head. 'I love it. It's my home. But I know it won't be there forever, and I have to start thinking about doing other things. There's only a finite number of books and we're coming to the end of them.'

'Well, you know what your father thinks you should do next.'

'That I should do the half-animated kids' comedy where I'd be playing a sixteen-year-old?' It was called *Dinky Daffy and the Detective Squad*; the character description had said 'she just loves to wear primary colours!'. That's all you need to know.

'You make it sound so juvenile! It's written by that man who wrote that adorable film you loved about the cat! Anyway, don't you want to go to Hollywood for a while? Wouldn't that be nice? A bit of sun on your skin, an ocean breeze? Shopping on Rodeo Drive? Where's this other one shooting again? Cork?'

'Outside of Galway,' I corrected her, but she waved her hand dismissively as if they were basically the same thing. 'I'm sure the film is going to be great and yes, it would be nice to go to LA and see the sun for more than a day at a time, I just don't know if I want to be playing a literal child again!' I ran my fingers through my hair, the heavy, straight, glossy dark locks of my signature style. I felt a rogue frizzy strand under my fingertips and yanked it out straightaway. I didn't want a hair out of place.

'You might as well do it while you still can!'

'May I remind you that I'm a whole twenty years old?' I said with a smile.

'Well, you'll always be a baby to me.'

'I think Hollywood can wait – at least until I'm old enough to have a Martini there, don't you?'

I gazed out of the car window at the Eurostar terminal as we trundled past St Pancras. I imagined jumping on a train and disappearing into the streets of Paris instead of going to this meeting. But that wouldn't be very Emily Montgomery of me.

'Mum, I'll always be a baby to *everyone* if I don't start taking more serious roles. People still see me as the thirteen-year-old girl I was when I first started playing Linderley.'

Mum twitched her nose as if she was thinking seriously about what I was saying. Maybe, just maybe, I was getting through to her on this.

'Well, darling, I just wish you would think more about the longevity of your career. You're so *young*, you've got so many years ahead of you. Don't you want to be set up for life?' This was an idea my parents kept coming back to, as if it wasn't enough that I was earning exponentially more than anyone my age doing a normal job. It was like they were trying to create a world where I wouldn't have to work past twenty-five, without considering the fact that I actually *wanted* to work, that to me acting was not just a wildly lucrative childhood hobby.

'I *am* set up for life,' I said with a shrug. I knew it was a crazy thing to be able to say at twenty, but Wonderwick and all the associated brand deals meant I wouldn't have to worry about money for a very long time. This was something I felt vaguely uneasy about, but I told myself it could be worse, I could have been an oil heiress or, just as bad, a Hollywood nepo baby. Mum raised her eyebrows at me sceptically. 'Anyway, I don't think we're going to be talking about my plans for the hiatus at this meeting.' I uncrossed and re-crossed my legs uncomfortably, shooting my mum a sideways glance. There was only one hot topic on the agenda for this meeting, and I was *not* happy about it.

'Everyone's so excited about this bloody kiss, aren't they?' She rolled her eyes.

I swallowed hard and tried to sound nonchalant. 'It's what they've all been waiting for.'

We pulled up outside the studio offices in King's Cross and before the car door was even fully open, a flashbulb went off in my face. 'Emily!' said a voice from outside the car. Better this than surreptitious photos with a long-range lens, I supposed. Better to know they're there than wondering where I was being photographed from and at what angle, because the fact remained, I was almost always being photographed from somewhere.

I untucked my hair from behind my ear just in case @Joe14573 had a point, and let it fall across my face. A little veil of privacy. It wasn't so much that I minded having my photo taken, I just preferred it to be on my terms.

'*Smile*,' my mum urged me as she smoothed out the chic grey herringbone wool coat that was draped over my shoulders, on top of the most perfect cream cashmere sweater and wide-leg black jeans with my signature Chanel flats. A very Emily outfit: sleek, classic and put-together.

We were escorted from reception by an assistant, even though I'd been there loads of times before. Always the same conference room on the highest floor, overlooking Coal Drops Yard. Same conference room, different film. This Wonderwick Woods instalment was the big one. OK, they're *all* big ones. Big budgets, big shoots, big expectations. But for me, the next film was . . . big for other reasons. Reasons that had me feeling nervous.

Everyone was already sitting around a shiny glass table when we arrived and the room was abuzz with conversation. I instantly felt calmer at the sight of my beloved publicist and best friend Chloe, her halo of peroxide blonde curls and her penchant for short, tight dresses with sky-high heels, her big mouth permanently painted in shades of hot pink, bright red, vibrant purple that somehow managed to *never* budge, no matter how many margaritas she drank. She was someone to be underestimated at your peril. The other side of her was my eternally star-struck manager Glen, followed by Lisa Halley, the senior vice-president of production at Legacy Pictures, aka the biggest production company in the world, and then Martin McBride, the director of three of the top-ten highest-grossing films of all time.

They all leaped to their feet at the sight of us. 'There's my favourite client!' Glen boomed at the same time Martin shouted, 'Emily! Our little star!'

This kind of reaction still caught me off guard. I know it's silly, but sometimes I just didn't feel like that person, that celebrity. It was like they were talking about someone else. I hugged both of them in turn before squeezing Chloe slightly longer than the rest. Lisa, the studio head, always scared me a little bit. She carried a crocodile skin Hermès bag which seemed just right for her: expensive, luxurious, in high demand. She had the kind of surgical enhancements that pre-fame Emily wouldn't have even been able to detect, but I had been in the business long enough by now to know that it was almost certainly the work of Dr Sam, the most discreet and light-handed surgeon in

Beverly Hills. We held each other slightly at arm's length in a stiff hug, and then it was time to get to work.

Legacy had ordered in catering from the excellent Japanese restaurant around the corner from the office, in a quantity so extravagant I felt guilty about the food waste just looking at it.

Pleasantries over, the room settled down into silence so we could get on with business. 'Emily,' Lisa said, fixing me with a shark-like stare, like we were the only two people in the room. 'We are just *so* excited about the next Wonderwick movie.'

'That's an understatement!' Martin brandished his napkin. 'Be prepared to go *stratospheric* with this one, Ems.'

'To the stratosphere!' Glen said, raising a glass with a slightly maniacal glint in his eye.

'To the stratosphere!' Mum gamely raised her own glass.

If I had known, when I turned up to my first-ever open audition – trying my luck against over a thousand other girls for the hotly contested part of Linderley Jones – what 'stratospheric' felt like, would I still have gone?

Because I knew why they were so excited. This was the film that the Wonderwick fans had been excited about since the adaptation was announced. The instalment where Linderley Jones and Rowan Clearwater *finally* kiss. Which for me meant . . . well, I couldn't put it off any longer.

I had to kiss Josh Sacco.

The most annoying, obnoxious, self-infatuated, tedious, person you could imagine. The nepo baby to end all nepo babies. *The* Josh Sacco. I'd filmed scenes where I was being chased by a tennis ball on a stick because the monster is being added in post-production, but *this* was going to be the real test of my acting capabilities.

'It'll be a completely manageable kind of stratospheric, though,' Chloe said, reassuringly, her eyes darting towards me. She knew I was just a *little* bit nervous about this film, but also knew that the hype building around it was only a good thing for me as an actor.

'Of course.' I shrugged, trying very hard to play it cool. Cool was not my default setting.

'Yes,' Glen said, drawing his chair closer to the table. 'We're keen to get a look at the final script ASAP.'

'I thought the last one I received *was* the final one?' I said, panic rising that we were set to start filming *the following week* and I might not be completely prepared.

'Oh it basically is! Don't worry about it. Your lines won't change between now and then, Ems.' Martin waved away our concerns. 'We're ninety-nine per cent of the way there, just ironing out—' he cleared his throat '—the details, you know, some of the, er, non-verbal elements.'

'Such as?' Chloe's eyebrows had crept so far up her forehead they had almost disappeared into her mop of blonde curls.

'Nothing major,' Lisa said, frowning slightly too emphatically, adjusting her Cartier Panthère watch.

I smiled and shrugged as breezily as I could manage. 'As far as I'm concerned, the kiss is the only potential issue, and it's written straightforwardly in the book so I'm not worried.' If I said 'I'm not worried' often enough, maybe it would come true. But the fact was, they *were* starting to worry me.

'Well,' Martin piped up, tossing the shell of an edamame bean onto his plate.

'Mmmm?' Chloe turned to him. It shouldn't really be my publicist's job to grill the director and producer, but unfortunately for me, Glen was a Martin McBride fanboy, so more often than not he struggled to hold him to account on my behalf.

'We're in discussions around whether we use an intimacy coordinator for this movie,' Lisa said smoothly with a blank smile.

'I don't think an intimacy coordinator is necessary for a kiss, right?' I asked.

Martin waved his hand expansively. 'We'll probably have to have one for hugs next.' He looked around the table, waiting for nods of agreement.

'It *is* just a kiss, isn't it, Martin?' Chloe said, fixing him with a gaze like an iron grip. The energy in the room shifted in a moment. Martin broke eye contact with Chloe and glanced sideways at Lisa.

'Actually . . .' He cleared his throat and set down his knife and fork.

'Mmmm?' Mum's nostrils flared. Always a bad sign.

'We were thinking,' Lisa spoke up, in that bold, forthright American way that studio executives do.

'What about taking things a little bit *spicier*, Ems?' Martin looked at me without blinking, and I could almost make out some dollar signs in his eyes. 'The fans love you and Josh! This is the moment they've all been waiting for! Why not give them what they *really* want?'

'This could be a great opportunity for you, Emily,' Lisa urged. 'You're not a girl anymore, you're a young *woman*. Why not turn that to your advantage?'

I tried to figure out quite what I wanted to say, but the discussion carried on without me. I knew it was coming, of course. I knew that was what we would end up discussing at this meeting. But it still felt weird. Me, spicy? Would anyone even buy that? *Them* telling me I'm 'not a girl anymore' and that I'm a young woman has a different ring to it than me telling my mum I want to do a small indie film instead of a big budget children's comedy. But the fact was, it was still true. I was growing up, and so was Linderley Jones.

'And what does Josh say about all of this? I assume you've already discussed it with him?' Mum cut in. She was right: nothing happened on Wonderwick without it getting past Josh and his high-powered Hollywood parents. If you produced some of the biggest films of the 2000s, your kid was pretty much guaranteed to be allowed to do whatever he wanted in the following decades.

'Oh, Josh is *totally* up for taking things to the next level,' Martin reassured her.

'I bet he is,' I murmured quietly. I knew Josh. He probably thought the whole thing was just hilarious – a new way of winding up silly, strait-laced Emily, now he had just about outgrown things like depositing a large (but harmless) spider in my dressing room on the first film, after we'd known each other for about three weeks, or changing the language on my phone to Mandarin.

'Darling,' Mum said, laying a hand on my arm. 'You know you don't have to do anything you're not comfortable with.'

'Yes,' Chloe agreed. 'I'm not exactly delighted about the way we've been ambushed with this.' She cut her eyes at Glen.

Glen raised his hands. 'Sorry, ladies, but I think it's a great idea. Giving you a, uh, shall we say, *saucy* edge will make you all the more bankable for future projects. It'll open you up to a whole new world of characters.'

I didn't remind him that the Edgar Malek movie he was trying to talk me out of in favour of a more lucrative project *also* represented a whole new world for me character-wise, that I was already there and didn't need to be 'saucy' or 'spicy' to do it. But I knew very well that it was what the fans wanted, and I was all about living up to expectations. Plus, knowing quite how much control the fans had over some of our creative decisions meant I was very much incentivised to comply.

'So, Emily.' Martin turned to me. 'What do you say?'

I thought of that thread on WeRateCelebs only that morning, the accusations that I'm frigid . . . uptight . . . stuck-up . . . and I couldn't help but wonder if maybe they had a point. Obviously it wasn't a *nice* thing to say and they certainly wouldn't have been saying it about me if I were a guy. But I knew that was the image I had in the media, I knew that's what people thought of me. Whether or not it was true or fair didn't really make any difference. 'Ears too big' felt like the least of my problems now and my 'ideal skull shape' (bleurgh) wouldn't get me out of this. I supposed it would be one way to prove them wrong . . . and to *really* test my acting skills. To be seen as a grown-up at last. Especially since Darcy Jackson was coming onto the next film.

I took a deep breath, set my shoulders and hoped desperately that I was doing the right thing. 'Whatever's best for Wonderwick.'

Chapter Two

'Babe, are you sure about this?' The array of jewelled cocktail rings on Chloe's fingers clinked against the glass of her Picante. 'Oh, cheers, by the way, to being the spiciest little nugget in cinema.' She raised her glass to me and I rolled my eyes while giving her the cheers she was clearly looking for. Everything felt that bit better when it was just us tucked up in a corner booth in Chloe's members' club, no more studio execs. I'd even managed to get Mum to head home, which was a feat in itself.

'Not the spiciest little nugget *just* yet. But yes, I'm sure,' I sighed. 'It's not like I could get out of doing the kiss altogether – it's in the book, I'm locked in, I have to do it, I knew it was coming, it's always been on the horizon. So why not make the most of it? Why not turn it to my advantage.'

'Fuck yes!' she said, bobbing her head as her curls seemed to move independently of her body.

'How spicy do we think is spicy?' I asked, taking a sip of my cocktail. 'As spicy as this cocktail or spicy like that chicken you had at Thai Diner in New York that made you beg a God you don't believe in for mercy?'

'Somewhere between the two, I'm thinking. And please don't remind me of one of my rare moments of humiliation. I still haven't got over Jake Gyllenhaal being at the *next table*! Not exactly ideal for one of my dream clients to offer to give me the Heimlich manoeuvre!'

'Good job you don't have a very distinctive look and a big reputation.' I bit my lip to stop myself laughing. 'He probably wouldn't remember you.'

'Ha ha. Anyway, this isn't about me.'

'Oh, but I like it when it's about you! It's more fun when it's about you! I don't understand why I'm the famous one and you aren't. You seem much better suited to it all than me.'

'Remember, babe, you're an actor. All the fame stuff is just a distraction. Your job is acting. And you're great at it. Which is why this Wonderwick spicy kiss, titty-touching extravaganza is going to be a breeze for you!' She shrugged.

I gasped in horror. 'Do you think I'm going to have to go topless? They wouldn't, would they?!'

'Oh they'd try, but there's no *way* they can make you. Maybe a hint of side boob if I read the vibe correctly,' she said, lightly. 'But just a hint, obviously.'

The thought of it struck fear into my heart, but I knew I had to push myself out of my comfort zone. I could do side boob, couldn't I? I swallowed down my nerves and put on a smile. 'Or maybe a bit of underboob?'

'Why not both!' Chloe raised her glass in the air. It was almost empty – classic Chloe, I could never keep up with her. I checked the time – we had a little bit of downtime before the party that evening and there was no one I'd rather spend it with than her. 'So, how are the studies going?'

'*Très bien*,' I said with my best French accent. 'I feel like I'm actually getting somewhere now I've started reading books and listening to podcasts.'

'Next thing you know you'll be getting Glen to broker deals for even *less* money in French indie movies.'

'Don't say that in front of my mum.'

'I think it's a very cool way to use your time between films.'

'It's my way of reclaiming my education from the world of on-set tutors. Who are great, of course, but it was all a bit rushed.'

'Oh, you don't need to tell me – I've seen it with my own eyes, people from the production team literally standing in the tutor room with a stopwatch so the child actors don't do a *minute* over the legal minimum.'

'I wish you'd been around when I first started on Wonderwick,' I said, wistfully.

'If my maths is math-ing, when you first started on Wonderwick I was in the middle of my first ever internship. I thought I was *such* a grown-up but I was only nineteen.'

'You've come a long way in seven years.'

Chloe had only been my publicist for the past couple of years, but in that time she had become my most trusted friend. That was the thing about being famous: you never really knew who wanted to get to know you because you're you and who wanted to get to know you because you're *You*. At least with Chloe I already had that business relationship, and she certainly wasn't one to care about how famous someone was.

'Says you!'

'Have I really, though?' I asked, a little awkwardly. 'I don't feel like I've gone anywhere at all. I'm still little Linderley Jones from the Wonderwick Woods series.'

'You're a gorgeous young woman, a baby style icon and a very talented actress. You're not just the kid who went to an open audition and fell into acting by chance anymore.'

For someone like Josh, life was all planned out: as the son of huge Hollywood producers, he was always going to go into the entertainment industry and none of his career was any surprise at all. But there was no grand plan for me. It just *happened* and now, seven years later, here I was.

'I know,' I said, taking the final sip of my Picante. 'It makes me the luckiest girl in the world.' I meant it: even amid the trials and tribulations of being part of a huge Hollywood franchise, I couldn't believe my luck.

'Stop talking about luck.' Chloe batted the idea away like it was an annoying fly in the room. 'Josh is lucky. You, my friend, are talented.'

'We'd better get going, my publicist will kill me if I miss the red carpet for the video-game launch,' I said with a smile.

She points at me as we slide out of the booth. 'Hey, make sure a book is poking out of your bag for @WhatsEmilyReading!'

'I'm not trying to force it, Chlo!'

'I know you're not, but it's still a cute, fun little thing, isn't it?'

'Yes, I guess it is,' I said, unable to disguise the delight in my voice.

@WhatsEmilyReading was a spin-off of one of the Emily Montgomery fan pages on Instagram, charting the books I was seen out and about with. Because I was *never* without a book. The idea filled me with horror. At first I thought they were just going to post for a couple of weeks and then the fun would wear off, but instead it gained traction, and with it more and more followers. So I decided to play along too – making sure I was always holding a book, or one was poking out of a pocket or visible from the top of my bag, something they could either instantly identify or have fun trying to figure out what it was. It had become enjoyable for me, too, in a way, to bring attention to books I loved or things that I thought had flown under the radar, being able to help debut authors, and in general just getting more people reading. I know, I know, it all sounded very typically Emily of me, but I couldn't change who I was at my core, and that was a reader. I read romance novels, literary fiction, thrillers, non fiction, fantasy, classics . . . anything, really. I always had done. That was what had led me to Wonderwick Woods, what had motivated me to go to an open audition all those years ago. I was the fan who had fallen into the pages of a book and come out the other side famous – and with a high-risk level for spending the rest of my life typecast.

As we walked through Soho to the venue for the video-game launch, I got Chloe to fill me in on her 'dating life' as we politely called it.

'What happened to the Spanish guy?' I frown at the mention of an Amelia, a DJ she hadn't told me about before.

'Ernesto? He was too . . . earnest-o. Always wanted to fly me out to Madrid and send me flowers and introduce me to his family.' She shuddered.

'But Amelia is just right?'

'Just right for now, anyway. The sex is incredible, she's just so *fun*, you know? Everything feels like an adventure with her, like we're properly exploring sex together.'

'That sounds . . . nice.'

'Yeah, it is, I guess,' she said, bemused at my choice of adjective. 'Anyway, what about you? Anyone caught your eye recently? Any of the male models at LFW? I bet I know some of their publicists, I could slide them your number.'

'Absolutely not!' I protested, shaking my head. 'I date vicariously through you.'

'You should think about, er, *not* doing that and maybe meeting someone *nice* yourself.'

'Are you saying that as my best friend or my publicist?'

She shrugged. 'Maybe both.'

Chapter Three

The launch of the *Wonderwick Woods: Creatures of the Forest* video game was kind of a bigger deal than I'd thought it would be. Not being a gamer myself, I hadn't realised *quite* how excited people were for it, and what an opportunity it would be to market the films – especially while we were between instalments. The red carpet was packed with photographers jostling for position and journalists and approved content creators standing by with their phones and recording equipment. Well, I say it was a 'red carpet' but the carpet itself was Wonderwick Woods green. That had become our thing: all the big events were accompanied by a green carpet. I'm pretty sure the studio had even trademarked the exact shade of green, *that's* how into it they were. As soon as I set foot on the carpet, the bulbs started flashing and cries of 'Emily!' rang in my ears. I made sure they got a few of me holding my copy of a new campus novel by a young Korean-American author which had been a big hit in the US but hadn't resonated as much here. Yet. Maybe a few more people would buy it if they saw me with it?

But unfortunately, I wasn't here to spread the good word about literature. Chloe guided me to the first journalist, a guy from a gaming magazine who wanted to know about the process of recording the voices, then it was a perky, cheerful journalist from British *Vogue* who I recognised from other events, and who, understandably, wanted to know about my outfit. That evening, I was wearing a strapless navy jumpsuit under an oversized cream silk blazer. Without the blazer, I would have felt *way* too exposed, but with it, I felt it made for a pretty elegant look.

'The jumpsuit is Stella McCartney and the blazer is MaxMara,' I told her.

'Interesting!' she said with a bright smile. 'Do you ever think of deviating from these, um, more well-established brands?'

'How do you mean?' I leaned in, trying to hear her better over the noise of the crowd as Chloe hovered behind me.

'Oh you know, just that other actresses your age are going for more, um, experimental looks or working with newer emerging designers. I was just wondering if that's something you're thinking about or if you're firmly committed to the heritage brands.'

'I . . .' I was a little taken aback but I didn't want to let it show. 'For me, it's not about a commitment to a brand but a commitment to wearing things that speak to me and my style, whatever that might be.'

'Thanks so much for your time,' Chloe said before steering me onto the next person.

'Heritage brands! Was she saying I dress like an old person?' I whispered to her as I was presented with a journalist from the big mainstream film magazine, a stubbly guy in a baseball cap.

He greeted me with a smile. 'Hey, Emily, I just wanted to ask if you're looking forward to starting work on the next Wonderwick film? I guess it's about to kick off, right? Everyone's in town by now!' Not the most original question but I could work with it.

'Of course, I'm so excited. This is actually my favourite of all the books in the series and it gives Linderley a lot of character development – not that I've been lacking it until now, of course! But it's just got a really different feeling to the other books as far as she's concerned, as well as some of the most exciting moments in the whole arc of the series.'

'Not to mention the romance,' he said, raising his eyebrows.

'Well, quite! I know the fans are looking forward to things ramping up a bit in this film and I *really* hope we deliver.'

'And I hear Darcy Jackson has signed on?'

'Mmmhmm! So exciting!' I nodded, a tight smile on my face.

'Thanks so much for your time.' Chloe firmly shook his hand and then it was on to the next and the next and the next.

Finally, we made it inside the venue, which had been decorated to resemble the Canopy Plaza, one of the most iconic Wonderwick sets. Stilt walkers in outfits inspired by the films (or, I suppose, the game? The book? Who knew at this point) crossed our paths and we had to dodge a rather enthusiastic fire breather. Cocktails in carved wooden cups trailing coloured smoke travelled past us on vast trays, and speakers blared a strange remix of one of the key themes from the original film score. Scenes from the game were projected onto the walls and the ceiling and it was all a bit mind-boggling, seeing Video Game Me dashing around in the Wonderwick world, all the trees and the habitats and the creatures enveloping us while we were sipping drinks and mingling in the VIP area. Or was I in the VVIP area at this one? Lisa from the studio and Martin the director raised their glasses to us from across the room but neither of us made any attempt to approach the other.

'I think they know they did well out of that meeting and don't want to push their luck,' Chloe murmured at me, then gasped with delight. 'Emily!' She grabbed my arm, her many rings pressing into the silk fabric of my blazer, her long, oval Builder In A Bottle-fortified nails digging into my flesh. 'It's Blake Shaw! What's he doing here?!'

Blake Shaw, the gorgeous, red-haired star of various high profile and very celebrated indie movies had graced the Wonderwick Woods video-game launch with his presence, for reasons I couldn't fully understand. What I *could* fully understand is that he was Chloe's white whale, both professionally and sexually.

'Maybe he heard you were going to be here,' I said, drily.

'Now's my chance! Either to poach him off Brian Leger or to rip his clothes off! You'll be all right on your own for a bit, won't you?'

Before I could even answer, she bopped off in Blake's direction, who, it must be said, was looking *very* handsome in an ugly-cool Loewe jumper I recognised from the Paris Fashion Week show. Which left me . . . somewhat alone. I could feel my cheeks heat up a little bit as I took a sip from my glass. It was starting to feel like there was a spotlight on me and everyone could see I was just standing around on my own. I took my phone out of my bag for something to do, and fixed my expression so I was deep in thought. Surely someone would eventually come up and talk to me? It felt as if I had been stood up and everyone knew it, like I was waiting at a table for a date to arrive but they never would. Where were the other cast members? Where was Max who played the rebellious inventor Alder? I couldn't see Tommy, famous for playing the serious and stoic Ash. Or Felicity, better known as my screen mother Imriel. I'd have even been happy to see Alexander Christie, the classically trained actor behind Vulpus, the sexually confusing shapeshifting fox.

A booming laugh filled the air from somewhere nearby and I turned to see a big, round table with *precisely* those four chatting over novelty cocktails, except for Max who was, as always, drinking a pint. Tommy must have said something funny to make Max throw his head back and laugh like that. I paused, unsure if I should interrupt the scene. They all looked so at ease, like one big happy family. I knew I couldn't make any of them laugh like that, for starters. How was it possible that I was a star of one of the biggest film franchises of all time and I was standing on my own at a party while my colleagues were hanging out without me?

'Emily!' Max caught me looking and waved me over like a madman. As I walked towards them, nerves creeping over me, the four of them started banging on the table in a drumroll to herald my arrival.

'Oi, budge up,' Max instructed Tommy, elbowing him in the ribs, so I could join them in the booth.

I shook my head. 'No, it's OK – I just wanted to come and say hello.'

'Join us,' Alexander said, standing up from the one chair facing the table and gesturing for me to sit.

'You don't have to give up your seat for me!'

'Oh, I was going to get a drink anyway,' he said, pulling the chair out gallantly. 'Can I get you anything?'

'No thanks, I've probably had enough already.' I sat as he strolled off towards the bar, looking every inch the gentleman in his suit. There was always such a divide on Wonderwick between the 'kids' and the adults – we didn't really mix that much on set, both camps sticking together, socialising together, so events like this were one of the few times we were all mixed up.

Felicity reached across the table to me and grasped my hands in hers. 'Darling, I've missed you.'

'I've missed you too,' I said, a little awkwardly. I've never been much of a hugger, a toucher, a *darling, I've missed you*, but the fact was that I *had* missed Felicity. I'd missed them all. It just made me feel so embarrassed to say it, like I didn't want them to know how much they meant to me. How much the whole thing meant to me.

'So, are we the cast representatives tonight?' I asked, desperately hoping Josh was still in LA for another couple of days before filming started. I wanted to postpone encountering him as long as humanly possible.

Max and Tommy frowned and look at each other like I was clearly mad, while Felicity just smiled politely.

'You're joking, right?'

'No, why?'

'Emily . . .' Felicity said, gently.

'You know what this party is *for*, right?' Tommy sounded uncomfortable, nervous, even. As much as he would get whipped up in Max's rambunctious behaviour, he was a sensitive soul at heart.

'Yes,' I said with an awkward laugh. 'It's the party for the video game.'

'That's not the *only* reason,' said Max.

Felicity muttered, shaking her head. 'I don't know why they wouldn't tell you, maybe they thought you wouldn't come after all the silliness in the media.'

'For God's sake, can someone just tell me what's going on?' I burst out.

Just then, Alexander reappeared sipping an Old Fashioned. 'Ah, there she is,' he said, his eyes fixed on the entrance, where, under a spotlight stood the closest thing I had to a rival, if your rival could be a person you've never met before.

Darcy Jackson.

Chapter Four

So that was why we were there. That's what this was all for. To introduce Darcy Jackson, fledgling actress and descendant of rock royalty Steve Jackson from The Sweats, to confirm her as the newest cast member of the franchise, to reveal her as Loreia Buckthorn, the fan favourite villain of the later Wonderwick books, daughter of none other than Lord Thorn, the OG Wonderwick villain from book one.

'She's not *really* your nemesis, is she?' Max asked from across the top of his cocktail. His upper-class accent hung on the word 'nemesis', making it sound like the most ridiculous thing in the world.

Felicity rolled her eyes and swatted at him with the back of her hand. 'Oh, don't be so silly, what are you talking about, *nemesis*?'

Max held his hands up in submission. 'I don't know, do I? No one tells us anything, do they, Tommy?'

Tommy smiled and shook his head, running a hand over his tightly cropped hair. 'Don't think we're important enough, mate.'

'There was that article, though.' Max glanced sideways at me.

'Max Rogers, you have been in this industry long enough to know that most of what's in the media is a load of bollocks!' Felicity chided him. Even off the Wonderwick set she seemed to inhabit a maternal role for all of us, despite her best efforts to remain regal and icy.

'Yeah, well, it's different when it's not about you, though, isn't it?' Max said with a completely straight face and the rest of us couldn't help but laugh, even me.

'What did the article say, anyway?' Tommy asked, flicking a nervous glance in my direction.

'Wasn't just one,' Max said through a mouthful of dyed green popcorn. 'Articles *plural*.'

I was fed up of being talked about, across and over, especially by some of my oldest friends in the cast. 'That I've been campaigning hard behind the scenes to get her blocked from being cast, that I see her as a threat to my position in the Wonderwick universe, that I'm scared she's going to be more popular than me, that I've been trash-talking her dad's music, that I got my "people" to make sure she was on the second row at any fashion week shows where I was on the front row.' I listed off all the silly accusations the gossip sites had made about me and Darcy. 'To name but a few.'

'But it's all a load of bollocks, right, Emily?' Tommy raised his eyebrows. He would often get involved in

Max's silliness but he was more peaceful by nature, and clearly wanted to draw a line under this for me.

'Right,' I said firmly.

Technically that was true. With one exception. I hadn't been campaigning to stop her getting cast in Wonderwick. I definitely hadn't been doing any trash-talking about her rock star dad or his discography. And I hadn't done any behind-the-scenes meddling at fashion week, I promise. But I did know she was a threat to my position in the Wonderwick universe. Not just in the story of the books, I mean. The fans had been making it clear for *years* that she would make the perfect Loreia Buckthorn, bringing it up at every ComicCon, mentioning it in every Wonderwick-related Reddit AMA, flooding official social media posts with replies about Darcy. It all started with *one* post on *one* Tumblr fan page where someone observed how close she looked to the way Sylvara Runequill had written Loreia in the books. Back then, it was a bit of a joke, she was just some rock star's kid, occasionally spotted at celebrity parties in LA. But then it gained momentum as she grew up and the two paths converged, and I would be lying if I said that it didn't rattle me a bit. Where does a bit of fan service end? With Linderley Jones getting reduced to a supporting role by the final film, and Loreia Buckthorn getting a spin-off series?

If you wanted to know what my real problem was, it was that Darcy was so deeply the *opposite* of me. How could I ever lose my reputation of being the good girl, the prim one, the stuck-up one, the safe one if people already believed that anyway, and now they would have a super-sexy, confident, daring, laid-back, cool rock star of a person to compare me to? I couldn't shake the feeling that I would always come up short, that I would always be just a little bit boring, a little bit too much of a goody two-shoes. Who would want *that* when they could have Darcy Jackson?

'Do you know the funniest thing?' I said, trying to keep my voice light. 'I've never even met Darcy before. There's all this gossip and we've literally never met.'

'Don't look now but I think you're about to get your chance,' Alexander whispered discreetly in my ear.

I barely had time to glance over my shoulder when Darcy was upon our table, complete with entourage: a man in a huge fur coat and a woman with a mane of neon-orange hair, both of whom were wearing sunglasses indoors and neither of whom spoke.

'Striking' was the word that most often got used about Darcy Jackson. Platinum blonde hair cut into a sharp bob. Six feet tall and never seen without a pair of vertiginous heels unless she was working out, which she did often – how else would she have the kind of ripped physique that inspired legions of fans to comment 'step on my neck' under every photo where you can see her toned thighs and biceps. She was like a real life Amazon, and absolutely nothing like me.

'Hey guys, I can't believe you're all hanging out without me!' She gave a sly smile, her dazzling white teeth glinting wolfishly in the low light. Her outfit was kind of crazy but also totally inspired: a way-too-long ultra-tight fishtail skirt with a matching bralette that barely covered her nipples and showed off her rock-hard abs. I had absolutely no idea how she came up with these looks or where you would even *get* such an outfit. All I knew was that the British *Vogue* reporter on the carpet outside didn't ask *her* about heritage brands. 'Isn't this party *so* cute? I'm Darcy, by the way.' She said all of this slowly, in a lazy drawl, her eyes heavy with black glitter like a galaxy behind aggressively spiky lashes. Note to self: eyelashes not sufficiently spiky.

She held out her hand to each of us in turn, and far from the limp, weak suggestion of a handshake I was expecting, she squeezed my knuckles in a bone-crushing grip that took me completely by surprise. Her vibe may have been laid-back but her handshake was all business.

'Nice to meet you, Darcy,' I said, trying to smile through the nerves. 'I'm Emily. I'm really looking forward to working with you.'

'I know who you are. And I look forward to working with you, too.' What did that mean? That I was famous or that she was bringing some kind of *energy* with her, just like I was?

'It's so great to meet you,' Max said, scrambling to his feet and offering her his place in the booth. 'Please, come sit with us, Darcy.'

'No, that's OK, babe.' She shrugged lightly. 'I just wanted to come say hi so we weren't all meeting for the first time on set. Me and my team are going to mingle. See you around.' She gave a little flick of the head to signal that the conversation was over and she and her fashion minions disappeared into the crowd.

She had barely stepped away from the table when the group erupted into chat. '*Oh, please, come sit with us Darcy*,' Tommy mimicked his friend in a high-pitched mocking posh tone. 'Is this what you're going to be like next week?' He shook his head at Max whose cheeks were glowing scarlet.

'What? I was just being polite,' he mumbled.

'I thought it was very gentlemanly of you,' Alexander said.

'She seemed nice,' I said, shrugging my shoulders casually, acutely aware of the heaviness of the blazer against my skin. I felt so covered up all of a sudden.

'I think the next film will be very interesting,' Felicity said archly, taking a sip of her cocktail, which she refused to drink out of the carved wooden mugs and instead had decanted into a Martini glass. 'Though I have to say, my friend's brother was Steve Jackson's PA for a while and said she was, and I quote, "fucking delightful", so you never can tell.'

Swiftly, Darcy was replaced by a breathless Chloe. This must have been a pretty big deal if it could tear her away from chatting up Blake Shaw. 'Shit, Emily, I had no idea! They've completely sprung it on everyone! I think it was meant to be a surprise to maximise the hype around the video game but bloody hell they could have given us a little warning.'

'It's fine,' I said to her, looking her intensely in the eyes. It wasn't really fine, and in fact what Chloe said only made it worse: I knew they hadn't sprung it on everyone. I knew that Tommy and Max and Felicity and Alexander and, presumably Josh (wherever he was) knew that this party was all about Darcy, but a decision was made to keep it from me. The idea that I was seen as either a diva or a sensitive little child both made me want to scream. 'I don't know why everyone is making such a big deal about it.'

Chloe's expression clouded for a moment before she fixed a smile. 'Of course, it's nothing! If anything, it's exciting to have a new cast member to liven things up.'

Liven things up was exactly what she'd done already: not only were my co-stars hunched over the table, talking a million miles an hour about their brief encounter with our new colleague, but the whole room seemed to be tracking her every move. Surreptitious glances over shoulders, sneaky photos on covertly positioned phones. The excitement was palpable.

'My thoughts exactly,' I said, resolutely. And for the second time today, I found myself saying, 'Whatever's good for Wonderwick.'

Chapter Five

'I can't say I think much of this little ambush,' Chloe said, folding her arms across her chest, before instantly unfolding them to take two cocktails in a mini cauldron from a passing tray and handing one to me. 'Words will be had on your behalf.'

'It's fine, and I think the more fuss we make, the worse it'll get. Let's just play it cool. Maybe someone *did* just forget to tell us.' I shrugged, knowing full well that was wishful thinking.

Chloe let out a sceptical snort, and we were saved from any more chat about Darcy by the appearance of Courtney Williams, one of the Wonderwick supporting cast who joined the franchise two movies ago to *great* chatter, not all of it good.

'Well, aren't you looking absolutely radiant?' Chloe said, drawing her into a hug before I did the same.

'More like luminous!' I added. Courtney beamed at me, running a hand over her hair, newly shaved short and dyed a fluorescent yellow-green that contrasted deliciously against her dark skin.

'I take creative inspiration wherever I find it and this summer I felt captivated by the unique shade of a tennis ball,' she said, twirling on the spot. Her gold lamé suit and bright white sneakers gave her even more of a sense of being a beautiful beacon in the dark of the party.

'Oh yes, I saw you were at the US Open! Was New York fun?'

'It was *crazy*, I still can't believe this is my life! It's like . . . a few years ago I was a teenager with no money and now people can't stop throwing free shit at me! Me? Courtney Williams? In New York? Watching tennis? On someone else's dime? Get real!'

'It's funny to remember that we all used to have normal lives, isn't it?'

Wonderwick changed everything for us as teens, absolutely everything. One day we were vaguely normal, maybe some of us had been in a couple of commercials or done a bit of theatre, but no one you'd recognise on the street. And then that part of our lives was over, and we were . . . famous people.

'Well,' Courtney smirked, 'not all of us.' It didn't take a genius to figure out who she's talking about. No one loathed Josh quite like I did.

'Speaking of which, has anyone spotted our favourite nepo baby or is he still in LA?' I asked, casually.

'I think he's around here somewhere.' Courtney craned her neck. 'I'm sure I saw him in a dark corner with a model.'

'A likely place for him to be,' Chloe muttered.

'Can't believe the gang's all back together next week!' Courtney was bouncy with excitement. 'And you've got some smooching to do!'

'Oh, don't! I'm trying not to think about it!'

'They want to make it spicy!' Chloe said, wiggling her eyebrows suggestively.

'Can you both shut up about the kiss! I'm trying to think about it as little as possible!' I said, a now familiar sense of dread pooling in my stomach.

Just then, we were approached by a tween girl who was being physically steered toward us by her mum. 'Hi, girls, I'm so sorry to disturb you but Jess wanted to ask if she could get a quick selfie. She was too shy to ask you herself.' Even through the dim light I could tell the girl's cheeks were beetroot red with embarrassment but I didn't doubt that she really wanted a selfie with us. She was wearing an enamel pin on her jacket that said 'TREETOP LIBRARIAN' with a stack of books, in reference to the iconic Great Archive from the treetop world, my personal favourite of all the Wonderwick sets and the inspiration behind reams of fan art. A library built into the hollow trunk of an ancient, towering tree, lined with bark-bound books and scrolls but also reading platforms carved into the inner branches, it was a bookworm's idea of absolute heaven (and a place I occasionally liked to hang out on set, much to the displeasure of the set builders and prop department).

'Of course, that's OK with me if that's OK with you, Courtney?'

'I'd love to!'

'Linderley and Clover are my favourites,' Jess managed to choke out. 'Especially Clover . . . I can't wait to see the scene in the next film where you almost lose Alder in the sinking sand. That's my favourite scene in the book, even though I've read it a million times I'm always scared it's going to end differently.'

'But it's so horrible! I don't know how I'm going to get through it, Jess!' Courtney grasped onto her shoulders with great enthusiasm. She always seemed to have such an easy way with fans, and they loved her in return.

'You can do it,' Jess laughed, coming out of her shell a little. 'And Linderley,' she said, turning to me, 'I mean . . . um, Emily, I can't wait to see the big kiss with you and Josh Sacco!'

'It's gonna be steamy!' Courtney interjected before I could say anything.

'Argh!' I covered my face with my hands, playing up my embarrassment but only a little bit, because the embarrassment was *real*. 'I'm glad you guys are looking forward to it!'

Jess's mum held her phone up to take the photo.

'Everyone say "Wonderwick!"' Chloe instructed us, and we all said it in cheesy unison before breaking into a giggle.

'Is the photo OK?' I asked Jess's mum, who showed the screen to Jess for approval.

'I can't believe I got a photo with Linderley and Clover! Sorry, I mean Emily and Courtney! Thank you so much! You guys are the best! And Courtney, I'm sorry about all that . . . you know . . .'

Courtney swallowed and nodded. 'I know. Thanks, Jess. It was nice to meet you.'

When they'd disappeared back into the crowd, Courtney let out a sigh. 'I'm glad there are more good people than bad in the world. It's nice to remember it sometimes.'

I wanted to squeeze her hand or give her some reassuring gesture but it just felt too intimate, so I said, 'I think you were really brave for getting through all of that.' *All of that* was the absolutely mad online backlash to a Black actress being cast as Clover. It didn't even matter that she's white in the book! But a vocal minority of the Wonderwick 'fans' (I hate to even call them that) decided it was a betrayal of the original books and that the film was trying to 'pander to the woke agenda'. Cue review bombing, online abuse, the classic racist fandom playbook, and Courtney was on the receiving end of it, aged seventeen.

Courtney chuckled, bitterly. 'What was the alternative? Quit the films? Die? I get through this shit because I have to get through it.' She glanced at me out of the corner of her eye. 'But, yeah, thank you, mate. Anyway, now I've done my community service and taken one or more selfies with a fan, I'm going to slide off home, get an early night and rest before the proper work starts.'

Once we'd said our goodbyes, it was just me and Chloe again. Courtney was seemingly the only person who had left the party and people were still continuing to arrive. The room felt almost too full, and as if the music had got even louder. Maybe Courtney had the right idea after all. 'You know you don't need to babysit me, right, if you want to get back to chatting up Blake Shaw?' I told Chloe.

'Well . . . he does seem to be making eyes at me across the room,' she said, her voice light with glee. I turned to see where he was standing and in exchange, Chloe whacked me with the back of her hand. 'Oh my God, Emily, don't be so obvious! We've got to play it cool!'

'Sorry!' I grimaced. 'I just can't believe how easy this is for you! It's like you wanted to meet him, you met him, and now he can't take his eyes off you!' It sounded so simple when I said it, but romance had never felt that straightforward for me. I found it hard to trust people's intentions. I'd had a few little relationships with boys over the years, tentative, fumbling things with other actors, but no one had really captured my attention. No one really felt special enough to distract me from work. When you're famous, relationships are never just you and the other person.

'Are you sure you'll be all right on your own?' Chloe asked.

'Of course, I'm a big girl. Consider yourself off-duty for the rest of the evening. Fly free, little butterfly,' I said, shooing her off in his direction

'I'll see you soon, though?' She glanced at me over her shoulder, already making her way towards her target. She was so confident! I wished she could bottle it and sell it to me. 'Let me know how the shoot goes! I'm always at the end of the phone if you need anything!'

I was alone again, but now everything felt too hot, too close, too loud. I needed a breather, just a little bit of fresh air and no one to talk to, no worries that I'm boring or disappointing or stuck-up or not as exciting as Darcy or as fun as Courtney or keeping Chloe from getting with her crush. I could treat myself to a little alone time, couldn't I?

Chapter Six

I stood in the passageway behind the venue and just let the sounds of the Central London backstreets wash over me. Further down the alley, one of the cocktail waiters from the party was having a cigarette. I took a deep breath. The lack of people talking to me and looking at me and wanting to see my reaction to Darcy felt like a holiday.

Unfortunately for me, the peace was almost instantly broken by an all-too-familiar voice through the darkness. 'Hey, Squirt! Is that you?'

There was only one person that called me that. The cocktail waiter wasn't a cocktail waiter at all but . . . Josh Sacco grinding the butt of his cigarette under the heel of his expensive Japanese trainers. Of course. The one person I didn't want to see right then. I think I would rather have encountered Darcy in this dark alley than *him*.

As much as I disapproved of meeting him here like this, it must be said that I very much approved of his outfit: a crisp white T-shirt tucked into black linen trousers with those brightly coloured sneakers and an embroidered satin bomber jacket. Money might not be able to buy you taste but it could clearly engage the services of a stylist.

'Hi, *Josh*,' I said, pointedly. 'Would it kill you not to call me that?'

He nodded at me in greeting. We didn't hug. I tried to avoid physical contact with Josh as much as humanly possible. 'Why? There's no one around to hear it.'

'I'm around to hear it!' I protested.

'Ah, you don't count, Squirt,' he said. 'I would ask if you've come out here for a sneaky smoke but we both know you're above that. So, what's up?'

I shrugged. 'Nothing's up, just taking a minute away from all the noise and the people. I wasn't sure if you were even coming tonight.'

'Are you kidding? I wouldn't miss this for the *world*.'

'I didn't know you were such a fan of gaming,' I said, as if I really thought that was what he meant.

'Come now,' he said, dropping his chin and looking at me very intently. A lock of dark curly hair flopped annoyingly over his forehead and under the overhead glare of the street light, his cheekbones looked even sharper than usual.

'What?' I feigned ignorance.

'Darcy Jackson joining the party? Literally and metaphorically?' He leaned against the wall of the party venue. Josh was always *leaning* against something, ever so casually, as if standing up seemed too much like hard work and he had to outsource it to a wall or a table or a counter.

'Oh, that.'

He threw his hands up. 'You've got to give the people what they want, and the people *really* wanted Darcy. My parents have been saying it all along.'

'It's going to be great,' I said, flatly.

'Really? You really think that? Or you're just saying that because it's what you think you're meant to say? You are allowed to rock the boat a little from time to time, Montgomery.'

This was how conversations with Josh generally went: me, always on the back foot, trying not to come across as pathetic or boring, him saying out loud the things that other people were thinking. Not for the first time I wondered how on earth we were ever going to make a romance storyline between Rowan Clearwater and Linderley Jones convincing.

'I really think that. It's clear that Darcy Jackson is going to give Wonderwick that extra little boost to cement its status among fans.'

Josh winced, his dark eyebrows almost meeting in the middle. 'Yikes! Did you copy and paste that from the press release or come up with it all by yourself?'

'Words all my own, I assure you.'

'Darcy was looking pretty spicy in that leather combo, right? Those abs made me want to put in a double session with my trainer tomorrow. The outfit should be more than enough to get people talking.'

'I should think so,' I said, trying to resist being drawn into a conversation about how sexy and exciting Darcy is.

'She went through her whole workout routine with me when we had brunch last week, it's intense as fuck.'

'You two have been hanging out?' I asked, almost involuntarily. Sometimes it felt like there was a whole world happening somewhere near me but just out of reach, a party taking place in the room next door.

He shrugged. 'She was in LA recording something at her dad's studio, I knew she was going to be in the next movie, so I sent her a message. We got pancakes. No biggie.'

'Sounds delicious.'

'So, uh,' he said with a smile, sensing that we'd come to the end of that particular conversation. 'What have you been doing with yourself since the press tour? Learning all your lines for the next movie, I guess? Plus maybe everyone else's too? Or have you dreamed bigger and started writing another Wonderwick book for Sylvara so the franchise never has to end?'

'I'm not even going to ask if you've read the script, I assume you have *people* to do that for you. Such a shame you can't outsource the acting part as well.'

'Ouch, Squirt!' he laughed. 'You're really rattled by this whole Darcy thing, aren't you?'

'I'm not *rattled*, everyone is just being annoying about it,' I muttered, darkly.

'Annoying? *Moi?* Never. Anyway, I can tell you're rattled because you haven't even mentioned the kiss. I think it's a good idea to take it steamier, don't you?' he asked, nonchalantly.

'It doesn't seem like it matters whether I do or not when you and your parents are making these decisions without me,' I said, pausing for breath, during which he clutched his chest with a mock-wounded expression on his face. 'But for what it's worth I think it's a decent idea. It certainly seems like the direction the fans want everything to go in.'

'You gotta be careful with fans, though. Give them this and it'll be full-frontal nudity and XXX-rated shit in the next movie.' He saw the expression on my face. 'I'm kidding! Jesus, learn to take a joke. Anyway, tell me how Emily fills her hiatus.'

I tried to come up with an answer that didn't make me sound completely insufferable, because I already knew what Josh thought of me. I could already see his face if I said, *I've been learning French and reading lots of books and going to fashion weeks* – the perfect mix of nerdy little good girl and utterly predictable.

'Oh, this and that,' I said, lightly.

'Wow, dark horse much?' Josh laughed and took a sip from his glass. 'Way to overshare!'

OK, he had a point. 'I'm sorry!' I covered my face with my hands. 'I just worry that everything I do sounds really boring to you, like I haven't been windsurfing in Sri Lanka or scaling the side of a mountain in Yosemite!'

Josh arched his eyebrows. 'For someone that claims to have no interest in what I do, you have a surprisingly detailed understanding of what I've been up to and where I've been up to it.'

I could feel my cheeks heat up and hoped desperately the lighting was sufficiently gloomy out here that they weren't visibly beetroot red. I should probably have chosen less specific examples of 'adventurous activities', shouldn't I? It was hard to miss Josh's big, splashy social media presence. He was always posting live from parties, beaches, clubs, taking photos with fans, being present and available and relatable in a way that just felt so alien to me.

I waved him away. 'Oh, you know what I mean. So, when did you get into London?'

He thought for a moment, the disorientation of long-haul travel whirring away in his brain. 'Yesterday morning, I think? I just checked into the hotel, did a bit of shopping, had dinner at Di Angelo's. You been?'

'I have actually, I went with Edgar Malek a couple of weeks ago,' I said, unsure if he would either know or care who Edgar was. 'I thought the amatriciana was incredible.'

'You went for dinner with Edgar Malek?' His eyes were wide with delight. 'Like *the* Edgar Malek?'

I laughed, taken aback by his enthusiasm. 'Why, are you a fan?'

'Wow, yeah, a little bit. I only think he's the most exciting director working today?' The enthusiasm coming off him was infectious, *almost* charming.

'Me too!'

'So, you two are hanging out now? What, is he your new boyfriend or something? Maybe you could put in a good word for me?'

I frowned at him, annoyed that was his first thought. 'No, he's not my boyfriend, don't be ridiculous. He's married.'

'Never stopped a lot of people in Hollywood.' He shrugged. 'So, this was a spot of professional networking?'

'Well, yes, actually,' I said, clearing my throat, conscious that I had to play it a bit cool so as not to seem like I was showing off. 'Anyway, what am I putting in a good word for you about?'

He seemed a little sheepish all of a sudden, an expression that I wasn't used to on him. I waited for him to speak. 'Like, I would *love* to work with him on something, some day. When the time is right, of course.'

'Oh!' I finally got what he meant. I can't say it had ever occurred to me that he would be interested in working with Edgar Malek. 'Right, yes, of course.'

'Unless you think I wouldn't be up to it,' he said, so quietly I almost didn't hear him.

I was genuinely taken aback by this. As long as I had known him, Josh only seemed interested in not only being in, but also watching, films with huge budgets and big, exciting sets, preferably with explosions or magic. 'No, no, it's not that, I just didn't know you were so interested in his work that's all. Well, I'll let you know how it goes if I end up working with him – maybe everything will fall apart before I sign the contract.'

'You're actually *working* with him?' he asked, not quite incredulously but more awestruck.

The pride and excitement I felt at being offered the role now felt a little embarrassing, like I needed to play it down for Josh's benefit. I nodded, quickly. 'Well, yes, I think so . . . If I do then I'll be shooting it after we finish the next film. It's filming in Ireland. I'll be leaving as soon as we wrap on Wonderwick.'

'Shit, that's huge, congratulations, Emily,' he said, pulling me into a hug, like he had forgotten we didn't do that. It was in his nature: he was a touchy-feely American type, and he squeezed me so tight I could feel the muscles in his chest. 'Tell me all about it?' he asked as he relaxed his grip on me.

'Well, it's a bit of a change from Wonderwick,' I said with a grimace. 'It's a kind of weird, uncanny, speculative thing . . . I'm still not entirely sure *what* it is but I'm excited to find out.'

'And are you the lead?'

'Not exactly, it's split quite evenly across three parts. So I'm the third of a lead,' I said with a shrug.

'You could have walked onto pretty much any big-budget movie you wanted but you had to go for this. I gotta say, I admire it.'

I smiled, almost against my will. 'Thank you.' I didn't want to let my guard down *too* much but

I couldn't look a gift horse (Josh being nice to me) in the mouth.

'But seriously.' He fixed me with an intense gaze. 'This is fucking cool and I hope you know it. Really fucking cool, Montgomery. This is real acting. Real shit. Not that what we do isn't real or isn't important or isn't good, but . . . this is something else. And I'm proud of you for it.'

Before I could figure out what I wanted to say in response to Josh's unexpected kindness, the door swung open and a few actual waiters – not actors looking for an improvised smoking area – poured out into the alleyway for a break.

'I guess this is our cue to rejoin the party,' I said.

He nodded and held the door open for me. 'Back to reality.'

Chapter Seven

I milled around the party, chatting to various cast members and people from the studio, occasionally checking in with Chloe. Someone high up at the gaming company made a speech, and I did a good job of pretending to listen while my eyes scanned the room for Darcy and/or Josh. Just to see what they were up to, you know? I couldn't spot them, which meant they could be off somewhere *together*. That was the last thing I needed, them forming a cosy little twosome or worse, dating. That'd really confirm my redundancy on Planet Wonderwick.

Finally, the speech was finished, and when Max tried to wave me over to have another drink with them, I shook my head and mouthed, 'I'll see you tomorrow.'

'I think I'm going to head off,' I told Chloe.

'You want me to get you a car?'

'No, it's fine, I can get my own,' I told her, requesting a driver on the fancy car service app we use. 'Look at me being all self-sufficient!'

'You're a strong independent woman, Emily Montgomery,' she said, placing her hands on my shoulders.

'Let me know if you need anything from me while you're on set, yeah? But you'll have Carrie and all your little mates so hopefully you won't get too lonely.'

It was all starting to feel very real, that filming for the next Wonderwick was just over the horizon.

'My guy's nearly here,' I said, looking down at my phone. 'I'd better go outside.'

'Love you!'

I headed out to the street where the official red carpet had dispersed but in its place was a swarm of paparazzi waiting to capture C-list celebrities or, if they were lucky, one of the Wonderwick cast, stumbling out of the party. I was greeted by a chorus of 'Emily!' 'Over here, love!' 'All right, Ems!' and a glittering of flash bulbs. I shouldn't have come out until my driver was actually here, but I was starting to feel a little partied-out. As well as the paparazzi there were a few fans waiting with phones outstretched for selfies, and of course I obliged while I had time. Sometimes it was necessary to engage the services of a private security company but I tried to do as much as possible in the 'real world'. I gave the horde of photographers my sweetest smile and strode off purposefully in the direction of a couple of waiting cars in the hope one of them was mine. It wasn't. I felt exposed, having to loiter here with the paparazzi so close by, but almost instantly the doors behind me opened again and—

Josh and Darcy emerged. Not hand in hand, not with his arm around her waist, nothing like that. But they *were* together. Leaving together. If the photographers were excited to see me, it paled in comparison to the absolute chaos that erupted when they realised it was Josh and Darcy. Although they weren't making physical contact, there was something so . . . conspiratorial about the way his head was bowed towards her, the little smirk on his face as she was saying something into his ear. In the bright outdoor lighting, her outfit was even more striking, her bleached hair even more icy, her body even tighter, her eye makeup even smokier. Fortunately, neither of them noticed me and in an instant my car pulled up.

As I slid into the back seat and greeted the driver, I hoped and prayed that the sight of the two of them leaving the party was so thrilling to the photographers that none of them thought to turn around and capture my reaction.

Chapter Eight

It was only when I got to the lobby of my building that I realised what a long day it had been. It felt like absolutely *days* ago rather than hours since I'd left that morning, and I said goodnight to the evening concierge, Tom, before heading up in the lift to the eighth floor. I slid my key into the lock and as the door shut behind me, I couldn't help but let out a sigh of relief that the place I came back to was all my own.

The calmness of the cool powder-blue walls with white trim greeted me like an old friend, and I set my keys and bag down on the table in the entrance hall next to the big glass vase full of fresh flowers before heading to the living room and sinking into the cream bouclé sofa.

I had only ever lived with my parents or in houses rented by the studio during filming, before I bought this place. I'd been away a lot, hotel and plane hopping while promoting the last film, *Wonderwick Woods: Into the Shadow Realm*. I always found myself wondering when I would ever really get to enjoy my first big purchase, paid for with the money I'd spent my adolescence earning.

I slid the big glass doors open, feeling the cool air hit my skin and the sound of cars on the street below fill my ears. Ahead of me, the vast expanse of Regent's Park spread like a black hole before the lights of the West End glittered in the distance. In the darkness, the park looked slightly ominous, but in the daylight it was my happy place, somewhere I could run in loops for miles without getting bored, and I had found that when you're running, people were less likely to stop you for a selfie. I couldn't help wondering where Josh and Darcy were now. Not that I minded, of course, they could do what they wanted. And besides, I probably needed to get over myself, stop thinking that everything they do is somehow going to affect me. But . . . what if it did?

After a few minutes of peace on the balcony, I headed back inside and resigned myself to the fact that it may be late, but I had a job to do. Through the wood-framed archway into the bedroom, I flicked on the warm light cast by the milky glass orbs overhead. Pulling both my Louis Vuitton trunk suitcases out from under my bed, I went about packing to head off to set in the morning.

I slid open the wardrobes, which moved seamlessly on silky mechanisms, and looked at the comforting sea of navy, grey, camel, cream and white in front of me. Pulling out a strategically chosen array of clothes, I ran my fingers over the beautiful pieces I would never take for granted – the silk slip dresses, the cashmere sweaters, the cotton jackets, the denim jeans cut exactly to my measurements, the things I didn't know if I necessarily deserved but totally treasured anyway. Next, I headed to my bookshelves (naturally the first thing I had unpacked in my new flat) and took . . . well, more than enough to keep me going for the shoot. Yes, they weighed me down but there was no substitute for a real book. I'd tried the digital reading thing after Josh hid my book one too many times, but it didn't feel the same. I missed the smell, the texture of the paper, the fonts, the joy of seeing the cover design, plus I didn't want Josh to 'win'. He was *always* winning.

When you've spent as much time on the road as I have, you get quite good at packing. The problem was that other than my clothes and my books, a lot of my other things were still in boxes – boxes that were artfully hidden in big cupboards rather than sitting out in the open, but in boxes nonetheless. I'd been getting by with a hairbrush that a beauty brand had sent me, but I missed the Mason Pearson brush that I knew was buried in a moving box somewhere, and I wanted to find it before I left.

The first box I started to dig around in was full of kitchen stuff, the second contained even more makeup than was already unpacked, and as I went rummaging in the third, I discovered it contained miscellaneous 'bits'. As soon as my hand hit the hard plastic, I knew exactly what I'd found. I couldn't help but smile as I drew it out of the box.

And there it was: my first ever photo pass for the Wonderwick set. Look, I may be a fashion girl *now* but once upon a time I was thirteen years old and thought I knew how to put together an outfit. Unfortunately that look was now immortalised for all time in the form of this photo, and I'll *never* get rid of it. I looked down at that face, my face, and tried to remember what it felt like before . . . all this. Of course I knew it was going to be a big deal – the Wonderwick books were huge, I was a devoted fan of them myself, and everyone had been wanting a film series for years – but I don't think I could have ever have known what it would all *feel* like. Back then, I only thought about it in terms of going to the set, doing the acting, and then going with my few school friends to see the film in the cinema. I didn't think about all the rest of it. The actual fame, the travelling the world, the sense of being in the public eye, the glamour and the insecurity.

But seven years ago I was not thinking about any of that, I was only thinking of what the best possible outfit would be for my first day of my new life as a *real* actress, which I decided would be an iridescent lilac top, a pair of khaki trousers and, for some reason, a choker. This photo didn't show my feet which was a small mercy, because if it did you would see a pair of cowboy boots, which had *not* experienced their renaissance at that point. My mum gently suggested I went for something a little more understated but I thought it was the coolest combination I had ever seen, and you couldn't have talked me out of it if your life depended on it.

Obviously, the outfit hadn't quite stood the test of time, but instead of being embarrassed, I felt a little swell of pride for my old self. Charging off to set with all my lines learned, an encyclopaedic knowledge of the books, a frankly wild outfit chosen for the occasion and with no idea what I was letting myself in for. *Good for you*, I thought, looking down at my photo. I would have been about thirty minutes away from meeting Josh Sacco for the first time, at which point my day, and perhaps life, took a nosedive, but I was happy that this moment had been preserved forever under frosted plastic on a Smithdown Studios lanyard.

As I climbed into bed, the Egyptian cotton sheets feeling like a luxurious cocoon, I was filled with a powerful mix of excitement and fatigue. Half of me wished we could have just one day off, just one day with no plans, no parties, no meetings, nowhere to be and nothing to do before we had to head to set. But the other half was raring to go, as fizzy with excitement to get to the set tomorrow as I felt the night before I headed off, a little thirteen-year-old girl, to enter the Forest of Wonderwick.

JOSH

Sure, it's not like I haven't given her ample reason to distrust me since then, but part of me wonders if Emily is still holding a seven-year-old grudge from the first time we met.

We've done four films since then, shot hundreds of scenes, travelled the world to promote it, but I can still remember the nerves and excitement of that first visit to Smithdown. I was fourteen and didn't know anything about anything, but of course I didn't want anyone to know that. Everyone else had chaperones from their family – generally parents or grandparents but sometimes older siblings who wanted to trade in their day job for the daily stipend and a brush with fame. Not me, though. My parents were too busy with other projects in LA, so the studio hired this guy, Matt, to follow me around and make sure I wasn't getting mistreated or whatever.

'Isn't this exciting?' Matt asked me, a big grin on his face. Just at that moment, a huge, grey industrial park zoomed past the window of the studio car. He'd been saying other stuff too but I hadn't really been paying attention. I'd been using jet lag as an excuse for the past few days when I hadn't been listening, and to be fair it was very early in the morning. But the truth was, I wasn't paying attention. Classic Josh! I just nodded in response. 'Nervous? It's all right to be nervous, you know.' He offered me a Polo from a roll he produced from his pocket. Matt always seemed to have something like this on him, as if the studio had told him I might be placated with weird British candy.

'I'm not nervous,' I assured him, but took a Polo anyway. What would I, Josh Sacco, have to be nervous about? I had practically grown up on a film set. My parents were some of the biggest producers in Hollywood. Sure, it was a big franchise, the biggest role of my career, but it wasn't like I was new to any of this.

But the truth was, I did feel nervous, for lots of reasons. One reason which made me burn up with shame was that I missed my parents and felt very alone in England under the care of Legacy Pictures. Look, now I can see that the idea of sending a fourteen-year-old child five and a half thousand miles away from home, without his parents, to do a job he was barely qualified for is insane. But at the time I thought it was my responsibility to just *man up* and get on with it, that any other kid would be psyched at the freedom, so I acted like it. And it's not like it wasn't fun, too. It was a lot of fun.

Another reason to feel nervous was precisely what Matt had already identified. I don't think the term *nepo baby* had been invented by the first Wonderwick film – thank God – but that's exactly what I was. Or . . . what I am. Either way, I knew that people on Wonderwick knew that my parents were not only big Hollywood producers, but were producing *this specific film* that I had been cast in. It felt like a heavy load to have to bring to set on the first day.

I had been on TV and movie sets before, of course, but they were *nothing* like this. Even the sound stages of Hollywood studio lots I had been on felt flimsy in comparison to the Wonderwick world that had been created at Smithdown. For us. And I was the male lead. No pressure.

Matt and I were greeted by a runner who gave us a whistle-stop tour of the set, introducing us to as many people as possible, from hair and makeup to carpenters to sound engineers to the background actors. It felt like every corner of every space contained someone working frenetically to get the project going.

Everyone I met at the studio that day was kind, friendly and professional, and I can't help but wish I had taken a leaf out of their books. But hey, what did I know? I was a teenager and simultaneously kind of an asshole and kind of terrified, all of which combined to really foreground the *asshole* side of things.

We stood outside one of the spaces next to the biggest sound stage that was being used as a green room until the trailers arrived and I could hear noises and curious banging sounds coming from inside.

'Well, that's the tour done. You want to chill for a bit? Do you need something to eat?' Matt asked me. I shook my head. 'I'm starving – you'll be all right on your own, won't you? I'll come back and pick you up to take you to wardrobe in, say, fifteen minutes?'

'Uh, no, I won't wander off. I'll be fine,' I told him but as soon as I walked in, I was almost knocked down by Max Rogers who had Tommy Wells in a headlock. Of course, at the time I didn't know they were Max and Tommy, to me they were just two boys fighting. One tall with a puff of dark blond hair and the other stockier, with thick dark eyebrows and a face that was kinda sweet.

'Woah!' I laughed, as they barrelled into me at great speed mid-wrestling-match.

They both looked up at me, panting. 'Sorry, mate! We were just trying to settle who gets the last doughnut,' Tommy said.

I frowned at them. 'I'm pretty sure there are more doughnuts at craft services, probably not worth fighting over.'

'Just a bit of fun, mate. I'm Max.' He grinned at me broadly while Tommy wrapped his arms around me and clapped me on my back so hard it felt like he was administering the Heimlich manoeuvre. 'And you're the famous Josh Sacco.'

'The Yank interloper.' Tommy released me and wiggled his eyebrows significantly.

'It's not that deep.' I tried to head off the topic of conversation with a casual wave of my hand but Max and Tommy wouldn't let it go.

'Oh yes it is! Sylvara Runequill was very clear about wanting an all-British cast for this and yet here you are snaffling up the male lead,' Max said.

'I guess I was just the right person for the job,' I said, a rush of anxiety in the pit of my stomach. I hoped *every* interaction with my fellow cast members wasn't going to be quite like this. Where were the naive little children who wanted to know all about life in Hollywood? Who were these bouncing, wrestling menaces? 'So, uh, are you two, like, old friends?'

'We actually met during auditions,' Max said, chewing on the doughnut, clearly the victor.

Just then, we were interrupted by another newcomer. Now *her* I recognised from the headshots I'd seen. Emily Montgomery. My co-star. Obviously, being separated by an ocean, we hadn't met in person during the casting process, and the video calls to check if we had 'chemistry' felt like a brief, tick-box exercise. Whether I liked it or not, Tommy was right: I was, indeed, the Yank interloper.

'Tommy and Max, the wig lady wants to see you two next,' Emily said in a bright, clipped, slightly bossy voice.

'Aye aye, captain.' Max saluted her and the two of them dashed off, leaving us alone in the green room. I took in my co-star, this girl with incredibly shiny, extremely straight brown hair, pale skin, eyes glinting at me curiously, one brown and one blue. She was wearing a truly bizarre outfit involving both a choker and cowboy boots which was strangely at odds with how otherwise refined and polished she seemed for a thirteen-year-old.

'You must be Emily,' I said, as confidently as I could manage.

She nodded. 'And you're Joshua.' The way she said it in her English accent made it sound like no version of my name I'd ever known.

'Josh, actually,' I corrected her. 'No one calls me Joshua, not even my mom.'

'Got it, I'm sorry,' she said, so seriously that it sounded like she wanted to take out a little notebook and write it down so she didn't forget.

And then silence fell. Without the lively energy of Tommy and Max to fill the room, it was like we were both standing there waiting for something to happen. We both looked down at our shoes or the bright white walls of the green room, as I desperately tried to think of something to say to her, this person I was going to be working with across several films for the rest of my teens and early twenties.

'So, which scene are you most excited about shooting?' Emily finally asked me. Although I was grateful she had broken the silence, I also found the question slightly excruciating.

'Uhhhh.' I furrowed my brow as if I was thinking deeply. Oh, yeah – that was another reason I was nervous. I kinda hadn't read the Wonderwick books. Outside of required reading, I'd never read any books growing up, we just weren't that kind of household. So not only was I not *completely* sure of my lines, often I would also not really understand the significance of something that was happening in the plot. Any proper fan would know it was a building block for something that would happen later, but not me. 'The scene where Rowan has to tell his whole family he's leaving to find the Heart of Wonderwick with Linderley. It's pretty emotional, but I think I can take it,' I said, feigning modesty but really I wanted her to be impressed that I was looking forward to taking on an emotional scene rather than one of the big action ones.

But no. She was not impressed. 'Isn't that the scene they had all the Rowan Clearwaters read for their audition?' Emily asked, keeping her tone light, but I could tell it was a very pointed question. This is a key Emily Montgomery trait. Not only does she always know what she's doing, she probably also knows what *you're* meant to be doing.

'I mean, sure.' I shrugged my shoulders. 'They just happened to pick my favourite scene from the script. I mean, from the book.' I had to hope the scene was actually in the books and hadn't been added by the screenwriter for the adaptation.

It was as if she could see right through me, and I hated every second of it. 'You *have* read the books, right?' She looked panicked.

'Of course I have, how could you even ask me that!' I was already starting to sweat under her laser beam gaze. What was with this girl?

She shook her head. 'I'm sorry, I didn't mean . . . I just want this film to be perfect. It's my favourite book, you know. I've dreamed of this since I was little . . . *being* in Wonderwick. I didn't know what that meant when I first had the thought, the idea of wanting to *be* in Wonderwick . . . I guess I thought of it in a sort of childish fantasy way, that one day I would wake up and I wouldn't be in my bed anymore but in a treehouse high off the ground, living in a forest with this group of friends who were kind of like a family but . . . now I guess it means being in this film.' Emily spoke with such sincerity and passion that it almost took my breath away. What would it feel like to care this much about a project? I couldn't imagine it. Of course I *wanted* to be there, wanted to do this movie, but for her it felt like it really meant something.

'That's cute,' I said, as dismissively as I could manage. I wanted to show her I was, I don't know, *cool* and that I didn't care and that caring was lame. Everything about this first meeting got my back up, and, let it be said once again, I was fourteen years old and even more of an asshole than I am now. 'But I'm just here to do a job.'

Emily looked wounded, which was exactly what I had hoped for. I needed her on the back foot so she didn't keep showing up how little I knew about Wonderwick. 'Well, if you . . . if you want to run lines or anything before we start shooting, just let me know.'

How did she know that was *exactly* what I needed and probably the last thing I would ever ask for? Look, if someone held a gun to my head that day, I promise you I would have known my lines. But I wouldn't necessarily have known the *context* for the lines or been able to recite them without a gun to my head. But we weren't starting filming that day, so I still had time. No big deal, right?

I sighed, obnoxiously. 'I'd better go. I've got a final fitting with the costume department,' I said. And then a thought occurred to me, a different way to put her in her place. 'But I see you've already been.' I side-eyed her outfit.

'And what's *that* supposed to mean?' Emily bit back, more sharply than I would ever have expected a girl in her position to do.

I puffed up my chest – probably – and affected an air of nonchalance. 'Oh, you mean this is just what you wear in everyday life? I thought you were going method, trying to get into character . . . inhabiting the role of Lindy Jones or something.'

'It's *Linderley*,' she said, rolling her eyes. She didn't try to fight back against what I had said, and before I knew it Matt had come to ferry me off to wardrobe, but when I looked back over my shoulder, I saw her looking down at herself, at her outfit, as if she was trying to figure out what she had got wrong.

That could have been the end of it, I could have apologised to her later that day or even the next. But for some reason, maybe because I was a teenage nepo baby from Beverly Hills, apologising didn't come naturally to me, so I didn't. And that interaction kinda set the tone for the next seven years.

Wonderwick Romance? Josh Sacco Seen Leaving Party With New Co-star Darcy Jackson

By Risha Logan for LondonNewsonline

No sooner was Darcy Jackson announced as a new cast member of the Wonderwick Woods film series than she was spotted leaving a party in the company of Josh Sacco. The pair, both twenty-two, attended the launch party for the new video game *Wonderwick Woods: Creatures of the Forest* in London, before leaving together in the same car. Jackson, daughter of Steven Jackson, lead singer of the Sweats, put to rest speculation that she would be cast as Loreia Buckthorn in *Wonderwick Woods: The Far Shores* when her role was announced earlier that day. Josh, son of Hollywood producers Rick and Amberlyn Sacco, was most recently linked to model and clean beauty entrepreneur Norah Mason, but their break-up was announced via Instagram story post a month ago. Jackson, known for her daring fashion, had already turned heads that evening in a leather two-piece from Gabi Moreno that showed off her enviable abs. Sources close to Sacco and Jackson refused to comment on whether they are in a relationship.

Chapter Nine

The 4.30 a.m. alarm came as an unwelcome intrusion, given I had only managed to get to sleep at three o'clock. It didn't matter how many times I'd done this, I would always feel so fizzy with nerves that I couldn't get any sleep the night before. I made myself as presentable and polished as possible, and at 5.15 a.m. looked out of the window to see a glossy black town car idling on the circular drive in front of my building. It was time to hit the road, and I struggled my two big suitcases out into the hallway. Finally, I made it outside where Mike was waiting for me. I couldn't help but smile at the sight of him, all big and hulking in a smart navy blue wool coat and leather driving gloves. There was something really rather *proper* about him.

'Hello, Mike,' I said, unable to contain my delight.

'Hello, stranger,' he said, opening the boot and heaving my suitcases in and grinning at me.

Once I was safely in the back seat, Mike looked at me in the rear-view mirror and asked, 'Where to, miss?'

'Smithdown Studios, silly,' I said, just like I said the first time we met seven years ago, outside my parents' house when my mum was still chaperoning me. Now, I was allowed to travel alone (despite my mum's best efforts), but the familiarity of Mike was like a warm blanket. Wonderwick had always tried to remain a tight and consistent team since the first film, and that extended to my driver.

'We're making a stop on the way, though, aren't we?' he asked as we set off, gliding along Prince Albert Road in the dark, the tiniest hint of dawn breaking through on the horizon.

'We are indeed!' I said, full of excitement at the prospect of picking up Carrie en route. I could get away with *not* having a Carrie, but if the studio was willing to pay for her, I would happily take an assistant. Chloe and Carrie were colleagues, but they were also my closest friends.

'Would you like me to put the radio on, Emily?'

'Yes, please,' I said, knowing without a shadow of a doubt that he was going to choose Classic FM.

He tapped a button on the screen without taking his eyes off the road, and the car was filled with the sound of violins.

At exactly the same time Mike asked me, 'Who's this?' I said, 'Verdi.'

'Am I that predictable?' Mike laughed.

'A little bit! But think of all the knowledge I've accumulated over the years!'

'This one was too easy, anyway. Let's see if we get anything more challenging.'

'I don't know if I'm up for challenging. I don't think my brain is working again yet.'

'You'll be back in the swing of things soon,' he reassured me. 'Anyway, I don't know if your brain has ever *stopped* working as long as I've known you. Seems like there's always something buzzing around in there.'

I smiled and looked out the window. He was right. There *was* always something buzzing around in there. Not least today.

I barely noticed we'd made it to Carrie's when we pulled up outside her flat, but the sight of her dragging her suitcase to the car with a huge grin on her face was enough to distract me from my thoughts for at least a few seconds.

'There she is!' Carrie drew me into an enthusiastic sideways hug in the back seat of the car as Mike rearranged the luggage in the boot. I inhaled the familiar scent of her perfume. 'Enough to make up for the ungodly hour. Not that I'm complaining! Film is all about the ungodly hours.'

Carrie had been my best friend at school, and it made me feel marginally more normal to have her around.

'Thank you for doing this,' I told her as we set off for Smithdown.

'As if,' she scoffed. 'Thank *you* for the work. Means I can postpone the post-graduation meltdown a little while longer.'

I felt a little twinge of jealousy at the word 'graduation'. It sounded so shiny and complete, the pinnacle of work and effort and real learning. I know I'm lucky to get to do this job, but I wondered if Carrie knew how lucky *she* was to have gone to university.

'Anyway, let's not waste time on my boring chat – what's going on in the wild world of Emily Montgomery?'

'Wild? Have you met me?'

'All right,' she conceded, 'maybe not wild but . . . glamorous?'

I sighed. 'Is it too early for you to have seen any of the stuff about Josh and Darcy?'

'What stuff?' Her eyes widened with intrigue.

'I don't know for sure yet what's going on, but the press are eating it up. There was this party last night for the video game and the studio sort of used it as Darcy's coming out party, she was wearing this really wild outfit and it felt like the whole party was for her, sort of. And then her and Josh left together.' I shrugged.

'Like *together* together?'

'Well, the paparazzi clearly thought so.'

'This is good, right? Building buzz for the film and all that?'

'Of course! It's really great timing! And the fans are going to love it, aren't they?' I said, a little too enthu-siastically.

Carrie eyes me with great scepticism. 'That didn't sound very convincing, Em . . . what's making you feel nervous here?'

'Am I really that bad at hiding it?'

'I mean, it helps that I know you, but . . . yeah, pretty bad. Talk to me?'

I covered my face with my hands and looked through my fingers at her. 'It's so embarrassing when I say it out loud.'

'Come on.'

'I guess I'm just scared of being replaced, you know?'

Carrie tilted her head to the side and narrowed her eyes at me. 'Emily, you're the lead, no one can replace you.'

'I know that's true in theory, but if everyone's been campaigning for Darcy to be in the films, and now she's in them, and then she's maybe going out with Josh, then it's basically giving the fans everything they want on a platter and I'm just this dusty old bore that they're stuck with in the lead role rather than this spicy and exciting new prospect.'

'First of all, you're not dusty, you're wearing new season YSL, and second of all, there's definitely room for both of you in this film. More than enough room.'

'In my head I know that's true but in my heart, I'm just feeling . . . pushed aside, somehow?'

Carrie thought for a moment, opening her mouth to say something then closing it again, her features arranging and rearranging themselves.

'What?' I asked her.

'Well, it's just . . . speaking of the heart, I mean, I just thought it was worth asking . . .'

'*What?*' Where was she going with this?

'It's not that you're jealous of the Josh thing, is it? I feel silly even asking it but, you know, just wanted to check so I definitely understand the situation.'

'The Josh thing?'

'Her going home with Josh, or whatever it was?'

'Am I jealous of that?'

'Yeah, I know it sounds crazy,' she said, shaking her head. 'I shouldn't have even asked. It makes no sense.'

I cleared my throat. 'No, it doesn't. Of course I'm not jealous.'

'OK, good, because I just thought maybe it's not just about Darcy being popular with the fans, but maybe about her being popular with Josh in particular.'

'Er, no,' I said flatly, my cheeks feeling hot with embarrassment.

'I mean,' Carrie said, her tone light, 'it would be completely OK if you fancied him. Lots of people do.'

'Fancy Josh?' I squinted at her, uncomprehending.

'Yeah, I mean, he may be annoying but he is also quite cute. That hair, those eyes, those cheekbones, that body . . .' she said, a little dreamily.

I knew this was what most people thought about Josh Sacco, but it was *not* what I thought about Josh Sacco. 'Absolutely not! He's a demon!'

'Cute demon,' Carrie murmured. 'Hot demon, even.' I thought Carrie's experience working on Wonderwick would give her a different perspective, I thought she understood what he was like! But no, she was just like all the girls mobbing Josh at events, taking sneaky pics of him skating topless on Venice Beach.

'No. This is absolutely not a thing,' I said, gesticulating wildly, keen to put an end to this.

'All right! If you say so!' Carrie said, defensively.

'I do say so.'

'And you're the boss. I mean, literally, you are my boss . . . so . . . yeah, not a thing.'

'I'm glad we agree on that,' I said, finally. 'But less of the boss stuff.'

'All right, boss,' she said with a sly smile.

I just rolled my eyes and looked out of the window. An awkward silence had descended upon the car that neither of us knew how to break. The jaunty Prokofiev tune coming through the speakers felt like it was mocking us. Was I blind to the fact that Josh had dark curly hair, deep brown eyes, a great bone structure and lifted weights every day? No. Did it change the fact he was a menace? No! To me, he was still the obnoxious American boy who turned up to the Wonderwick set completely unprepared, and not just because I chose to remember him like that, but because he literally still was that person. Sure, he had been a bit nice to me at the party last night but only because he wanted me to put in a good word with Edgar Malek about him. It didn't change the fact that we have a seven-year track record of finding each other irritating.

Finally, she broke the silence. 'I solemnly swear not to bring it up again.'

'Thank you,' I said, not wanting the whole shoot to feel awkward between us. 'I appreciate it.' I paused for a minute, trying to think of a way to make it clear I wasn't annoyed with her. I really wasn't, but my words often had this way of emerging from my mouth sounding sharper or harsher than I intended. 'And I appreciate you.'

'I appreciate you, boss,' she said, grinning. 'So, are you excited for this one?'

'I'm always excited to come back. It sort of feels like home to me.'

'You've probably spent more time there than you have in your actual home over the past seven years.'

'I'd hate to do the maths on that but you're probably right.' I grimaced.

Her eyes filled with delight. 'This one's even more exciting because of the—' she said, before abruptly cutting herself off.

'The what?' I frowned at her, before realising. 'Oh, you mean the kiss?'

'Yeah, but I thought after what we talked about you wouldn't want me to mention it.'

'That's different! That's just the film!'

'I know that! I just thought . . . I mean, how are you feeling about it?'

'I'd rather not do it, but like I said, it's acting, isn't it?' I nibbled the skin on my lip before remembering I was going to be on camera in only a day or so. It wouldn't be very Emily Montgomery to have flaky lips, now, would it?

'Maybe the kinda bad vibes between you will make the whole thing even hotter,' she said, almost breathless with enthusiasm.

'For the audience, you mean.'

She furrowed her brow. 'Yeah, of course. For the audience. Because there's obviously no way it could be hot for you.'

'No way,' I said, resolutely, shaking my head.

Because this kiss was not going to be hot, and I definitely didn't fancy Josh Sacco.

Chapter Ten

Arriving on the set of Wonderwick felt like coming home. I'd been here so many times and it never got any less exciting. Wonderwick took me out of school when I was in Year Nine but for me, the start of a new film felt like a new term after the summer holidays. Mike deposited us in the sprawling car park and it was time for the fun to begin.

Costume fittings, hair and makeup trials, chats with various heads of department, discussions about stunts, negotiations over where I would have to be at what time, what I wanted in my trailer, if I had any special requirements for catering . . . those were the last-minute things that would be taking place to prepare us all for *Wonderwick Woods: The Far Shores*.

But before I got too deep in pre-shoot prep, I couldn't help but swing by 'my house', just to check on it. Camila, the production designer, was a cinematic legend and her work on Wonderwick was some of her best, translating the style, the look, the feel of the books onto screen in such precise detail that it provoked gasps of delight in anyone who visited the set. The ramshackle under-ground cottage that Linderley Jones and her family lived in was as familiar to me as my own childhood bedroom. The heavy, dark, carved oak furniture, the wood-burning stove, the pantry lined with almost luminescent jars with cloth coverings for lids. Craggy walls with alcoves cut into them to serve as shelves, piles of firewood stacked on the floor. Cast iron pans (as replicated in a Wonder-wick merch collaboration with Le Creuset, a full set of which were sitting in one of the boxes in my flat) and hand-woven baskets hung from the ceiling, while piles of meticulously crafted fake vegetables were stowed away in little cubbyholes overhead, accessed by knob-bly wooden ladders. At the centre was a fire, often roar-ing and crackling in the films, but now quiet and cold, waiting to spring to life when needed. A cauldron was suspended above the empty hearth, and strung across the middle of the room was a washing line heavy with clothes in wool, cotton and linen. Everything here spoke of the natural world, of the raw hands of a worker, of rosy cheeks warmed by the fire. I knew every inch of it.

On the sound stage next door, I found my bedroom. Well, Linderley's bedroom. A room to inspire a thousand teenagers to go full cottagecore. I sat down on the ochre gingham bedspread (Wonderwick x Piglet in Bed – exclu-sive to John Lewis) covering sleigh-style bed and looked around. Dried flowers hung like bunting from the dark wooden rafters on the low ceiling, books towered in piles on shelves and on the flagstone floor, which between the books and the Turkish rug, was almost invisible.

'Thought I might find you here,' Courtney said, sitting down next to me on the bed. 'I was looking for you.'

'Oh?'

'Have you heard about the tattoo?'

I frowned at her. 'Whose tattoo?'

'Josh, of course, who else?'

'Oh no, what's he done?'

'*Massive* tattoo of a roaring lion on his left bicep. Basically covers the whole of his upper arm.' Courtney grimaced.

'That is *so* Josh Sacco. Has Pyotr had a meltdown?' Josh's makeup artist, Pyotr, was a highly strung Russian man with the sharpest eyebrows you'd ever seen. He would absolutely not appreciate this.

'Mini meltdown, apparently it's not quite as big a job as I thought it was going to be, but it's still half an hour's work *every day*.'

'Why would he do this?!'

'Because Josh Sacco. Act first, think later.'

I shook my head. 'Even by his standards this feels . . . impulsive.'

'Impulsive is his middle name.'

'It's actually Carmine, but, yes, exactly.'

'I'm happy I could be the one to break the news to you that Josh is causing trouble before we've even started shooting.'

'Thank you for giving me this gift,' I said, with a smile. 'But the thing is, I don't *want* it to be like this. I don't want to be proved right about him over and over again. Just once, I want him to surprise me by acting like he takes this job as seriously as I do.'

'Babe, no one takes it as seriously as you do.' Courtney nudged me. 'Anyway, gotta go, Wigmaster General wants to see me. I may have turned my hair into a tennis ball but that doesn't matter when you wear a wig! Zero extra work for anyone to deal with!' Courtney bounced off to the hair and makeup department, and I went off looking for Josh and the troublemaking tattoo.

Before I managed to locate him, Tommy and Max came barrelling into me at high speed. 'Josh's tattoo is fucking *sick*,' Max reported, eyes wide with enthusiasm.

'Yeah, you're gonna hate it!' Tommy chuckled.

'Give me a chance to see it first,' I sighed.

'He's that way.' Tommy pointed towards craft services, the area with an endless supply of food and drink for the cast and crew. Likely place for Josh to be if he was on set, but I have to say, I was surprised he *was* on set. I assumed he'd still be in bed.

As the two of them had informed me, Josh was in conversation with Jamila, one of the camera operators, by craft services. The way things are set up when we're filming in a studio means there are actually not that many places that actors – especially main cast like Josh and I – can really 'mingle' with crew or cast members who aren't our specific friends. We're always cocooned in our trailers, assistants bringing us our coffees, dressers bringing our costumes, hiding out in our heated E-Z UP tents between takes when there's not enough time to go back to our trailers. But *everyone* passes through craft services. It's just a catering tent, really, but it exists outside of normal mealtimes and you can get coffee or drinks or snacks or whatever. It's a good place to scope out what's going on in different departments or pick up gossip.

Josh glanced over his shoulder for a second and there I was, just staring at him like a creep. I looked away, pretending I was looking for something in my bag, rummaging long enough that by the time I looked back up he should be deep in conversation again but . . .

'Hey, Squirt.' He had instantly appeared by my side, his skin tinged with queasy grey and his eyes bleary and pink. Not quite the dashing male lead of Wonderwick just yet.

'Hello, Josh. A little worse for wear?'

'You could say that,' he said. 'I assume you stuck to water? Or are you more of a Shirley Temple girl? Remind me.' Despite the hangover, a sparkle appeared in his eye at the prospect of making fun of me.

'I had a drink. But I know when to stop if I have work the next day.' If he wanted to play the bad boy, I was perfectly happy to play the good girl.

Josh refused to take the bait. 'It was a fun party, huh?'

I felt a knot of anxiety form in my stomach thinking about last night, about the Darcy ambush, about all the feelings it stirred up in me, about her and Josh leaving together. 'Yes, it was nice to see everyone again.'

'You'll be sick of the sight of them in no time.' His voice was hoarse and his energy less exuberant than usual. He was chewing slowly on a pain au raisin, his square jaw working away at it. 'These are pretty good. I think they've changed catering companies.'

'I thought you swore by one of your mysterious green juices for a hangover?'

'Already had it. This is the main course, and then I'm going to go scrounging for dessert.'

'It's half past six in the morning, I don't know how you do it.'

'Where there's a will, there's a way, my friend. I thought I was going to die on the ride here, I had to have the window open the whole way and stick my head out like a dog.'

'And did you . . .' I said, nonchalantly. It was remarkable how hard acting could be when you were trying to do it in your own life rather than as a job. 'Did you come alone?'

A lazy smile crept across his face. 'Montgomery, what the hell kind of question is that?'

'I was just making conversation!' I said, as innocently as I could manage.

'Well you can nip *that* in the bud.'

'Oh?'

'You're as bad as the damn tabloids! Just because we left the party at the same time it doesn't mean we went home together. Anyway, why would it matter if we did?'

'It wouldn't! I assure you.'

'You're just being nosy, aren't ya?' He was definitely more lively now than at the beginning of the conversation. It seemed that my failed attempt to extract information from him was helping him shake off his hangover. 'Don't want anyone to know about *your* private life, whatever it may be, but you want to know all about your old pal Josh. Am I right?'

I was about to leap to my own defence when the sound of animated conversation punctured the room.

'Well, it's cold, so I don't know what to tell you,' came Darcy's voice. She was holding a coffee cup and speaking in that trademark drawl, which somehow managed to make it sound even more menacing, as if she had all the time in the world to toy with this junior employee.

'I'm s-s-sorry, Darcy,' stammered a runner who looked absolutely terrified.

'Either it was cold when you got it for me or you stood around chatting to your little friends for such a long time that it went cold. Which is it?'

'I'm . . .' She swallowed, trying to figure out the right answer. 'I'm sure it was hot when I poured it.'

'So you were just wasting time between getting it and bringing it to me? Is that right?' Her face was hard, her eyes narrow and sharp.

'No, no, it's not that!' the runner protested.

Other people had started tuning into the conversation by this point, eyes shifting towards the two of them.

'Aw, shit,' Josh muttered, shaking his head. Before I knew it, he was standing between the two of them. 'Say, Darcy, we can figure this out, can't we?' She looked at him, a hand on her hip. 'I'm sure there's a steaming new pot of coffee waiting for you on the table right now, and I'm sure . . .' He turned to the runner. 'What's your name?'

'Madison,' she whispered, awestruck by his intervention.

'I'm sure Madison didn't let it go cold on purpose, right?'

'Right.' Madison nodded like she was drowning and had just been thrown a life vest. 'I'll be really careful in future, I promise.'

'Well, that's great,' Josh said, before turning to Darcy. 'It's just coffee, right, Darce?' She looked taken aback, like she hadn't been expecting to be challenged.

'I guess,' she said, warily.

He clapped them both on the shoulder at the same time. 'Glad we cleared that one up!' Everyone resumed their conversations, and, blow-up averted, Josh came back to finish our conversation.

'She should get her own coffee if she's that bothered about it . . .' I said under my breath, not wanting to be the next person on the receiving end of Darcy.

'Oh, she's all right really.'

I rolled my eyes. 'Come on, it's day one and she's already bullying the runners. But you handled that pretty well.' I hated giving Josh any kind of compliment but it seemed like it might be due.

'Well, I know things can escalate when people go unchecked for too long,' he said with a knowing smile.

'Anyway,' I inhaled, ready to tackle the main event. 'Show it to me.'

'Awfully bold for so early in the morning,' Josh widened his eyes, pretending I meant . . . something else, which I most definitely did not mean.

'Josh! You know what I'm talking about,' I said, nodding in the direction of his left bicep while trying not to blush too deeply.

'Oh, you mean this little thing?' He grinned, yanking up the sleeve of his T-shirt to reveal, exactly as Courtney had described, a *huge* roaring lion head. 'Cool, huh?'

Whether I wanted to encourage him or not, I couldn't help but laugh at the sheer scale and audacity of the tattoo. This was the problem with Josh: he was like a naughty schoolboy, and even if he drove you insane, once in a while you just had to give it to him despite yourself. 'Josh! It's enormous!'

'That's what she said,' he quipped, pulling his sleeve down again, and I rolled my eyes.

'What possessed you to do it?'

'It looks sick as hell, and don't you pretend it doesn't, Squirt.'

Just then, we were interrupted by Carrie tapping me on the shoulder. 'Juliet wants you in makeup.'

'Juliet?' I frowned at her. 'Juliet isn't my makeup artist. I've always had Edith.' I would assume that Carrie had made a mistake but this wasn't the kind of mistake Carrie would make.

'I'm sorry,' she said, swallowing. 'I don't know what to tell you other than that Juliet is asking for you.'

'No, of course.' I said before heading off to the hair and makeup department.

'See ya around.' Josh nodded at me before throwing the last of his pastry into his mouth and catching it like a performing seal.

I made my way to the hair and makeup department, a sense of unease in my chest and any amusement over Josh's tattoo quickly evaporating as I heard footsteps approaching me around a corner from the opposite direction. I knew before she even turned the corner that it would be—

'Oh, hey,' Darcy drawled.

'Hi again,' I said, trying to keep the nerves out of my voice.

'Wait, did we . . . ?' She squinted at me through bloodshot, hungover eyes.

'We met last night at the party,' I reminded her.

'Oh, sure, of course we did,' she said with a throaty laugh. 'I have a memory like a sieve.'

I shrugged. 'No problem. I guess we'll be seeing a lot of each other.'

'You're in a house, right? Not in the hotel?' she asked, referring to the division between 'main cast' who get provided with private houses in the surrounding towns and villages, and the rest of the cast and crew who get put up in a hotel.

'I'm in a house,' I said slowly, frowning with confusion. It was as if she didn't quite realise I was the lead and I didn't know how to tell her.

'Oh, cool, I'm in Winterbrook but I don't really know where that is . . . I'm not up on my British geography.'

'It's pretty close to here. I was in a house there on the second film. This year I'm in Gables Cross.'

She shrugged. 'I have no idea where that is. But if it's close, we should all hang out. Find one of your cosy British pubs to drink in. It doesn't seem fair the rest of the guys in the hotel get to have fun while we're all separated, you know?'

'Right.' I nodded.

'Or are you not much of a boozer?' Darcy asked, narrowing her eyes at me curiously.

'No, I'm happy to have a drink, any time!' I said, brightly, knowing I need to befriend this girl. 'Well, I'd better get going. I'm due in hair and makeup.'

'I just came from there. Edith's a sweetheart, isn't she?'

'She's the best,' I said, a fierce sensation of possessiveness clutching at my heart.

'See you around.' Darcy raised a hand, the huge cuff of her oversized shirt so big that you could only see the tips of her fingers.

As soon as Edith saw me, she drew me into a warm, tight hug.

She held me at arm's length, looking me over. 'More beautiful than ever. My little dolly. Well—' she looked at the ground '—not my little dolly anymore. I can't believe I'm losing you to Juliet. Not that she's not great at her job – she is – I'm just going to miss you and those lovely eyes.'

'What?' My stomach dropped.

'Look, my love, it wasn't my decision. She needs a lot more makeup than you, so it was decided I would do it.'

'Who does?' I asked, even though I knew the answer.

'Darcy Jackson,' Edith said, raising her eyebrows significantly. 'The great disruptor.'

'Of course,' I said, quietly.

'Well, Loreia's makeup is a lot more elaborate than Linderley's. Either way, that's how we're doing it. I'm sorry, Emily, I loved being your makeup artist. It felt like such a calm way to start the day, just you in my chair before the chaos of the set,' she said, looking genuinely pained. 'It'll just be for this film, I'm sure of it. Anyway, Juliet is wonderful, I taught her everything she knows. '

'No, of course, I completely understand,' I said, flipping into professional mode. No feelings allowed.

'It makes sense. I hope you enjoy working with Darcy, too, Edith.'

She drew me into another hug, which made it feel like we were wrapping, rather than the first day of a new film. When she released me, she cocked her head to the side where Juliet was waiting for me and said, 'Suppose it's time to hand you over.'

I nodded, and put on my best brave face at losing the principal makeup artist. Juliet was delightful, warm and inviting, and between her, Alessandro the wig master, and George, my hair stylist, we went over the plan for this film. They all talked around me, everyone buzzing with ideas and excitement but I just sat in the chair and looked at my reflection in the brightly lit mirror, thinking, *You were right. Darcy is bad news.*

Chapter Eleven

By the time Mike drove me back to the house that night, my brain felt completely frazzled. This was already feeling like a *very* tumultuous shoot and it hadn't even started.

'Sorry.' I shook my head. 'I'm not really in the zone this evening, am I?'

He looked at me in the rear-view mirror. 'You've had a busy day, I don't blame you for being a bit quiet. It'll be nice to have some time to yourself this evening.'

'It'll be wonderful,' I said, dreamily, picturing the quiet of the house, unpacking my suitcases which got deposited there this morning, cooking something delicious with the provisions the studio supplied. As we pulled into the drive, I could see the lights were on downstairs. 'That's strange.'

'I must have left them on when I dropped off your cases.' Mike frowned. 'Not very environmentally friendly of me . . . they've got me driving this electric car and I'm still leaving the lights on!'

'It's all right,' I said, hopping out of the car. 'See you in the morning!'

'You have a restful evening, Emily, and I'll see you tomorrow.'

'I will!' I kept my tone bright but the truth was, I was already getting a sinking feeling about why the lights were on, and as I approached the door, the noise from inside only made matters worse. Refusing to ring the doorbell to my own (albeit temporary) home, I opened the key safe with the code the studio had emailed me, finding only one of two sets of keys in there. I let out an involuntary sigh and let myself in.

'She's home!' my dad called at the sound of the door closing behind me and within seconds my mum swooped down on me.

'Hello, darling! How was it?' she asked, but before I could answer, she gestured around the hallway of the house. 'This is nice, isn't it?! Even bigger than the last one!'

'Only the best for our Ems, isn't that right?' Dad beamed and squeezed me himself.

'Did you let yourselves in with the spare key?' I asked, trying not to sound annoyed. I'll admit it: I had historically struggled to set boundaries with my parents, but this time I hadn't even had the *chance* to set them. I didn't even know that this was a boundary I needed to enforce; ask before inviting yourselves in?.

'Yes, love, I'm still copied on some of your emails from the studio so I had the code! We thought we would surprise you on your first night in the house!' Mum looked at me and her expression drops. 'Why, aren't you happy to see us?'

Of course I should be happy to see them! They're my parents! But gosh was I looking forward to some alone time.

'I bloody told you we should check with her first, didn't I?' Dad said before I could reply, nudging Mum with his elbow.

'I thought it would be a nice surprise! I didn't know we weren't wanted,' Mum said, tightly.

'It's not that! I'm just tired and I don't want to be disappointing company.' That seemed to be enough to satisfy her.

'Oh, you could never disappoint us, darling!' The pressure of being an only child was at least doubled in my case by being not just an only child, but an only child who had achieved something most parents could only dream of. It could be a bit much sometimes.

Over dinner, Mum cut straight to the chase.

'Have they told you anything more about this kiss?' she asked.

'No, but I'm sure it's all under control. It doesn't change the script I have. I think we're filming it towards the end of the shoot.' The thought of it made me feel a little queasy with nerves, knowing the added pressure I felt to make it 'spicy' enough, to justify my place in the Wonderwick Universe, to show that I wasn't just a chaste, stuck-up actress playing a chaste, stuck-up character. I could be sexy, too.

'So there's still time to get Glen to sort it out? Get them to keep it like it is in the book?'

'I've been thinking about it and I don't know if that's totally necessary,' I said, calmly. 'It might be good for the film . . . and for me, too.'

'You don't want to be giving yourself away like that, do you?' She looked aghast.

'Mum, it's hardly like I'm doing full-frontal nudity,' I laughed. It was like she couldn't see that her stressing out about it would only make *me* stress out about it, rather than reassure me that it was all going to be just fine, nothing scary or out of my comfort zone.

'Hmmm, well, give these Hollywood types an inch and they take a mile, that's what I say.'

'I'm not going to do anything I don't feel comfortable with,' I reassured her.

''Course she's not, Ruth. She's a big girl, she can make her own decisions,' Dad piped up.

'You've changed your tune!' Mum scoffed. 'It wasn't two weeks ago that you were trying to persuade her what project to do next.' She was right, of course.

'So you're gonna do that Irish film, then?' Dad asked, shaking his head but smiling at the same time.

'I'm sorry, Dad, I just can't do . . .' I swallowed, the name of the film almost too stupid to say out loud. '*Dinky Daffy and the Detective Squad*. I need something a bit more challenging next. And anyway, I really don't think I would pass for sixteen.'

'They clearly thought you would! Didn't hear any objections from that casting director!'

'I know . . . but the main reason is that I want to try something different.'

'I don't understand what's wrong with doing more of what you're already good at,' Mum said.

'Maybe I want to find out what else I could be good at?' I offered, hopefully.

'It's your decision, Ems, it's always your decision. I was just telling you what I thought would be the most lucrative, you know? Of course I think you should be chasing the big Hollywood money! Then you can retire when you're twenty-five,' he said with a wink. This was always his grand desire for me – that I manage my money in a way that means I can *retire at twenty-five*. He was a financial adviser, so spent all his time thinking about other people's money, including mine.

'I like my work! I'm not looking for a way out!' I protested.

'Anyway.' Mum leaned in, conspiratorially. 'What's that Darcy Jackson like?'

I swallowed, trying not to let my anxieties around her show, even to my parents. 'She's nice enough.'

Mum wrinkled her nose. 'She doesn't seem like a very *serious* actress, does she?'

'Bloody LA socialites,' Dad chipped in.

'I guess if the producers think she's up for it, then she must be.'

'Or her dad leaned on them,' Mum suggests. 'We know that's how things get done in Hollywood.'

'Well, I have to work with her, so I should probably try to be her friend. Not that we have much in common, but . . .' It was then I noticed that both my parents were sipping from wine glasses. 'Which one of you is going to drive home?' It wasn't the longest drive in the world but it was already getting late.

They looked at each other and then back at me.

'Well, we were thinking we would stay here and keep you company on your first night. It's such a big house and you're here all on your own,' Mum said. I couldn't muster the energy to fight them, and realistically there was no way they were going to be leaving now. 'I've made up the bed in the room opposite the master bedroom.' Well, that was that then. A sleepover with my parents.

'All right,' I said, trying not to sound too weary. 'Thank you for making dinner.'

'You know, I can stay longer if you want me to,' Mum said, expectantly. 'Just because Dad has to go to work, doesn't mean I have to leave.'

'I think it's probably better if I just focus on the job for now, Mum.' I tried to give her a reassuring smile. 'Mike's picking me up early again tomorrow so I might not see you when I wake up.'

But she was determined to give it one more shot. 'And you're quite sure you don't want me to come along tomorrow?'

I looked at her, my eyes pleading. 'It's my workplace . . . it's the first day of shooting . . . I'm an adult?' I said, slightly disbelieving I had to say it at all.

'No, no, of course.'

I instantly felt terrible but I couldn't back down, otherwise they would just move in here full time and I would never be able to grow up.

'I'm going to unpack . . . don't want to be living out of suitcases for the whole shoot,' I said, standing up from the table, not looking either of them in the eye. No matter how lightly I tried to tread on the stairs, as I headed to my room I still had the sensation of being a sulky teenager.

I set about unpacking my suitcases, hanging my clothes in the wardrobes, filling drawers, trying to make the place look a bit more homely. My mum was right, the house was big, and part of me wondered what it would be like living here all alone for the duration of the shoot. Well, I certainly wasn't going to find out tonight. Finally, I flopped on the bed, which had already been made for me, and wondered if I should go back downstairs. Instead, I unzipped my suitcase and extracted a book, a classic Swedish thriller the second assistant director Maria had recommended to me on the last Wonderwick film. I read a few pages and was instantly sucked in, and before I knew it an hour had gone by. I took out my phone to WhatsApp Maria and tell her how much I was enjoying it, then got sucked into Instagram and started scrolling, idly clicking on Max's Close Friends story. One minute ago he had posted a video so noisy my thumb instinctively found the 'volume down' button, and once I had got over the audio assault on my ears, I realised what I was looking at.

Max, Tommy, Josh, Courtney and Darcy were at a bar in Shoreditch. Together. Without me.

While I was hiding from my parents in my bedroom, my colleagues were out partying. I mean, really, have you heard of anything more pathetic? I was clearly considered so boring and uptight that they didn't even think to ask me if I wanted to go. I was twenty years old! I should have been out with them! God! This was the worst, the absolute worst. Things needed to change around here. I mean, I know I said all I wanted was a quiet night at home to decompress, but if the choice was between feeling like the resident goody two-shoes and having to dance on a table in a club, I think I had reached the point where I'd choose dancing on the table.

The truth was, I felt like I had been forced into a role I had never really agreed to. I mean, yes, I loved to be prepared, I loved to work hard, I loved to learn and read and do things properly, and yes, I liked the people around me to take things as seriously as I did, but . . . there was surely more to me than that? At least, I thought there was. How could I shake off this image? How could I break out of this role that I'd ended up in? I never auditioned for this.

Just then, there was a knock at my bedroom door. 'Em?' my dad's voice called from outside.

'Come in,' I shouted back, throwing my phone onto the bed.

'I just wanted to say goodnight before we turn in.' He smiled. 'Sorry for . . . you know . . . I think we thought it would be nice . . .' He looked a little sheepish and I instantly felt terrible for being ungrateful. And yet! They still should not have let themselves into my house!

'It was nice,' I reassured him. 'I'm sorry, I'm just figuring things out at the moment and maybe one of those things is . . .' How could I even explain it? 'Doesn't matter.' I shook my head.

Dad lingered by the door, and I could tell he had something on his mind. 'There was just one more thing,' he said. 'You're all right if I move some money around, aren't you? Just temporarily? I mean, you're not short at the moment?'

'No, that's fine.' I shrugged. 'What's it for?'

'Interesting-looking new fund that I've got a couple of clients to invest in. Thought I might as well see what happens with some of your money too?'

'Sure!' I said, brightly, trying to make up for the lukewarm reception to my parents coming over.

'Great, you're a star. Night night, my darling girl.'

'Night, night, Dad.'

I lay in bed, trying to sleep but finding my brain whirring away, trying to problem-solve, figure out what

I needed to do. Eventually the tossing and turning got too much and I took out my phone.

'Emily?' Chloe said, urgently when she picked up. 'Are you all right?'

'I'm fine!' I said, realising the time was verging on the antisocial. 'Sorry, I know it's late.'

'For you it is! Not for me, don't worry about that. What's up?'

'I'm wondering if I should try to be a bit more . . . I don't know, adventurous?'

'OK,' she said, slowly, trying to interpret me.

'I just wonder if I'm getting a bit . . . stale, you know? Clothes, boys, partying, all that.'

'Emily!' she chided me. 'Don't be silly.'

'I'm not! I'm serious. I don't mean anything crazy, but . . . maybe something to keep me a bit fresh in the way people see me?'

She thought for a moment. 'Well, I'm sure there are lots of boys that would gnaw their arm off to go out with you. I bet I can think of someone for a strategic alliance, shall we say.'

'Like a showmance?'

'Exactly! It's nothing serious, and obviously we'd make sure you liked each other, but that could be something to keep you in the public eye, right? Boost your profile outside of Wonderwick?'

I was nervous, but just about desperate to give it a go. 'Sure, I trust you.'

'Phenomenal! I love playing matchmaker! Leave it with me, I'll come up with a sexy little list for you! Emily, you are truly full of surprises. Anyway, you feeling OK about shooting tomorrow? Everything under control?'

I didn't have the heart to tell her that this exact conversation was a product of me feeling that everything was *not* under control. 'Totally,' I said. 'I'll let you go. I suppose I should be getting some sleep.'

'Leave it with me. You've got a big day ahead!'

And didn't I know it.

Chapter Twelve

The cavernous sound stage at Smithdown Studios was electric with activity. The sound of hammers driving the final nails into one of the new treetop sets, the speed with which various black-clad headset-wearing professionals dashed between sound gear and scaffolding. Everything felt possible. And more importantly, I was prepared. Not for the kiss. I still wasn't prepared for *that*. But in every other way, I was ready to go.

I'd arrived bright and early that morning and headed straight for craft services to pick up something to eat, crossing paths with Martin the director en route who boomed an enthusiastic, 'Morning, Ems!' at me.

As I milled around the table, trying to detect the juiciest orange in the pile, I tuned into the conversation going on between two of the costume team.

'Oh, but she's *so* gorgeous, isn't she? So striking.' I knew instantly who they had to be talking about. I held my breath and stood very still, hoping they wouldn't notice me.

'Stunning, utterly stunning. I can't believe they actually got her. I hear she's being paid an absolute bomb, nearly as much as Josh and Emily.'

'She really brings *something*, doesn't she? A bit of excitement.'

God, was this going to be my life now? Overhearing endless conversations about how gorgeous and thrilling Darcy Jackson was?

'I suppose you have to be gorgeous and exciting if you have an attitude like *that* . . .'

I craned my neck, desperate to hear more but they'd already headed off back to the costume department. I returned to my trailer to eat my orange in peace, feeling the magic of the day slightly dampened by the presence of Darcy. The basketball hoop that Josh had installed outside his trailer on *Wonderwick Woods: Beyond the Forest* was already seeing some action, two of the props guys taking turns to take a shot. He'd found the endless sitting around too much to bear, and the games of cards weren't quite enough to stimulate him, so he'd installed the hoop and a small gym in his trailer.

My trailer was clean, tidy and peaceful, filled with my favourite candle that smelled of warm cashmere and vanilla. I could shower after my runs, I could prep in there until it was time to get to work and on breaks it was the perfect place to curl up with a book. Wow. I really am the on-set party animal.

The first scene we were shooting was a busy crowd scene using one of my favourite sets. I knew it wasn't *real* of course, but just like the ramshackle Jones house, the Canopy Plaza was a pure delight to behold. On the first film, I had no idea how the production designer and the set builders had managed to create something so utterly magic, and how the visual effects team had made it even more extraordinary in post-production. Although my character, Linderley, was a ground-dweller, Josh's character, Rowan, lived in the treetop society. At the heart of their world was the huge Canopy Plaza, part of the sprawling treetop habitat connected by wide, swaying, vine-laden bridges. No detail was left out of the design, and I always looked forward to shooting the treetop festivals, market trading or important information-gathering meetings that would take place there.

We were trying to shoot a tracking shot that went from a bird's-eye view of the Plaza in peak festival mode, getting closer and closer in until it found Linderley and Rowan in covert conversation with a trader who had heard from a travelling salesman that Lord Thorn's daughter Loreia Buckthorn had ascended to power in their kingdom and was hell-bent on revenge for her father's death. The default setting of the Canopy Plaza was already a visual delight: strewn with beautiful hanging paper lanterns in gently glowing shades of red, orange and yellow, while streamers made from shimmering leaves draped down from the highest branches and tree-dwellers crowded around huge communal tables made from giant slabs of polished wood. Because the scene took place during a festival, it looked even more amazing than usual, turning into a bustling bazaar where vendors sold magically floating candles, enchanted wind chimes that could play a different song in the breeze to match the mood of their owner, carved wooden toys that seemed to come to life in a child's hand. Acrobats swung from branch to branch, as below them musicians played ocarinas and wooden drums as tree-dwellers met in merriment at the festival, drinking from elaborately carved wooden chalices and dancing across the skybridges.

All of which is to say, not only was it wonderful to look at but it took a *lot* of coordination. A lot of background artists (or extras) were required to fill out the scene, all of whom were now loitering in the E-Z UP tents that actors waited in between takes, decked out in their tree-dweller attire.

Finally, I was summoned by Jonas, the first assistant director, who basically ran the show. Josh was already sitting at the corner of the polished wood table, and did not look at all well. He smelled of stale cigarettes, which fortunately wouldn't be a problem for the cinema audience but *was* a problem for me.

He nodded at me in greeting. 'What's up,' he croaked out.

'Hungover?' I asked.

'Uh, maybe just a little,' Josh said with an irritating smirk, his white teeth glinting in a lopsided smile. 'Been having too much fun.'

Before I could ask if the fun was with Darcy or a different girl altogether, Humphrey Attleborough plonked himself down in his seat to complete the trio of us that would have dialogue in this scene.

'Greetings, old friends!' he boomed at us. A rotund mid-fifties actor in a collarless hemp shirt with wooden buttons and billowing trousers, Humphrey played Hornbeam, who often acted as a conduit for news between Wonderwick Woods and further afield.

'Hey, Humph.' Josh slapped him on the back in greeting.

'Hello, Humphrey!' I rose to hug him and no sooner had I sat back down than Juliet, my new makeup artist, was re-powdering my jawline and one of the costume team was checking Humphrey's shoulder for makeup marks, which of course I knew better than to leave.

'Ready and raring to go? Prrrrimed to hear the terrible news from beyond the kingdom?' he asked, rolling his rs in that theatre actor way that had made him a national treasure. The dresser placed a pair of round glasses on his face, and he became the Hornbeam I'd known since the original film.

'I certainly am!' I said, gamely, while Josh just gestured his hand in a *could go either way* motion. He was bleary-eyed and I desperately hoped he would magically snap out of it when we started shooting.

'Has someone been imbibing too abundantly? Naughty, naughty boy!'

Checks and then final checks were called, and finally, the sound I had been waiting for: Jonas called action. Above us, cameras moved in an elaborate dance, gliding elegantly to create the bird's-eye effect, weaving their way down into the Canopy Plaza, through thronging crowds eating, drinking and being merry, then following a barmaid carrying a tray of drinks towards the table, finally settling on the group of three hunched at the end.

'Hornbeam, you're sure?' I breathlessly delivered my first line of the shoot.

'Have I ever been wrong before?' Humphrey replied in his sonorous voice, leaning forward conspiratorially.

'Then we need to start preparing for a fight,' Josh said, pounding his fist on the table. The only problem was, that wasn't the next line.

'Cut!' Jonas called, wearily.

'What did I do?' Josh asked, bewildered.

'There are at least two lines before you say that,' I sighed. 'You're *meant* to say "And this isn't just some ground-dwellers causing trouble – no offence, Linderley" and then Hornbeam says, "I heard it from the most reliable source, I assure you," and then you say the line about the fight.'

Josh's cheeks flushed.

'Need a spot of the hair of the dog, old boy?' Humphrey nudged him, producing a hip flask from his trouser pocket.

'I wouldn't say no.' Josh swigged from it. 'Just this once,' he added, seeing my expression. Everything was reset, and we tried again.

'Hornbeam, you're sure?'

'Have I ever been wrong before?' We delivered the lines identically to the last take. All we needed was Josh to—

'And you didn't hear this from some ground-dweller, right?'

'Cut!' Day one and Jonas's patience was already wearing thin.

'Shit, sorry, I know, I know.' Josh shook his head in irritation as the shot was reset around us. The extras were talking amongst themselves, shooting glances in our direction.

'Josh, get it together,' I hissed at him while Humphrey had his wig adjusted. I didn't need everyone else to hear it but I needed Josh to hear it. I couldn't let today set the tone for how Josh was going to behave for the rest of the shoot. He took up too much oxygen on set as it was, and I couldn't live like this for the next three months. I didn't want to be counting down the days on what was meant to be my dream job. 'You can't keep turning up to set hungover! It's embarrassing! And you're making work for people who already have more than enough to do!'

'Christ, Emily, you're not my mom, you're not Martin, you don't need to always be riding me so hard,' Josh said, exasperated.

A hot wave of embarrassment swept over me. I was doing the same old stuff I would *always* do. It was hard to remember I was meant to be trying out a whole new easy-going persona on this film when Josh was messing around like this.

'OK, I'm sorry,' I muttered, not looking him in the eye.

'You just make things worse, you know? I feel stressed as shit knowing you're judging me the whole time. Maybe if I didn't feel like I was under a microscope all the time I wouldn't make so many mistakes.'

This was too much. 'How is this on me? This is *your* mistake. And anyway, I'm not *judging* you, Josh, I'm just asking you to learn your lines! It's the bare minimum!'

'All right, all right, whatever.' He shook his head, dismissively. 'Let's go again.'

Jonas made sure the shot was properly reset, and we went again. Finally he got the line right, but that was just the beginning of having to shoot and reshoot the usual eight or nine or even twelve times. Such a lot of work for such short snatches of film. By the time we were finished, everyone seemed exhausted.

Maria, the second assistant director whose job it was to coordinate the production schedule, was striding towards us with the next day's schedule.

'Change of plan,' she said, handing us each a call sheet. 'We'd originally planned to shoot the river scene next week but the forecast is fucking abysmal and the next two days seem like our best bet so we need to switch things around. From tomorrow, we're on location.'

'Got it.' I nodded, resolutely.

Thanks to the reliably unpredictable British weather, the production would rearrange itself to accommodate the elements. So much of Wonderwick was filmed indoors with meticulously calibrated lighting to give the effect of being outside, but there were still several key scenes that had to take place outdoors. The iconic sets like the Great Archive, the High Council's Sky Lodge, Linderley's house and the Canopy Plaza were possible, if not easy, to replicate on huge sound stages but the river less so. Fortunately, there was only one scene in this film that took place there, but that could still mean multiple days of filming.

Josh looked a little flustered. 'Uh, all right,' he said, looking down at the call sheet, something he was not known to do habitually. 'See you there.' He gave her a charming, roguish smile but I knew him and I could see right through him: he was going to have to spend the evening learning lines for a different scene.

The first day had been so exhausting I almost fell asleep in the car back to the house.

'If you don't mind my saying so, you look shattered,' Mike said, looking at me in the rear-view mirror.

'I feel it,' I said with a weak smile. 'But it always feels like a silly thing to complain about. So many people would kill to be where I am now. Oh, and we're going on location tomorrow, did they tell you?'

'All under control, don't you worry about that. It's out near your parents, isn't it?'

'Yes, in that sort of direction.' I was faintly troubled by the implication that maybe I should go and see them after we wrap tomorrow, or even stay there overnight.

We sat in silence for a moment, before Mike said, 'It'll get easier. It's always strange at first but everything sorts itself out, every film.'

I smiled. He was right. Surely this was just first-day teething problems, right?

Wrong.

Chapter Thirteen

The afternoon sun drenched the riverside in a golden glow, the autumnal leaves looking almost fake in their perfection. The light danced off the deep but slow-moving river to create a sight so magic it could have been plucked straight from Wonderwick itself. That is, if you were to overlook the abundance of E-Z UP tents, lighting technicians, grips, gaffers, camera operators, PAs, sound technicians, set dressers, costumiers and many, many more people buzzing around the set. It was only a short scene, Linderley and Rowan, separated from the rest of the group, trying to find a way to cross the river once Loreia Buckthorn has destroyed the bridge. We'd shot scenes with Darcy the day before, but today it was just Josh and me. The problem was, we were time-limited, only being here for two days and yesterday things had, as always, taken longer than expected.

'All right people, let's get things going,' Martin called.

Josh and I went over lines as the final checks were being carried out around us. Josh proving that he had come prepared and wanting to get the scene right was surely an improvement on how things had been going so far. It wasn't a complicated scene, just the two of us going back and forth on our strategy as we stood on the outskirts of the forest, daunted by the river in front of us. The previous day, which had gone without a hitch bar Darcy insisting on incessant cigarette breaks, had involved a much more labour-intensive action sequence with special effects green dots. This should have been a walk in the park by comparison.

'Action!' Jonas shouted, and we shot some takes on the banks of the river, delivering our lines with various intonations, levels of urgency, the usual. After a few takes, they needed to reset the lighting as the sun was starting to set. It was too far for us to go back to the unit base, so we were whisked off to an E-Z UP tent complete with heater to keep us warm while we waited.

Josh was leaning back in a folding chair, his legs sprawled out in front of him. 'Don't you think the scene is kind of static?' He took a swig from a bottle of water.

'What do you mean, static?'

'I don't know, kinda boring? Don't you think we should add a bit of movement? A bit of dynamism?'

'Can't we just keep doing it the way it's written?' I sighed. This was very Josh, acting on impulse and expecting everyone else to go along for the ride.

'Fine.' He shrugged, dragging the tip of his beaten-up brown leather Rowan Clearwater boot across the bottom of the tent. 'But don't you think we've done enough takes your way? Now we can try it my way and see what ends up in the final edit.'

'It's not a competition.' I couldn't help rolling my eyes.

'Maybe not to you, Squirt.' Josh nudged me with his elbow, grinning.

'Right.' Maria stuck her head into the E-Z Up. 'We're ready for you.'

Josh and I were herded back to the riverside, lighting reset, our faces powdered, everything under control for another few takes of the same section of script we'd just been shooting.

Once again, Jonas called action, and we were off.

'There must be a way!' I called out to Josh, delivering the first line.

'I know,' he said, but instead of looking out across the river, brow furrowed, hands on hips, he started to prowl the bank. 'It's just a question—' he started stepping on stones, testing the water '—of finding it.'

'We might not be able to cross it but a horse certainly could,' I said, for the seventh time that day, trying to infuse it with the same sense of urgency I had given it on the first take.

'You're right!' Josh turned to face me, about to deliver his next line, but with all of his moving about he had ended up with one foot on a perfectly smooth stone.

It might as well have been a banana peel.

No sooner had Josh's foot slipped on the rock, he instinctively reached out to me for balance, and right then, all the momentum transferred from me to him, Josh now upright on a much more even patch of grass (precisely where he should have been in the first place) and me losing my footing. But I didn't grab onto Josh. Instead, I fell backwards. Straight into the river.

The shock of falling, of hitting the water, made me gasp, filling my mouth with water. I was only underneath for a moment but that was enough to leave me coughing, spluttering, desperate for air when I resurfaced, furious, a second later. Thank goodness I had the presence of mind to tread water, because I was seriously out of my depth. As I pedalled my legs and pushed myself towards a big, stable-looking tree root to hold on to, the fury built in me that I had been humiliated and, frankly, endangered like this all because of Josh.

I felt a hand reach down towards mine and when I looked up, there he was. Josh. All of his workouts paid off as he pulled me out of the water with relative ease, leaving me drenched and furious, the crew all surging towards us, calls being made to the medic tent, calls being made to I don't know who. And was that . . . my mother? Surely not. I didn't have time to wonder, anyway. I needed to give Josh a piece of my mind.

'I can't live like this anymore, Josh! I don't understand how I'm meant to work with you when you're so committed to just doing your own thing, marching off down your own path, shooting scenes how *you* think they should be done. At some point every day for the past seven years on set you have made me feel like a bore or an idiot when all I'm doing is my job, while you're always bringing some new scheme or plan to mess with the perfectly good work everyone else is doing. You're lazy, you're immature, you have absolutely no integrity and I'm sick of it.' I glared at him with white-hot fury, waiting for him to laugh in my face. All around me was quiet, everyone having realised that something juicy was happening, that I wasn't in immediate danger and the medic could wait. When I finished speaking, quiet murmurs broke out among the crew, but Josh just looked at me, bewildered. So much for all my resolutions to be more exciting or sexy or cool or fun.

'Emily,' Carrie said, bundling me into a huge blanket. 'Let's get you back to the trailer, OK?' I turned back and looked at Josh. He was still standing there, trying to figure out what had just happened.

'All right,' I said, starting to shake with the adrenaline.

'Darling!' came my mum's voice. So she *was* there. I couldn't deal with any of this right now.

It wouldn't be so bad if it was the first time it had happened. But it wasn't.

JOSH

OK, so the problem with me fucking up on set is that it wasn't exactly my first rodeo. And it wasn't the first time Emily had been the one on the receiving end of my mischief. I had, shall we say, *form*. Now I was old enough to know better, but the first time? I was still a stupid kid. It went something like this:

We were close to the end of the third movie, *Wonderwick Woods: Into the Shadow Realm*. The set was dark as the night, the dry ice was swirling to make it all extra atmospheric, the only illumination was a huge fake moon that broke through the branches of the fake forest. We were ready to shoot one of the final scenes, where we're alone in Wonderwick Woods with God knows what creatures lying in wait to ensnare us, and we're equipped only with swords. They were these huge wooden things that had been given to Rowan and Linderley by one of the forest mages. They were props, of course; there was no reason to give us real ones – both as actors and as actual children, the highest standards of health and safety are always followed on set, especially here in England. Anyway, there we were under the light of the moon, about to pick our way across mossy boulders and knotty tree roots.

'OK, kids, I know it's been a long day but once we've got this in the can you're free to go, so no messing around. Right, Josh?' Martin, the director, told us (or rather me) firmly.

'Right,' I said, probably with a smirk.

Jonas, the assistant director, yelled, 'Action,' and we were on.

'Which way?' I delivered my first line, looking wildly around the forest set, trying to decide which direction we needed to escape to.

'That way!' Emily yelled, shrilly, pointing off into the distance. 'I think I can see light over the trees, that must be east!'

'Gods, I hope you're right, Linderley!' I said, looking back over my shoulder before tearing off in the direction she'd pointed, weighed down by the stupid prop sword.

'Cut!' Jonas yelled, and for an instant I worried I had messed my lines up again, but they just needed to fiddle with the lighting again. This was only the first take, and knowing Wonderwick we'd probably have to do it another ten times before Martin was satisfied. I was already sick of carrying that dumb sword around, so I took it out of its sheath and started swinging it around like a lightsaber. I mean, you would, wouldn't you?

Emily rolled her eyes at me, like she had probably done about a thousand times already that day. 'Can't you just stand still for one minute?'

'No can do, Squirt,' I said, not looking at her, my gaze concentrated on the end of the fake sword.

She just made that huffing noise she so enjoys and before we knew it, the lighting guys had reset the overhead rig, all was well, and we were ready to go again. I put my sword back in its sheath, poised to hear Jonas yell 'action' but instead, Edith the makeup artist dashed forward and started powdering Emily's nose. I guess she was looking a little shiny, or whatever.

Cue me making Emily's huffing noise and taking out my sword again for one more little skirmish with an invisible Darth Vader. Except this time, I got a little too into it and started gathering great momentum, spinning around while holding the sword in both hands. And then my grip loosened and it was only in one hand. And then I kind of lost complete control of the situation and it was in no hands at all. Instead, it was flying through the air and much like in a cartoon, time seemed to slow down. It was like I knew the sword was going to hit the overhead lighting rig. It was my bad luck that it was the *only* place it was ever going to land. It wasn't going to fall to the floor and rest on a mossy boulder. It wasn't going to spin off and hit the studio floor. It was only going up. The seconds between the sword leaving my hand and the sword hitting the overhead lighting rig felt like minutes, enough time for me to do something even if I couldn't get the sword back into my hand.

Edith had just turned her back on Emily, her nose sufficiently powdered and now directly under the lighting rig. I used the moment I still had left to reach forward and yank Emily towards me, roughly pulling her by her costume before the crash came. The sword made noisy, chaotic contact with the rig before pulling the whole thing down under its weight and speed. It came down in an instant, hurtling towards the set below and to the exact spot where Emily had just been standing. When it hit the ground, glass shattered and sparks went flying across the set, chaos erupted, the whole production team going into panic mode.

Emily and I just stood, frozen, my hand in a vice-like grip around her wrist, only a couple of metres away from the mangled equipment and broken prop sword, shattered under the weight of the rig. Staring at each other in disbelief, it was clear Emily still didn't really understand what had happened, or that it was my fault.

For a moment, everything was quiet on set, and then it *really* wasn't. The sound of everyone talking, moving, shouting at the same time hit us like a wave.

'What the fuck were you playing at, Josh? What did you think was going to happen? Don't you know better?' Jonas almost screamed at me. Then Emily understood.

'Why did you do that?' she stammered in a whisper, her eyes shining with fear.

Why had I done it? Because I was bored, stupid, obnoxious, arrogant. Because I didn't take anything seriously. Any of those work. But I couldn't say that. I couldn't admit I was wrong. I knew my parents would hear about this. But I never really had to take responsibility for anything on Wonderwick, and I wasn't going to start then.

'What are you talking about? I saved your life,' I scoffed, going back into douchebag mode. 'You'd be mincemeat if it wasn't for me.'

'What is wrong with you?' Her voice shook with anger. 'Everything is a joke to you, isn't it? Or maybe it's just that *I'm* a joke to you.'

Before I could respond, she was spirited away by her mom, who glared at me with a ferocity that could have turned me to stone.

Whatever Emily may think, I still feel terrible about it to this day. I mean, I nearly killed her for Christ's sake, and the idea I might have put her in danger again, on this movie, makes me feel like the biggest piece of shit alive.

Chapter Fourteen

Carrie did a good job of whisking me back to the unit base via a frankly unnecessary trip to the medic tent without having to face too many people.

'Ugh!' I burst out, sipping the hot chocolate she seemed to have conjured out of thin air. I was wrapped in blankets and sitting in front of a space heater in my trailer as everyone else figured out what we should do next.

Carrie grimaced. 'I'm sorry, pal. But we're lucky, it could have been worse. And you really did give him a good talking-to! I'd be surprised if he did it again in a hurry.'

'He'd better not. I honestly thought he'd grown out of it by now, but—'

We were interrupted by a knock at the door, and before I could even tell them to come in, the door swung open. 'Darling! And Carrie! So nice to see you!' She swooped down first on Carrie then on me.

'Mum.' I held my arms out to hug her so she didn't feel too rejected when I asked, 'What are you doing here?'

'Oh, well, I didn't have much on so I thought I would swing by while you were on location! See you in action! But I didn't quite expect *that* much action.'

'Neither did I.'

'I'll leave you to it, figure out what the plan is,' Carrie said, making a hasty getaway from the trailer as my mum narrowed her eyes.

'Aren't you happy to see me?'

'Of course I am, it's just, you know, slightly bad timing,' I said delicately. 'This isn't exactly me at my best, is it?'

'Too bloody right it's not,' she said, shaking her head.

'What's that supposed to mean?'

'I know you two don't see eye to eye about most things, that's nothing new. But you have to be able to work together, and sometimes that's going to mean you taking the high road when he's messing around.'

'Messing around?!' I asked, incredulously.

'Emily, darling, you are his *colleague*. I know he can be hard work, but it's not your place to talk to him like that. His parents are the producers!'

'And you think that means he should just get away with everything?'

'No, I don't! But it's not up to you! You talk about him like he's a naughty schoolboy, and sometimes you talk *to* him like that as well!'

I exhaled so hard it felt like I was going to breathe fire. But she was right, and I knew it. 'Fine.'

She folded her arms across her chest. 'Darling. You've been at war with him since day one of the first film. A lot of it I understand, but some of it I don't. All I'm saying is, make life a bit easier on yourself, eh? Not everything is your responsibility. There's a whole team out there getting this film made. You shouldn't have been put at risk today, no way.' She shook her head resolutely, and then she softened. 'But I can't have you working yourself up like this over someone as silly as Josh Sacco. You're my little girl, I just want what's best for you.'

'And sometimes you have good advice,' I said, finally smiling.

'Only sometimes?' she asked, but then Carrie was back with a respectful knock on the trailer door.

'Martin's just going to use one of the takes you guys already did . . . I think the vibes are too chaotic now to go again and the light is becoming a problem, so you're done and we're back at Smithdown tomorrow.'

I let out a little snort of disapproval. I hated the idea of just making do: I wanted every take to be the best it could be. But I wasn't the boss, Martin was, and he thought we had a take we could use, so I had to let it go. And maybe I had to let things go with Josh as well. Of course he hadn't pushed me into the river on purpose.

After we wrapped for the day, I didn't want to be on my own, spending the evening stewing in my own irritation at both Josh and myself. In a way it was good that my mum had chosen today to drop by, so we could get dinner together and maybe take my mind off the whole thing.

'Thank you for coming, Mum,' I said, stabbing a salad leaf with my fork that evening. 'It's actually really nice to see you.'

'I can be around more if you like?' she offered, but I shook my head. 'I know you don't need a chaperone anymore . . . I thought you might be annoyed at me for coming by the set.'

'Of course I'm not annoyed.' I kept my tone gentle but remembered how unwelcome my parents' presence felt on that first day on set when I just wanted some time to myself. 'I'm just . . . trying to figure out my life as an adult, I guess. It's not about pushing you away, it's about giving myself the space to find things out for myself. Does that make sense?'

Mum nodded. 'We're always here for you, darling.'

'How's Dad?'

At that, my mum's expression changed, just for a second, a little flicker. 'Oh, he's fine, you know, just busy!' She waved her hand in a way that was just that little bit too casual.

'All good I hope?'

'I assume so, he just seems a bit overwhelmed with work stuff, you know how it can be when he gets busy.'

'Are you sure?'

'I'm sure, darling! Don't grill me like that!' She laughed, and everything seemed normal again. 'So, are you going to bury the hatchet with Josh tomorrow?'

'I'll sort it out, nothing I can't handle.'

'Darling.' She put her hand on top of mine on the table. 'You're Emily Montgomery. There's nothing you can't handle.'

Chapter Fifteen

Carrie greeted me with a coffee from craft services before I had even made it to my trailer.

'You know I can get my own coffee?' I asked her, smiling, despite the ungodly hour.

'I wanted an excuse to be here when you went in your trailer,' she said, her eyes glowing with delight.

'Why?' I frowned, taking a sip of coffee and pushing open the trailer door to find . . .

Flowers, on every surface, as far as the eye could see. Which, in a trailer, is not that far, but still. Flowers on the table, flowers on the work surface next to the sink, flowers on the windowsills. Glass vases were overflowing with wildflowers that looked as if they had just been picked from a meadow and expertly arranged for my delight. Shades of cornflower blue, the zingy red of a poppy, a spray of gypsophila, all harmonised to create a sense of abundance and natural beauty. A card in a powder-blue envelope was lodged in the middle of a huge lilac hydrangea.

I knew the erratic scrawl on the envelope immediately. A little nervously, I opened it.

> *Dear Emily,*
>
> *I'm so sorry for yesterday. I know these flowers won't make it up to you, but I wanted you to know how serious I am about being sorry, so please accept them as a symbolic gesture that cost me a ton of money. But for real, I'm sorry. Thank you for putting up with me.*
>
> *Josh*

'I think we're going to have to move these before Lou gets here with my costume. There's barely enough room for me in here as it is,' I mumbled, slipping the card back into the envelope, not knowing what else to say. Clearly I wasn't the only one who had spent the night regretting how things had gone.

'Isn't it incredible?!' Carrie gasped, outwardly expressing what I just couldn't bring myself to. 'It's like the proposal scene in *Gilmore Girls* or something.'

I swallowed hard at that. 'Yes, they're beautiful.'

'They're from Josh, right?'

I nodded, a little too overwhelmed to be able to speak. Was it possible that, although delivered in the heat of the moment, I had been right to say what I said?

'Yesterday was not great . . .' She looked at me out of the corner of her eyes. 'But this seems . . . like a fresh start?'

I paused for a moment, thinking. 'It's certainly the first time he's ever tried to, I don't know, *make it up to me* after he's done something wrong.'

'And do you think this could represent, quite literally, a new leaf?' she suggested, optimistically.

'Let's hope so,' I laughed. 'OK, Lou will be here any minute so, er, let's try and redistribute these among the trailers – take them to hair and makeup, the production office, visual effects, the prop workshops . . . oh, and can you get some to Big Phil in security, his wife would love that bouquet with the poppies.'

'Aye aye, captain.' She saluted me and set off with two vases as I sat down in front of the makeup mirror and gazed at my reflection. Tired, undoubtedly, but nothing that coffee wouldn't fix. And something more. Maybe hopeful? Was it hope I was feeling? Yes, that must be it. Hope.

My thoughts were interrupted by a knock at my trailer door. 'Ems, I know you're always around early so just wanted to let you know I'm ready in makeup when you are,' Juliet called.

I opened the door, and her eyes widened at the sight of the flowers.

'Bloody hell, what's all this, then?'

'I'm on a redistribution mission,' Carrie said, reappearing from her first trip. 'Here.' She handed a vase to Juliet. 'For makeup! Not to stereotype or anything but you'll probably appreciate them more than props did. Here, take two!'

'They're gorgeous!' Juliet's eyes lit up, cradling one vase under each arm like twin babies. 'Who on earth are they from? Secret admirer?'

'No,' I laughed, shaking my head. 'Josh. To apologise for yesterday.'

'Pretty extravagant way to apologise,' she said as we made our way from my trailer to hair and makeup. I relieved her of one of the vases and we walked side by side past Josh's trailer. 'He must be feeling guilty.'

'I guess so,' I said.

The makeup trailer was buzzing with activity, full of my fellow actors with an early call time. Felicity was in the chair on the other side of me, deep in conversation with her makeup artist about some new miracle cream that she hoped would keep her young forever. Courtney was gossiping to Wen, another of the supporting cast, about a cute new grip who had come onto this film. I sat down in my chair in front of my mirror while Edith sat in the chair next to me, where normally Darcy would be. She greeted me with a warm, 'Hello, love!' and played on her phone while Juliet got to work.

After a while, I realised Edith was still on her phone and Darcy was nowhere to be seen.

'Not that you shouldn't be relaxing as much as possible, but isn't Miss Darcy meant to be here by now?' Felicity asked Edith from the other side of the mirror. Naturally, my ears pricked up.

'Oh, she is,' Edith said looking up from her phone.

'Naughty girl,' Felicity said, archly. 'You wouldn't keep people waiting like this, would you, Emily?'

'I'm not saying anything.' I mimed zipping my mouth shut. After being called out for scolding Josh, the last thing I needed was getting a reputation for complaining about Darcy.

'I heard you gave Josh a good talking-to yesterday,' Felicity said, getting up from her chair. 'Good for you. We can't let the boys think they run the show.' She gave me a squeeze on the shoulder before heading out of the makeup trailer. This was the general feeling I had about my outburst at Josh: I wouldn't do it again, but I didn't necessarily regret it.

'Ooh, crew WhatsApp group says Darcy has graced us with her presence. Jen claims she'll be here any minute . . . assuming she doesn't get sidetracked,' Edith said. 'I would say I quite enjoyed that slow start to the day but it just means I'm going to have to work double hard to get her ready vaguely on time.'

Finally, Darcy materialised clutching a pale purple iced drink. 'Hey,' she said to Edith as she slid into the chair. Naturally, she did not apologise for being late, instead slipping AirPods into her ears and scrolling on her phone as Edith tried to work around the downward head-tilt of someone whose gaze is locked on a screen.

It was only then I noticed everyone in the room was sort of looking at each other and smiling slyly. Interesting.

I was almost finished when Darcy took out one single AirPod, gestured at the flowers on the windowsill, the one surface of the room not covered in makeup, skincare, hairdryers, eyelash curlers and anything else the hair and makeup team carried around in their bag of tricks.

'What's with the flowers?' she asked, flatly.

I was about to answer when Edith excitedly told her, 'Josh sent them to Emily.'

It was like a cloud passed over Darcy's face. 'Oh?' She took a sip from her blueberry matcha, her icy blue nails so long they almost curled around the straw.

I cleared my throat a little awkwardly. 'Just . . . after yesterday, the whole thing on set. I think he felt a bit bad,' I told her.

'Huh,' she said, before pausing. 'Maybe I should be more of a bitch,' Darcy drawled. The room, which had already gone quiet as everyone strained to listen to our conversation, went deadly silent. I'm pretty sure I even heard Edith gasp. 'Then maybe someone would send me flowers.' I flinched, involuntarily. 'I mean, not that you're a bitch, or whatever. You know what I mean.' She waved her hand dismissively.

I took a deep breath. Confrontation wasn't in my nature but I was getting fed up of her. 'Darcy, you can think what you want, but all I can tell you is that *you* wouldn't have enjoyed a dunk in the river.'

'It's a film set, how bad can it be?' she said, as if there isn't a rich history of people literally dying on film sets.

'All those flowers seems like a bit of an overreaction. But that's between you two, I guess. Your weird little thing.'

The moment was broken by Jen coming to check if Darcy was ready. Of course, she wasn't, but I was, and I walked back to my trailer with Jen.

'It's funny, before this film I'd always heard how *nice* she was.' Jen shook her head. 'And she's been nothing but trouble. Between her and Josh it's like herding cats.'

Just then my phone screen illuminated with an incoming call from Chloe. I'd told her about the mess of the previous day just in case anyone on set didn't know better and leaked it, though I doubted any of them would. 'Sorry, Jen, I've got to take this,' I said, shutting myself in my trailer. 'Hey, Chloe.'

'How's my girl doing today?'

'Better than yesterday, Josh has been trying to make it up to me, which is . . . a change?'

'Very mature of him. But actually he's not the gorgeous boy I wanted to discuss with you.'

'Oh?'

'What do you think about Ben Sage-Whittle?'

'As an actor?' I sensed she didn't mean as an actor.

'As a potential strategic alliance. Not right now, this is Wonderwick time. But in the future. I think you two could be a good match?'

'That's . . . very flattering,' I said, trying not to actually giggle. Ben was really quite gorgeous, a little bit older than me, a pretty, posh boy with a straightforwardly handsome, open face, a thatch of sandy blond hair and piercing blue eyes. He'd been linked to a lot of high-profile girls, mostly actresses but also a couple of singers, a model. And now, maybe me? 'Do you think he'd be . . . you know, interested?'

'Well, I can do some investigation, can't I? But I think he would be delighted to be seen on the arm of one Emily Montgomery. Anyone would, babe!'

'I appreciate your faith in me, Chlo.'

'Gotta dash, I have a meeting in precisely one minute but I just wanted to run it by you! So you could live with that? Little matchmaking with you and Ben?'

I swallowed, nervous at the thought of a public romance. I'd done it before, a few years ago, with another young actor, but it was nothing serious and fizzled out after only a few weeks but still managed to generate lots of tabloid headlines. Clearly no one thought it was a bit weird to be writing endless articles about two seventeen-year-olds going out together. But I did need *something* and maybe this was that something. Ben was a serious actor, had been in various well-regarded films already and his star was only rising. I could do a lot worse. Plus, he was cute, and we would make sense together. Two slightly buttoned-up British types, a bit posh, a bit awkward.

'Sure, I'm in,' I said, as gamely as I could.

'That's the spirit! Mwah, love you, babe. Speak soon!'

'Bye, Chloe.' I always felt better after talking to Chloe, like everything was just a game, that there was this whole world going on under the surface that might not be totally based in reality. It was comforting.

I sunk into the sofa and waited for my costume to arrive. As my eyes settled on the one remaining vase that Carrie had left, the one with the hydrangeas, it took me a minute to realise I was smiling. Because the flowers were beautiful. Not because of Josh. Obviously.

Chapter Sixteen

'Hey, Emily.' Ben Sage-Whittle got to his feet and hugged me. He smelled good, maybe something like Terre d'Hermès. Ben was very tall, a great Viking of a person, and he towered over me in a way that felt vaguely thrilling.

'Hi,' I said, a little breathily. 'Sorry, I know this is so silly and awkward.' I slid into the green button-back leather seat opposite him at Soho House on Dean Street.

'Oh, not at all,' he said, waving away my nerves. Chloe and his publicist had set up this little encounter so we could check that we didn't totally hate each other, which I thought seemed sensible. 'All part of the fun, isn't it?' He sat back in his chair and smiled at me, running a hand through his fair hair, all soft and floppy. He looked so relaxed, like he owned the place. It put me at ease, like this was just something people did all the time. And I was reassured that there would be *big* trouble if it looked like any of the other members were taking photos of us. I suppose that's why people like Ben joined clubs. A place to go and not be bothered.

We ordered coffees and got down to talking. 'So, is this the sort of thing you do all the time?' I took a sip of my oat flat white.

'Of course not,' he laughed, then paused and looked at me out of the corner of his eye. 'Why, do you?'

'No! I think I've just been single a while and Chloe thought this would be a nice little bit of "romantic intrigue" or whatever she likes to call it. What's your excuse?' My nerves were wearing off, and I seemed to be absorbing a little of Ben's natural confidence.

'In the politest possible way, I think there's a feeling that going out with you will bring me a degree of . . . how should we say . . . populist appeal?' He said with a raised eyebrow.

'Oh, I don't think there's anything wrong with being popular. I hope some of the Wonderwick magic rubs off on you.'

He took a sip of his coffee. 'And it doesn't hurt that you're very pretty, of course.'

'Well, I suppose that helps, doesn't it?' I said, lightly, but inside I felt all fluttery. I supposed when it was essentially a glorified business transaction it was easier to be straight-forward. I was used to overthinking everything, holding back, being unsure, but clearly this was going to be *much* easier. Maybe I should get Chloe to broker all my relationships.

'So, you're filming at the moment? How's it all going?'

Now that was a big question. I couldn't tell him the truth, obviously. He was a *proper* actor and if he knew the stuff I had been putting up with from Josh then he would never take me seriously. It would be as if I was tainted by association. 'Well, it's probably slower going than anything you're used to. It's the only thing I've ever done so I don't know any different, but actors who come from . . . well, you know, independent films and theatre, things like that, I think they struggle a bit with how little we can actually get done in a day.'

'You've really only done the Wonderwick series?' he asked, incredulous. I nodded. 'You have the vibe of someone who's done, shall we say, more serious work.'

I wasn't going to bother trying to convince him of the merits of Wonderwick, so I figured I would pull out my current trump card. 'I'm on the next Edgar Malek film,' I said, shrugging lightly. I hadn't actually pulled the trigger but I was about to get Glen to commit me to the project, and I wanted something to prove to Ben that I could be as serious as him.

'Damn.' He smiled and threw up his hands in defeat. 'Well, you've got one up on me there. I read for it but they gave it to bloody Tom Dwyer in the end.'

'Tom's good. I saw his Stanley in *Streetcar* a couple of months ago.'

'He's a nice guy, you'll have a good time,' Ben said, sitting back in his chair, his long legs crossed in front of him. 'I'm just jealous, that's all.'

'Of him getting the part?'

'And him getting to spend time with you,' he added, smiling. 'I've had worse offers of . . . what was it your publicist called it?'

'Strategic alliance,' I laughed.

'Right.' He nodded. 'I always thought you had something about you.'

'Well, thanks,' I said, taking a sip of coffee and setting the cup down on the saucer. 'But you can't just drop something like that and expect me not to ask for specifics!'

'Oh, just a lot of so-called up-and-coming actresses for the most part but there *was* this one time . . .' He looked around to check no one was sitting too close.

'Go on,' I said, my interest piqued.

Ben dropped his voice and leaned in. 'Well, let's just say a famous *momager* floated the idea with my publicist for some *cute red carpet moments* and that we are definitely spelling cute with a K.'

I gasped. 'No!'

'So you see how this—' he gestured across the table '—makes a little bit more sense?'

'I do. So, what happens now?'

'I suppose we can tell the matchmakers that once your Wonderwick duties are over, we can regroup. We've met, we know we get on, I like you, you like me, we can let nature take its course, right?' he said with a sly smile. 'Nothing too formal or serious, just . . . something fun and mutually beneficial.'

I checked the time on my phone. 'Well, now that's sorted, I actually have to go – I have a meeting on Broadwick Street in five minutes,' I said, picking up my bag. I didn't really have a meeting, I just wanted to keep this short and leave the mystery hanging in the air.

'Well, this has been fun,' he said, rising to hug me goodbye. I could see our movement was drawing attention from people at nearby tables, all of them pretending they weren't looking. 'Huh, it's working already.' Ben kissed me on the cheek, which I hadn't been expecting, and the surprising feeling of his lips against my skin made a little shiver of delight run through my body.

'Definitely working for me,' I said, trying to inhabit a confident new persona as I strode out onto the busy street. I couldn't wait to tell Chloe her vision had come to fruition. I didn't necessarily *feel* like the kind of actress who did the whole 'showmance' thing but I could give it a bloody good go, couldn't I?

Chapter Seventeen

I was reading in my trailer a week later when I heard a knock on the door.

'Come in?'

The door swung open to reveal a Josh Sacco vibrating with tension. 'Have you seen my—' he started, before looking around my pristine trailer and shaking his head. 'Never mind.'

'Your what?'

'Don't worry about it, this is my shit to deal with,' he said, resolutely.

'Go on, try me.' I put my book down and gave him my full attention.

He closed his eyes and breathed in heavily. 'Emily, you're going to be so mad and I need you to resist the urge to lecture me.'

'OK,' I said, slowly.

'I can't find my script.'

'Oh, that's not so bad!'

'No, like, I-I think I might have lost it. Somewhere . . .' He gestured vaguely towards the outside world. We both knew that would be bad news. A whole Wonderwick script just floating around out there before we've even wrapped? Josh knew it would be bad news, I didn't need to lecture him.

Instead I tried to reassure him. 'It'll turn up, it's probably in your trailer.'

But Josh wasn't really listening. 'Uh, yeah, maybe,' he said, raking his hands through his dark curls. 'Don't tell anyone, OK?'

'I won't, I promise. And I'll keep an eye out for it.'

He didn't seem reassured. Our scripts were watermarked with our names so if they did go missing, the production team would know who to give a good bollocking. The best case scenario was that it was just lost somewhere in his house or trailer, the second best was that he'd left it lying around on set and someone was going to find it and hand it in, and the worst-case scenario was that it would end up on eBay . . . or in the hands of the *Daily Mail*.

Later that afternoon, the crew were setting up the next shot, and a few of us were sitting around in an E-Z Up tent, playing UNO. Even Josh had deigned to join in, after previously claiming he could never look at an UNO card again after we overdosed on it while shooting the first Wonderwick film. I wanted to ask him about the missing script situation but couldn't do it in front of everyone.

'Max! No!' I wailed after being the victim of a +4 card. 'I'm dying here!'

'Come on, pick 'em up.' Josh pushed the pile towards me with a huge, annoying grin on his face. 'What? Don't look at me like that, it wasn't my fault!'

'Ugh!' Dutifully I did as I was told and picked up four. Classic Max. 'Remind me never to sit next to you again. Somehow you always end up with the naughty cards.'

'What can I say? I'm God's favourite. Anyway, you take this too seriously!'

'All's fair in love and UNO, pal,' Eve, one of the supporting cast who I liked but didn't know very well, chimed in as the game carried on. Things descended into chaos quickly, Eve somehow in possession of a hand full of +2 cards, leaving Josh groaning at every turn and the rest of us cackling with delight.

The flap of the tent opened and Darcy stepped in. She cast a sceptical eye over the scene in front of her.

'Hey, Darcy!' Max said cheerfully.

'I was just wondering what the noise was all about.' She shrugged, coolly. Darcy was rarely seen in an E-Z Up with other actors: she had her own private tent, because *of course* she did.

'Just playing UNO,' Tommy told her.

'What's that?' she asked. Who hasn't heard of UNO?!

'It's . . . I mean, it's a card game?' Max offered.

'C'mon, Darcy, you can join us.' Josh gestured to an empty folding chair. But before she could answer, it was time to head back to the set.

'Someone should tell her that just because she's playing a bitchy villain she doesn't need to go full method,' Eve whispered, giving me a sideways glance as we walked over to the sound stage. I giggled, admiring her audacity.

As everything was being set and checked around us, Carrie waved my phone at me, the screen illuminated. 'Glen's calling. Shall I answer for you and tell him you'll call him back?'

'No, it's OK, I think I have a second,' I told her, taking the phone and answering it. 'Hey, Glen.'

'How's my favourite client?' It was safe to assume he opened all calls like that.

'Great, I can't talk for long. What's up?'

'I just wanted your final, final answer. What's it going to be: *Orientations* or *Dinky Daffy and the Detective Squad*?'

'Oh, Glen, I'm going to break your heart.'

The sigh could be heard from outer space. '*Orientations* then?'

'Yes. I think it's time to get serious.' I thought it was a little bit funny that all the conversations we'd had at the kick-off meeting for this Wonderwick were about how I was a grown-up now, a woman now, that that was what people wanted from me and I should be prepared to give them, but when I wanted to apply that to something *other* than a 'spicy' scene, it was somehow a surprise to them.

'Couldn't you get serious *with* a ton of money?'

'Glen, fifteen per cent of something is better than fifteen per cent of nothing,' I said, more assertively than I felt.

'True. It's your decision!'

'When Edgar Malek gets that Oscar nod and you're asking to be my date on that red carpet, it'll be worth it' I laughed.

'Let's pretend that's a remote possibility to get me through this inevitably paltry negotiation about your compensation. Everything OK on Wonderwick so far?'

I paused before answering. 'It's a weird one.'

'In a good way or a bad way?'

'Too soon to tell . . . but nothing for you to worry about, you know the series is a juggernaut at this point,' I reassured him, and we said our goodbyes.

'Hey.' Max caught me just as we were about to start rolling. 'A bunch of us are going to take cars into London tonight for some drinks and dancing. You in?'

'Ummm . . . is this a Darcy plan?' I asked, tentatively.

'Yeah, but she said I could invite you.'

'Did she actually?'

'Well, she said, "Yeah, sure, whatever," when I asked so that basically counts.'

I swallowed. I should say yes. 'Sure, why not?'

Max nodded approvingly. 'Sweet, man. We'll head in after we wrap.'

I'd said yes! I was going out with them, just like I'd said I wanted to. Progress!

A slow afternoon and many, many takes later, I was heading back to my trailer to change for the night when I ran into Josh.

'Any word on the . . . you know?' I raised my eyebrows at him, as if there was any doubt over what I meant.

He bit his lip and shook his head. 'I don't know what to do, man. I feel like such an idiot.'

'Do you want me to come search in your trailer with you?' I offered, not quite knowing why.

'God, I don't know, maybe? In fact, definitely,' he said, and we headed off in that direction. As we walked, Josh stopped dead and looked down at his phone.

'What the hell?' he muttered. I stopped and turned back to him. He held up the screen to me. On it was a text from a number that wasn't saved.

Script is probably pretty valuable. If you want it back bring a grand in cash to the Royal Oak pub in Wyton, 9 p.m.

I looked at the time at the top of the screen. That was only an hour away. Josh furrowed his brow. 'Who the hell is it? And how do they have my cellphone number? None of this makes any sense . . .' He gasped and looked at me. 'Shit.'

'What?'

He smacked his hand against his forehead. 'I'm such an idiot. I must have left it in the taxi last night when

I was coming back from Darcy's. We'd been running lines together and maybe I had too much to drink . . .' He flicked his eyes up and met my gaze. 'Don't say it, please.'

'I'm not saying anything! I think you should report this taxi driver to the police for extortion!'

'I can't do that . . . it's not worth it.'

'Well, what do we do, then?'

Josh sighed. 'I guess I pay him.'

'Do you want me to come with you?'

'No way, there's no point both of us missing the fun.'

'Josh, I really don't like the idea of you going to meet this extortionist on your own.'

Before he could answer, my phone screen illuminated with a text from Max:

Where you at?

I typed back quickly:

So sorry but I'm kind of tied up with something! Hopefully next time!

Maybe I was never meant to have a night out.

'Anyway,' I said, looking back up at him. 'Do you have a thousand pounds in cash?'

Josh thought and scratched his head. 'I mean, I could probably cobble it together. God, how do I explain this to Yuri? Drive us to a pub in the middle of nowhere, wait for, I don't know, ten minutes and then drive us home?' Josh didn't want to lose the good opinion of his driver any more than I would want to lose Mike's good opinion of me. I understood.

'Send Yuri home and we can get Mike to drive us. He won't judge you. Promise.'

Josh nodded.

Ten minutes later we were in the car on the way to the Royal Oak in Wyton.

'Are you sure about this? Maybe he's dangerous.' Mike looked back at us in the rear-view mirror.

'I don't think he's dangerous. Just trying to make a quick buck,' I reassured him. And it was true: this was clearly a chancer who'd managed to exploit a drunken idiot in his car. 'If he wasn't trying his luck he could have asked for a lot more money and given you a longer deadline to find it. He just wants a quick payout.'

'What if he asks for more?' Josh asked, panic in his voice.

Obviously Josh could afford more, but it was the fear that it would never end. 'We'll cross that bridge when we come to it. It'll be fine,' I said.

'All right, but the slightest sign of trouble you tell me and I'll wring his bloody neck, you hear me?' I could tell Mike didn't like this one bit.

'Oh, loud and clear,' said Josh, the first smile I'd seen on him all day. 'Mike, you're a prince.'

'Just doing my job,' he said stiffly, as if he offered to murder someone on my behalf every day.

'Dvořák,' I said, as the sound of his 'New World' Symphony serenaded us via Classic FM.

'Huh?' Josh replied, but Mike and I just smiled at each other in the rear-view mirror.

A taxi was parked in the pub car park when we arrived. 'Don't you worry, I'm making a note of the registration number,' Mike said as we exited the car.

We tried to slip into the pub as unobtrusively as possible. Maybe it was a mistake for us to come as a pair. 'Would you remember him if you saw him?'

'Yeah, he had, like, ginger hair and glasses . . . pretty distinctive,' Josh said, his eyes scanning the room. 'Bingo.' He pointed towards a dark corner where a ginger man was sitting alone at a table, doing a very bad job of acting casual. His leg was bouncing nervously but when he caught sight of us he straightened himself up in his seat and puffed out his chest like he was a hard man.

We sat down in front of him.

'Hand it over,' I said, straightaway. What was the point of me being there if not to take control of the situation? Catch him off guard?

'You got the money?' he asked, his eyes darting from my face to Josh's. He seemed baffled to be faced with the two kids from Wonderwick but determined to get his payout none the less.

I held up a hand to Josh, telling him not to produce the wedge of banknotes he'd been able to, in his words, 'cobble together'. 'You got the script?'

''Course I do,' he said, sliding something heavy and rectangular in a plastic bag across the table. I took a look inside and then showed it to Josh. It was his script, JOSH SACCO printed on every page. I could feel the relief wash over him.

'How do I know you haven't photocopied this?' I asked the taxi driver.

He looked confused. 'Well . . . I don't know how you know. I just haven't.' He frowned with such intensity that it was clear the idea had never occurred to him. 'Now, I've held up my end of the bargain, you hold up yours.'

'Not exactly a bargain,' I snapped. 'This is called extortion.'

He snatched the bag back off the table and I knew instantly I'd overstepped. 'If you're not going to pay up I'm sure there are a lot of little Wonderwick nerds who will.'

'No, please,' Josh said, his voice trembling. 'I've got the money.' He produced the roll of banknotes.

I held out a hand to the man. 'Hand it over.'

He could sense Josh's desperation. Damn! Why hadn't we discussed strategy? 'On second thoughts . . .' he said, leaning back in his chair and holding the plastic bag against his chest. 'Who's to say a grand is a fair price?'

'You are. You asked for it. We brought it,' I told him.

'Maybe I didn't realise the value of what I had,' he said, trying to affect a pose of nonchalance, but I knew he didn't have the nerve. His leg was nervously jiggling again.

I banged my fist down on the table, not caring if I attracted the attention of the few other customers. 'Listen up, pipsqueak. We are very grateful that you found Josh's script in your car and for that kindness, Josh is willing to give you a thousand pounds to say thank you for looking after it for him. Because if you were holding it hostage in exchange for money, well, that sounds like extortion to me, and we have your phone number, your car registration number, and access to a lot of powerful lawyers. It wouldn't be hard to make your life very, very difficult.' I stared him dead in the eye before turning on my sweetest smile, the one I used at premieres. 'But that's not what you're trying to do, is it?'

He shook his head like a wet dog shaking off water. 'No,' he said, sliding the script back across the table. He really was just a stupid chancer. I almost felt bad for him.

'Give our nice friend here the money, Josh.' He did what he was told. 'Now, everyone happy?'

'Sure am,' Josh said, much more calmly than I knew he felt.

'Yes, all right,' the man said, counting the money.

'It's all there,' I said, assertively. 'We'll be off now. Pleasure doing business with you.'

We walked out of there as discreetly as we could manage. It wasn't until we were back in the car that Josh let out a sigh of relief and I realised my whole body had been tense until that moment. We started laughing.

'Success?' Mike asked, turning over his shoulder to look at us both. But we were laughing so hard we couldn't get a response out. Josh choked out 'Pipsqueak!' and that made me lose it. Eventually we calmed down and Josh held up the script victoriously.

'I couldn't have done it without Emily. I'd have lost my mind with stress. She just . . . took control of everything. She saved my ass.'

'I'm glad you know that, young man,' Mike said with a curt nod.

We arrived at Josh's studio house, and he held up the bag. 'Better not forget this!'

'I don't think Mike's going to extort you even if you do leave it behind,' I said, drily.

Josh got out, and leaned down to speak to me across the back seat. 'Emily,' he said, looking at me through the open car door, 'you're a real pal, you know that?'

I felt my cheeks heat up. 'Any time.'

He looked down at his watch, a heavy silver analogue thing, definitely vintage. 'You know, the night is still young. We could go and meet the guys in London? Might be fun? To celebrate our great success tonight. Even if we do a little pit stop to change we could still be there by midnight?'

Of course, my natural instincts were to say no, that we'd already done more than enough tonight, but deep down, I knew I wanted to. More than I wanted my warm bed and its soft sheets and a cosy night's sleep. Josh and I felt like a team, which in turn felt sort of magic, and I couldn't help but want to prolong it.

I shrugged nonchalantly. 'Sure. Let me go home and get changed and I'll see you there.'

A lopsided smile transformed his face. 'For real? OK! Don't go letting me down, though?' He knew what I was like.

'I won't.'

'Mike, you're a prince among men, take the rest of the night off and I'll get us a car service.'

Mike looked back at me in the mirror for my approval. 'Are you sure?'

'Positive,' I told him.

'I'll pick you up in an hour?'

I nodded. 'See you soon.'

Josh closed the car door and we drove off, back to my house in Gables Cross.

Mike and I sat quietly for a moment, letting the sound of Holst's 'Jupiter' fill the car. 'I know he's a bit silly,' Mike said, as if we'd just been speaking, 'but he's a good lad, really.'

I watched the orange glow of the street lights whiz past out of the car window. 'I hate to admit it, but I think you might be right.'

Chapter Eighteen

I tore through my wardrobe like a whirlwind, looking for the perfect outfit. What would be perfect about it? I didn't know, but I knew it would strike me when I saw it. Aha! A dark chocolate-coloured heavy satin YSL mini-dress with long sleeves and a high neck was the one. Not just because it was super short, made even shorter by the addition of a deep brown leather belt, but because of the suspenders. Had I ever worn a dress with suspenders and stockings before? No. But I knew it was perfect for this occasion. The high neck and the super-long sleeves gave it that air of strictness and formality that maybe people had come to expect from my outfit choices, but the several inches of exposed thigh between where the dress ended and the stockings began were decidedly new, and *very* spicy. I would pair it with the pointiest heels I owned, put a quick loose wave in my hair and do a lightly smoky eye.

When Josh knocked on my door at the agreed-upon time (not late! On time to the minute!) I suddenly felt a wave of something like shame pass over me. Did I look ridiculous? I'd chosen this outfit, done my makeup, done my hair in such a rush and when I looked in the mirror I loved what I saw . . . but it wasn't the Emily that everyone knew. Would Josh take one look at me and barely conceal his amusement at me trying to dress *sexy*? But I didn't have time to change. I had to commit.

I opened the front door, and it was the first time I had seen someone's jaw *actually* drop. Josh stood agape on the front steps of my temporary house, surprisingly smartly dressed in head-to-toe black. It was as if we were completely different people to the ones who had been facing down an extortion attempt in a pub only an hour ago. Awkwardness crackled in the air, but I had to say something. 'You look nice,' I told him, as assertively as I could manage. My skin prickled with embarrassment at my ridiculous attempts at dressing 'sexy'. I wasn't sexy, and I knew it.

'Uh, thanks.' He blinked at me in confusion. 'What's . . . I mean, this is . . .' I hadn't expected my outfit to be causing a scene already, but Josh seemed to be completely overwhelmed by my attempts at spicing things up. He cleared his throat. 'This is a new look for you.'

Better to get it out of the way. 'And what do you think?' I asked, feeling my cheeks flush.

Finally, he spoke. 'Emily, you look incredible.'

Relief swept over me. We walked to the waiting car and he gallantly held the door open.

We chatted on and off during the journey into London, alternating between an easy back-and-forth and a peaceful silence, as if the silly rigmarole of the evening so far had allowed us to move past something that had been hanging over us for years. I couldn't say for certain, but every so often I was sure I could feel his eyes on me when I wasn't looking.

We reached our destination around midnight, just as Josh had predicted, and were greeted by a couple of paparazzi loitering around the entrance to the underground club on the edge of Chinatown.

'Smile for the cameras,' Josh said as we breezed past the doorman. We were used to it by now, just a regular part of our everyday lives.

Down the stairs, we found our castmates and a few members of the crew on the dance floor, a couple taking a breather at a round table nearby. The energy was high, and a cheer went up when they spotted us from across the room, which, in turn, made everyone *else* look in our direction too.

'Maaaate!' Max lurched towards us, beer sloshing over the top of his glass. Even somewhere this fashionable couldn't tempt Max away from his beloved pints. 'You came! Both of you! And Emily, what is this new look we have going on?' There was only a tiny hint of a mocking tone to his voice, and mostly he seemed surprised and impressed that we had turned up at all.

'She looks fuckin' sharp, doesn't she?' Josh said, casting another appreciative eye over my outfit.

'You know what?' I said, tucking my tousled hair behind my ear. 'I feel it.'

Darcy was in a booth with one of her fashion minions, surveying the scene and drinking a fluorescent cocktail.

'Damn, girl!' Courtney sidled up to us and clasped me in a tight hug as I was wondering if I was expected to go over and say hi to Darcy. 'You look *insane*, I'm obsessed! I'd given up on you coming and here you are, looking like a whole meal! Here, we've got a bottle,' she said, leading me over to the table where champagne was chilling on ice. I was going to pour another glass for Josh, but he had migrated to the bar with Max and Tommy. After spending so much of the evening with him, I felt a tug of disappointment that I now had to share him with everyone. I swallowed *that* thought down with a mouthful of champagne. There was only one thing for it: hit the dance floor.

I danced and danced and danced. I danced with Courtney, with Max, with Tommy, with Maria, the second AD, with Jurgen, director of photography, all of us giving ourselves over to the night, trying to shake off the pressures and trials of shooting a film like *Wonderwick*. I wasn't used to letting myself go, dancing unselfconsciously, feeling that cathartic rush of a cocktail in one hand and a sense of infinite possibilities in the other. The truth was, my outfit was making me feel like a new person. Or not exactly a new person, the same Emily but more energised, more open, more . . . *something*. The whole time I was dancing, my glass being periodically topped up by invisible hands, as much as I tried to lose myself completely in the moment, I felt a prickling consciousness of where Josh was at all times. By the bar, chatting to the boys at the table, taking selfies with fans, and then . . .

'Hey, you.' There he was. 'Having fun?'

I nodded, suddenly feeling the effects of the champagne. 'I'm glad we came. Thanks for making it happen.'

'It's been a fun evening, right?' he asked, a smile creeping across his face. The music was so loud he had to lean close to my ear, the heat of his body radiating against mine.

'Yes, all of it,' I said into his ear. I leaned back and we just looked at each other for a moment, looking each other right in the eyes, as if we were waiting for something to happen, daring the other one to move first. And then the music shifted, a beat dropped, and the spell was broken.

'Fuck, I love this song!' Josh grabbed my hand and we danced together, my body close to his but with a cautious distance because really what the hell was happening? *This* wasn't happening, this was just a weird madness that had taken over us this evening. *This* wasn't a thing. Instead, we danced. But I couldn't deny the electric spark I'd felt, or thought I'd felt, between us in that moment.

Finally, it was time to head home. The group of us stumbled up the stairs and the club spat us out onto the street where a fleet of cars was waiting for us. Along with the photographers that had been there on the way in, who seemed to have multiplied in number while we were dancing, no doubt tipped off that the whole cast *including* Josh and I were there. And my outfit certainly didn't hurt.

Before I could make it to the car, one of them stepped forward, and sort of went down on one knee, shooting me from below, *almost* but not quite upskirting me, but still in the realms of plausible deniability.

'Woah!' Josh said, slipping a protective arm around my waist and holding up a hand to the photographer. 'Getting a little too close there, pal.' And then under his breath he murmured, so no one else could hear, 'You sell that to anyone and I'll ruin your fuckin' life, you hear me?'

Everything had happened so fast that I hadn't fully registered the feeling of Josh's arm around my waist, guiding me to the waiting car. But everyone else clearly had. The sound of shutters going off, the sight of members of the public holding up phones to photograph or video the moment, all signalled to me that something unusual was happening. And yet the moment he took his arm away to hold open my car door for me, it felt like something was missing.

Josh leaned down and spoke to me through the open car door. 'See you tomorrow. It's been a trip.'

JOSH

It was only a couple of years ago but feels like ancient fucking history by now.

I stepped onto the red carpet for the premiere of the last movie, *Wonderwick Woods: Into the Shadow Realm*, and there Emily was.

She looked . . . different. I mean, I'm no fashion critic, but the looks she had chosen for the first couple of premieres were interesting to say the least. Strange combinations of dresses and shoes, bags in the shape of watering cans or the addition of a huge necklace or her naturally straight hair forced into curls. This time, everything was just simple. Just right. Just perfectly her. A black dress with a square neck, tight on the top and then flaring out at the waist. Hair sleek, tied back in a low ponytail. No crazy necklace, not even something small and dainty, instead the neckline of the dress framed her collarbones and the soft skin of her chest like a work of art. She looked, in a word, amazing.

The problem was that I felt *something* and I didn't like it. Any time I felt these *somethings* towards Emily, I tried to crush them down, like a garbage compactor, because really that's what these feelings had to be: garbage, because I was a garbage person with garbage feelings.

My date for the evening was some model I was seeing for about ten minutes – that's what you're meant to do when you're nineteen years old and a big deal in Hollywood, right? But Emily went alone, and the whole evening I wondered what it would be like if I told her how amazing she looked. No, not amazing. After careful consideration I decided that wasn't the word I wanted to use. The word I wanted to use was beautiful. Did I tell her how beautiful she looked? No. Did I make some stupid crack about how she couldn't get a date for the premiere? Yeah, yeah I did.

Because that was who I was, and that was who Emily was. We had our roles and we stuck to them. She was a good person, serious and dedicated to her work. She held herself and everyone else to a high standard, and what did I do? Fuck around and only occasionally find out, because I was so often insulated from the *finding out* part by my parents' position. So even though when I saw Emily that night I felt this pull towards her, this unsettling sense that I found her beautiful, captivating, enchanting, whatever the hell you wanted to call it, I knew the place for me was right next to some girl I barely knew who spent the whole movie checking Instagram. No, that's not quite right, what she was actually doing was scrolling back through her *own* Instagram.

That was what I deserved, and that was the person Emily saw when she looked at me. An unserious, spoiled Hollywood brat who had made it his business to wind her up, troll her, prank her, make fun of her. How could I stop being that person? That was what I wanted to know. Was it even possible, or was this just who I was destined to be, forever?

Tonight as we left the club, I got a little taste of what it would feel like to have my arms around her, and I wanted more.

Chapter Nineteen

The morning's shoot had been tedious, all stops and starts – even more than usual. The mood onset was fractious, everybody getting frustrated and blaming every other department for the problems. Not only were several key cast members nursing hangovers, but even the people who hadn't been out last night were aware of the increased press attention that Josh and I had drawn. Better that than a news story about Josh's script ending up online, I supposed. Instead of taking myself off to my trailer, I'd come to hide out for a bit in one of the reading platforms carved into the huge tree at the centre of the Great Archive set. Are we meant to hang out on the sets? No, but if this was the only act of rebellion I ever made on Wonderwick, it was probably allowed.

Of course I knew it was fake, that all the books were fake, that I wasn't really in a vast, sprawling library carved out of ancient trees, but the way the set designers had made it come to life meant it *felt* real. It felt like being held by the branches of an enormous oak, surrounded by thousands of hand-crafted tomes. Even without the magic, twinkly golden light that the lighting team created when we shot, it still felt remote and peaceful. I'd taken a photo of myself reading a new book (the final instalment of a series by a Black American sci-fi author) in the Great Archive and posted it to my Instagram stories so @Whats-EmilyReading would have some new material. I was a few chapters in when someone called to me from below.

When I leaned over the side of the reading platform, I saw it was Josh.

'I can't believe you've gone public with your little hangout spot,' he said. 'I thought I was the only one who knew you came up here and now you've shared it with your millions of followers!'

He started climbing one of the ladders up to my nook.

'To what do I owe this visit?' I asked as his face appeared at the top of the ladder. I moved over so he could share the platform with me, and realised I had gone so far to create space between us that I was squished up against the fake tree bark.

'Say, Montgomery, what do you think of a drink tonight?' Josh asked, a little apprehensively.

I grimaced at the thought of another night of drinking, another night of weird ping-pong with my emotions. 'I don't think I have another a big night in me,' I said. Better to be on the safe side.

'Who said anything about a big night? But if you're sure you don't feel like it, I totally get it,' Josh said, scratching the back of his head.

'Oh, sorry, what were you thinking?'

'Uh, I meant more a cosy pub kinda vibe? You know, like our last, uh, extra-curricular activity but without the side dish of extortion? There's a place in Kingsdown that has a real fire . . . I thought it could be, I don't know, *nice*?' The way we were sitting side by side meant he didn't have to look me in the eye, instead casually gazing off into the distance.

We were making more of an effort with each other, and I didn't want to let my weird feelings the night before get the better of me. 'That actually sounds great, Josh. Who's going?' I wasn't sure if I was up for spending social time with Darcy as well as professional, but would take one for the team if necessary.

Instantly, his face froze. He opened his mouth and closed it again and looked a bit like a chiselled goldfish. 'Um, uh, actually . . .'

'Yes?' I raised my eyebrows at him.

'I was thinking maybe it would be nice, just me and you? Call it corporate bonding or whatever,' he said breezily, but he couldn't quite shake the awkwardness of having to say it out loud.

'Oh!'

Josh frowned at me. 'Unless that would be weird? I don't want it to be weird.'

'No, it wouldn't be weird at all!'

'Great!' The relief in his voice was palpable. 'See you there at eight? It's called the White Hart in Kingsdown.

Give Mike the night off, I'll get Yuri to drop you home. Consider it payback for the lift the other night, right?'

'I'll see you there.' I nodded as he descended the ladder. I didn't know why Josh was so keen for us to hang out, but I couldn't reject an olive branch like this. Maybe this would be the film where we became friends at last? Or if not friends, then . . . not-enemies? 'I think we're nearly good to go again, if you're ready to rejoin the real world?'

Back in the real world, my phone was ringing.

'Ben's keen. Like *keen* keen,' Chloe said before I could even say hello. 'Your saucy little minx outfit last night has really got things moving! Whose idea was all that anyway? Josh putting his arm around you all possessive! I thought it was up to me to come up with press moments!'

'Oh, it was nothing,' I told her. I couldn't quite bring myself to admit that the whole thing had been completely organic, not to mention a little swoonsome.

'Well, you're clearly doing something right. Keep up the good work!' she said, before hanging up. It struck me then that this was how I was mostly thinking about it, like work. I needed to get my head in the game and remember how very gorgeous and dashing Ben was.

That afternoon, Darcy stalked past Carrie and me as we picked up coffees from craft services.

'It's like she's *trying* to be bitchy, you know? The way she walks, the way she doesn't make eye contact with you, the way she talks, it's all so fucking contrived,' Carrie said.

'It does feel a bit like she's trying too hard, doesn't it?' I murmured. 'I thought she was meant to be nice.'

'Well, that's what I heard too! Load of bollocks.' She shook her head before sipping from her cup.

'Josh asked me out for a drink later,' I said, like it was so weird I couldn't keep it to myself.

'Just you two?' She frowned at me. Of course, she hadn't known about the bonding over the lost script, and I wasn't going to tell her about it, so it probably seemed even weirder to her than it did to me.

'Yep.'

'Like a date?'

'No!' I said, quickly. 'Not like that!'

'Are you sure not like that?'

I turned to face her. 'Carrie, in what world would that ever make sense?'

'Look, don't ask me, stranger things have happened.'

'It's just a drink!' I protested.

She screwed up her nose sceptically. 'We'll see.'

'Well, apparently I'm destined for Ben Sage-Whittle,' I said, breezily. 'Josh wouldn't even get a look-in.'

Chapter Twenty

That evening, bang on time, Josh arrived at the White Hart. I had been tempted to try another more daring look after the success of last night, but settled for a classic chocolate brown sweater and belted Levis, a look I could picture 1990s Julia Roberts wearing. I wanted this to be the cosy evening he had promised.

'Well, mine's a Guinness, how about you?'

'That's a very intriguing choice for you, Josh,' I said with a smile.

'I'm full of surprises, what can I say. What am I getting you?'

'I'll have what you're having.'

When he returned with two glasses, he nodded down at my book on the table, which I stowed in my bag. 'Can't be too careful, there are book thieves around. Cheers,' he said, clinking his glass against mine.

'I'm glad you've grown out of that particular habit,' I said, drily. 'Very restrained of you.'

'I always gave them back! I mean, I coulda held them ransom like our old friend the taxi driver . . .'

'That's true, I suppose. Then you moved on to filling in every square on my crosswords with the letters J, O, S and H.'

He grimaced. 'Did I? God, what a jerk! I can't believe you had to go and literally hide to get away from me!' he said, shaking his head.

'Ah, today it wasn't about you, I just wanted to read in peace.'

'And provide content for that Instagram account about your reading material, of course.'

'You know about that?'

'I'm one of @WhatsEmilyReading's many followers!'

'You are not!'

'Er, there was a whole thing on the Wonderwick fan Reddit about me following the account, and also, I can read, ya know,' he said with a roguish grin. It was good to see him back to his playful self. It had been kind of unnerving, to see a stressed-out and serious Josh, but part of me had liked seeing another side to him. 'You should do something with that.'

'Like what?'

Josh shrugs. 'I dunno, just feels like something you're clearly passionate about.' He threw a peanut into his mouth and crunched it, thoughtfully. 'You could start a book club. Or . . . I don't know, a production company? Buy the rights to interesting shit, try to get it made.'

I couldn't help smiling, a warmth filling my chest that he'd even suggest something like that. It was never going to happen, I had no idea how to be a producer, but it was still a nice thing to say. 'I don't know if I'm up to the challenge but that's a good idea.'

'I'm full of 'em, what can I say.'

I bit my lip. 'Josh, I'm really sorry I was so hard on you before.'

He waved the thought away. 'Don't apologise, I was a total jerk. That's one of the reasons I thought we should, you know, have a chill, no-drama drink together. Just to really cement the fact that the old days are done.'

'They are, aren't they?'

'Thank God.' He shook his head, raising his eyebrows. 'I can't live like that anymore. I'm surprised I got away with it for so long, you know?'

'Not with me, you didn't,' I said with a laugh.

'Well, that's my point. For so much of my life nobody ever called me out on my shit. Then I got into films, and people only *gently* called me on my shit because they didn't want me to run home and tattle to my parents that they were being mean to me, or whatever. But you *always* called me on my shit, not because it was your job but because you really, actually cared about the thing we were trying to do. It took me too long to realise it, I guess.'

I nodded, wanting him to say more. 'What did you realise?'

He laughed and shook his head, not looking me in the eye. 'God, it sounds so fucking stupid when I say it out loud.'

'Try me?' I urged him.

'I think I understand what it feels like to care about stuff?' he ventured, cautiously.

I couldn't help but smile. 'That's a good place to start.'

'I know, I know, it sounds completely ridiculous, I can't help it. But after the whole . . . debacle at the river, when I knew I should just stick to the script but instead I wanted to screw around, try out doing shit *my way*, whatever the hell that means. Anyway, when I saw what a total mess I'd made of the whole shoot, how much time I wasted for everyone, how, rightfully, upset you were at me, I just thought, what's the point? Like, why am I doing this? And I didn't have an answer. I guess . . .' He swallowed, looked thoughtful, but didn't say more.

'No, go on, I want to hear what you have to say,' I urged him.

'I guess I kept doing it because it was what I'd always done, you know? Force of habit, or some shit? But I never, like, thought about whether I really wanted to keep doing it, and now I've realised, maybe I don't?'

'That's a good thing to realise.' I nodded, encouraging. Obviously I thought it was a good thing: I didn't want to get pushed into a river again, but more than that, it seemed like it was actually good for Josh, too.

'It's just hard, you know, when you're stuck in this role that you've been playing for years,' he said, looking at me. 'And I don't necessarily mean Rowan Clearwater, you know?'

'I do know.' I nodded.

The conversation flowed easily, a fluent back and forth that we'd never been able to achieve before. It was as if there was an invisible force field around us: no one came up to us asking for a selfie or to tell us they loved or hated Wonderwick. It was like we were in this funny little bubble, in the warm glow of the fireplace.

'What's next for you? After Wonderwick, I mean.'

'Going home for a while.' Josh stretched out, leaning back in the chair and folding his hands across his stomach, relaxed and comfortable in front of the fire like a big, friendly dog. 'I'm doing *Deep Water 2*.'

'The submarine one?' I had seen the first one and struggled to see how a sequel was a good use of anyone's time, money or energy.

'Right. Those guys must be pretty unlucky to have a disaster on a submarine not once but *twice*.'

'And this time they're even unluckier because *you're* there,' I said, unable to hide my smile.

Josh gasped in mock horror. 'Emily Montgomery, I thought you'd changed.'

'I have, I promise! I'm—' I started saying, before stopping myself. 'I'm almost glad you pushed me in that river. Otherwise we might not be here.'

Josh nodded, holding my gaze. 'And here is . . . kinda nice, isn't it?' His glance flicked down to my mouth and back up to my eyes, and there was something in that tiny motion that made my stomach feel fizzy. In the soft light from the candle on the table and the roaring fire, I could almost understand what all those girls saw in him.

I swallowed, overwhelmed with the moment. 'Yes.' I took a sip from my glass.

'Oh,' he said, reaching out towards my face. 'You've just got a little . . .' He cupped my jaw in his hand and gently wiped something off my upper lip. A little foam from the Guinness. He retracted his hand, but my face felt hot with his touch and I just blinked at him, stupidly. What was I supposed to do now? For a beat we just stared at each other, waiting for something to happen.

But the clanging sound of a bell shattered the moment. 'Last orders!' called the barman.

'Oh, uh, you want something?' Josh looked around, startled.

I shook my head, my mouth a little dry. 'No, that's OK. I should probably be getting home.'

'I guess so,' he said, looking at the time. 'Yuri's gotta get to bed, too.'

We didn't speak on the drive home, both of us just looking out of the window at the twenty or so minutes' worth of passing scenery. But far from an awkward silence, it was comfortable. Hard earned, like we'd spent the past seven years scrapping for the right to be able to just sit next to each other in the back of a car. Josh was one of the only people in the world who could understand what things had been like since we got cast in Wonderwick, what it was like growing up in the public eye, everyone having an opinion on your outfits, who you were or were not dating, what project you should sign onto next, what X, Y or Z meant for your reputation, how much money could be wrangled out of this brand or that agency.

Part of me just wanted to keep sitting here next to Josh in the back seat forever, but Yuri eventually pulled up outside my house, sitting dark and empty on the suburban street.

'Well, thanks for the ride,' I told Josh, leaning back down to speak to him through the open car door, just like he'd done last night. 'See you tomorrow, I guess.'

'Thanks for the drink,' Josh said. 'And, you know, for giving me the time of day after . . . well, everything, ever.'

'Any time.'

I looked over my shoulder as I turned the key in the lock. Josh was still there, waiting to make sure I got inside safely. The sound of a car window opening punctuated the quiet evening stillness on this empty street, and Josh stuck his head out. 'Night, Emily.'

I waved to him as I pushed open my front door. 'Night, Josh. See you tomorrow.'

As I closed the door behind me, I leaned my back against it and closed my eyes, standing in the dark of the hallway. With great reluctance, feeling my heart beat a little quicker in my chest, I couldn't help face the facts. It was looking dangerously as if I had joined the legions of girls across the world who had a crush on Josh Sacco.

Chapter Twenty-One

I didn't want to speak too soon, but it was starting to feel like my co-star was a whole new Josh. It had been a few weeks and he had managed not to mess anything else up, didn't seem like he was arriving with a hangover, he knew his lines, hadn't lost any more highly valuable items, and most importantly, didn't push me into any more rivers.

I'd finished in makeup and had swung by craft services for some breakfast to eat in my trailer, picking up Carrie on the way, when I was greeted by the sight of Josh dunking a ball into the basketball hoop outside his trailer. He was, for some reason, shirtless, his skin retaining its LA tan despite several weeks in the British gloom.

'Hey, Emily!' he called to me, and I raised a hand in greeting. He raised his in return, his bicep flexing almost involuntarily to produce a fairly startling effect. 'Hey, Carrie!'

'I feel like Josh is around earlier and earlier these days,' I murmured to her as we entered my trailer, trying not to dwell too much on Topless Josh.

'Christ, is that all you have to say about what we just witnessed?' Carrie whispered to me. 'He's so ripped! That body, my God!' she added. 'Shouldn't be allowed.

'Carrie! No! Do *not* encourage me to look at him like that!'

'I wouldn't dream of it.'

'Anyway,' I said, trying to get her back on track. 'Do you think I'm right, about Josh being . . . better?'

'Everyone's talking about it, how he's got *way* more punctual all of a sudden. No one's waiting around for him anymore, he's always *right there* when you need him. He's even been reading the call sheet – Maria couldn't believe it. She'd been putting silly messages in there as a joke, knowing no one actually read it properly, and he went up to her and told her it wasn't very likely that Elvis Presley was visiting the set that day since he'd died in 1977!'

'Well! That's certainly a turn of events,' I said, sitting down to my fruit salad. 'While we're on the subject of, shall we say, human behaviour—' I didn't want to call it gossip and this sounded more respectable '—when I came in this morning, Darcy was getting out of a local taxi rather than being dropped off by her driver. Do you think she'd stayed at Josh's?' The fact he'd left the script in a taxi after hanging out with her had played on my mind, I had to admit.

'Oh no.' Carrie shook her head knowingly. 'I'm already up to date on this, girlie. The assistants' WhatsApp group was *aflame* this morning.'

'And you weren't going to tell me?'

'I was building up to it! Anyway, Darcy had to come by taxi this morning because she was *so awful* to her driver yesterday that he refused to drive for her anymore, told the company how awful she had been, they refused to let another one of their drivers be "subjected to that sort of behaviour" and threatened to leave the whole production driverless if she didn't apologise.'

I gasped in horror at the thought of being rude to Mike, the person who cheerfully bookended my days for months on end, come rain or shine. 'So now she has to take a taxi?'

'Well, only for today, the hope is she'll say sorry. Do people like her *say* sorry?' Carrie grimaced.

'This is crazy! I mean, this is a company that's used to ferrying around celebrities . . . if they can't handle Darcy then she must be pretty bad.'

'She was having loud phone conversations in the back seat mocking what he was wearing! She yelled at him for being on time, said he was rushing her! I even heard she had a go at him for observing the speed limit because they were going to be late when *she* had kept him waiting for forty minutes!'

'I wonder if she thinks this is some kind of girl boss persona,' I mumbled, trying to understand what would motivate someone to act like this.

'I think she's just a bit of a dick, mate.' Carrie shrugged, stealing a strawberry off my plate. 'Anyway, you're due on set in ten, let's mobilise!' She clapped her hands and jumped to her feet.

Later that day, I was sitting and reading in an E-Z UP tent between takes when Tommy came in and joined me.

'Has Josh's new-found professionalism cramped the party style a bit?' I asked him.

'Well, it's certainly a new look on him, I'll give you that,' Tommy said, running a hand over his closely shaved head with a big paw-like hand. 'But what do you mean about partying?'

'You know, the lot of you going out after we wrap, getting the drivers to take you into London and all that,' I said, as lightly and casually as I could manage.

'You say that like we've been doing it all the time!' He laughed.

'So, you haven't all been going out in the evenings?' I asked, holding my breath. 'Hanging out together? Like when we went to that club in Soho that night?'

'Er, not really. Sometimes me and Max will go to the pub and play darts with some of the crew while eating scampi fries but that's about it. That night out we had when you wore those suspender things was kind of a rarity.'

'Oh.'

'Speak of the devil,' Tommy said as Max opened the flap of the tent and entered, holding a giant milkshake.

'Ruh roh!' Max said in a Scooby Doo voice, taking a sip of the milkshake. The sight of it made me smile, him in his borderline steampunk costume clutching this iced monstrosity. He sat down in a spare chair across from Tommy and me.

'We were just talking about post-work fraternising. Emily's feeling a little insecure,' Tommy said, switching into naughty boy mode as soon as Max was in the picture.

'Why? You think we've been hanging out without you?' Max asked.

'Well, I *know* you were hanging out without me. That night everyone went to Shoreditch just before we started shooting?'

Tommy furrowed his brow, trying to remember what I was talking about. 'Oh, that? Were you not invited?'

'You bloody were there!' Max protested, before having second thoughts. 'Weren't you?'

I shook my head. 'I wasn't! I really wasn't! And I assumed it was . . . I don't know, intentional. That Darcy had organised some big thing to show how cool and fun she was. And that no one wanted me there.' I wanted the ground to swallow me up for even saying it out loud but for some reason it felt like the right moment to get it off my chest.

'Get outta town.' Tommy pushed gently at my shoulder. 'Everyone thought everyone else had asked you. No one was trying to leave you out.'

'And was it not fun? Why haven't you all been out since?'

'Eh, it was all right. The place she took us to was kinda not my vibe. I don't know if it was really any of our vibes, to be honest. I kind of prefer the darts and scampi fries in the pub.'

'Those are some top quality nights, mate.' Max lobbed the empty cup into the bin. 'Wouldn't change 'em for the world.'

'It was like she was trying too hard, you know, trying to make it all *wild* and *crazy* when we just wanted to hang.' Tommy shrugged.

'Much as I hate to admit it, it would have been way better if you'd have been there.' Max sucked pensively on his straw. 'Might have actually had some good chat rather than just posing for endless photos with stupid drinks.'

I rolled my eyes. 'You don't have to say that just to make me feel better. I know I'm not fun like Darcy, no one has to pretend for my sake. I promise you won't hurt my feelings,' I said, although I knew that was a lie, and that I was *very* capable of getting my feelings hurt over stuff like this.

'It's not even like that,' Tommy laughed. 'It's not even about people not wanting to hurt you or wanting you to feel secure. It's just that she can be well annoying and you're, er, *not*. I mean, not all the time, anyway. At least you take a break once in a while. She's an always-on kind of annoying.'

I laughed despite myself. 'Do you really mean that?'

'Er, yeah,' they both said, simultaneously, before Tommy added, 'It's like she's putting it on, like she's so awful it must be acting.'

'And you're really not just trying to make me feel better?'

'When have we *ever* tried to make you feel better?' Max asked, incredulously. He had a point.

Maria stuck her head in the tent and sighed, exasperated, at the sight of the three of us sitting around. 'Tommy, you're meant to be rehearsing the fight with the combat coordinator!'

'Oh, shit, is that the time?' He quickly leaped to his feet and was out of there.

'Anyway, I'm gonna dash to the medic tent to ask about a boil on my bum,' Max said, engaging in the time-honoured tradition of taking any random non-film-set-related ailment to the medics while you were here. 'Catch you later.'

'I'm sure they're really going to enjoy that.' I grimaced.

'What? It could be worse, I could be showing them my—'

'Max!' I put my fingers in my ears.

'God, you're such a prude!' He laughed and dashed off in the direction of the medics. Good luck to them.

Maybe Darcy wasn't quite so popular, maybe everyone wasn't hanging out without me. Maybe I wasn't so perceptive after all.

'Crew WhatsApp group is on *fire* today,' Carrie murmured to me as we stood watching one of the monitors that afternoon. They were filming a scene in Alder's workshop, another vividly realised space plucked directly from the book, festooned with tiny little cogs and contraptions in wood and metal completing almost-impossible movements. Max's character, Alder, was showing Rowan and Cinder (also known as Josh and Eve), some new tracking device he had been working on. Linderley was elsewhere, sneaking around the High Council's Sky Lodge in disguise, so I wasn't needed for the scene.

'Oh?' I asked, sure that it would be some internal crew politics that I was never meant to know about in the first place.

Carrie glanced down at her phone. 'It seems Miss Darcy is getting a stern talking-to,' she said, reading intently. 'Turned up late one too many times, I guess. Word on the street is she was summoned to Jonas earlier . . . Martin must have outsourced his dirty work to the first AD.'

I grimaced. 'Yikes, I wonder what's going to happen. They can't, like, get *rid* of her, can they?' I secretly hoped they could.

'Eh, they could, but they won't. Way too late in the day for that, plus it would cause a huge media shitstorm.' She reached out and touched something at my collar. I was still wearing my Linderley Jones costume, which today consisted of a creamy-coloured shirt with a Peter Pan collar tucked into a voluminous gingham skirt. 'Your stitching's coming undone, you'd better take that to costume.' I looked down and saw she was right, a trail of thread was hanging off and the bottom of the collar was coming loose.

'Ooh, thanks for that. I'll go and get another one now.'

'If you change out of it in your trailer I can take it for you?' she offered. Carrie was always trying to save me from doing various jobs, but I liked having something to do and often enjoyed an excuse to walk around.

'It's OK, I'll go myself.'

I wandered off in the direction of the costume department with their mannequins and racks and sewing machines, spare buttons, Wonder Web, everything the human mind could conceive to use for a costume and everything else you might need to repair it. I traded one of my Linderley shirts for another, and headed back to find Carrie and hopefully everything would be ready to shoot again. As got near the sound stages, I heard loud, rapid footsteps coming towards me from round the corner, accompanied by a distinct sound of sniffing.

'Oh!' I said, as someone barrelled right into me. 'Darcy!'

She didn't look at me, just muttered, 'Sorry,' and carried on. Instinctively, I turned around and reached out to grab her wrist.

'Darcy? Are you OK?'

I looked at her, her makeup streaked all over her face. That must have been *some* talking-to from Jonas.

He was known for his flat, Scandinavian effect, but I'd never known him to make someone cry before.

'I was . . .' She sniffed. 'I was going to tell you to leave me alone but . . . then I remembered . . . I don't have to do that anymore.'

'What are you talking about?' I asked, baffled. 'Do you want to go somewhere quiet?' I racked my brains for somewhere we could talk undisturbed. 'We could go to my trailer?'

She nodded, and I bundled her out of a back door I knew connected with the car park that our trailers sat on.

Once the door of my trailer closed behind us, the floodgates truly opened. Darcy was openly wailing. 'I've been so awful,' were the first words I could make out. 'I'm sorry, Emily.'

'What's going on? Please, just . . . help me out here?'

Darcy took a deep breath and steadied herself. 'I thought this was what I was *meant* to do, you know?' Even without the tears, her voice sounded . . . different somehow. More lively, less laconic. More like, well, a normal person. 'I thought I was meant to be some rebel, some rock and roll girl, that that was what people wanted from me. Or what they expected of me. So I played up to it, didn't I?' She reached for another tissue from the box I had pushed across the table at her. She blew her nose loudly, something I never thought I would live to see Darcy Jackson doing. 'But I took it too far. I knew

I was taking it too far.' She shook her head, the shame of it palpable. 'I should have just put a pin in it when the whole thing with the car company happened. I was *so awful* to him and it caused such a fuss in the production I honestly thought I was going to get sacked. But then nothing *did* happen so I just . . . kept doing it. Kept my image up, you know?'

'But why?' I asked, baffled.

'Emily, you don't get it. You know who you are! You're just *you*! You have no idea what a fucking super-power it is to just be yourself. But I . . . I don't know. I thought I had to be someone else for the fans. They seem to love the idea of me being this spiky little ice queen and I felt like that's what had got me cast as Loreia, so I figured I should just keep doing that. I guess I thought that people would take me more seriously if I acted like a diva, that I would get my way more, get a reputation for being someone you didn't mess with. I don't know.' She shook her head, covering her face with her hands. 'I thought it was *cool* to be like that.'

I sighed and handed her a tissue. 'Oh, Darcy. Wonderwick isn't like that! A lot of us are just normal people who ended up here by chance. Plus Josh,' I added for accuracy. 'But no one is looking for Hollywood divas on this set. It's just not like that! It never has been!'

Darcy smiled, weakly. 'I wish someone had told me that before. That I wasn't in some kind of competition to be the number one star of Wonderwick.' So it wasn't all in my head. She had been, in her way, trying to assert herself against me. 'I'm going to make it up to everyone. Give a personal apology to everyone I was rude to. Order pizza for the whole crew. Never let myself get wrapped up in something like this again.'

I liked this Darcy. 'I think that's a good idea.'

'Thanks for the chat.' She sniffled, standing to leave my trailer. 'I'm sorry I called you a bitch that day in the makeup trailer. I honestly couldn't believe I said it. But, as I think I've made abundantly clear, I'm always taking shit too far . . .'

'Oh, I thought . . .' I started.

'What?'

'It sounds silly, but I thought maybe you were jealous? I know you and Josh, like, hang out . . .'

She gave me a half-smile, her gaze direct but relaxed. 'Babe, are you in some Tumblr-proof alternate dimension? I'm queer, I'm barely interested in men at all, even the pretty ones.' She shrugged. 'Josh is a friend. He was always trying to get me to chill out with the whole . . . you know . . . madness. But did I listen? Nope.'

I must admit, I had heard something like this on the grapevine over the years, but she and Josh just seemed so *intimate*. 'But why not just say it? I feel like the fans would absolutely *love* that: queer Loreia Buckthorn!'

Darcy shrugged. 'I want to leave some things for myself, you know? Not offer everything up to the world, to the fans.'

I nodded. 'It's a weird world, isn't it? It all gets a little confusing – what's real and what's not, who you are and who your character is, what you want and what the fans want . . . but we're in it together, Darcy, I promise.'

She looked like she was going to cry again, but instead grabbed me and clasped me to her chest like I was a life raft on the *Titanic*.

'Thank you, Emily,' she whispered into my ear.

Once Darcy had left my trailer to begin her process of making amends with everyone she had thus far wronged on set, I lay down on my sofa and stared at the ceiling. It struck me that what I'd said to her was true: none of us knew who we really were. We were, what, twenty or twenty-one years old, most of us had grown up in the public eye whether through Wonderwick or famous parents, no wonder we were all absolutely riddled with insecurities that came out in a variety of ways.

Knowing that Darcy wasn't quite the person I had thought she was didn't necessarily solve my problems: the fans still adored her, she *was* sexy and glamorous and exciting in a way that I was sure I could never be, but at least now she felt more like a person. I could deal with a person.

Wonderwick Love Triangle? Josh Sacco and Darcy Jackson CANOODLING in Romantic Evening at Hot London Restaurant

Only weeks after being photographed with his arm around his Wonderwick co-star Emily Montgomery, Josh Sacco has been spotted enjoying a romantic candlelit dinner with newcomer to the franchise Darcy Jackson.

The pair were seen canoodling in a corner booth at Sashiko, the new restaurant from celebrity chef Michi Ito. Onlookers said the pair were seen leaning in to whisper into each other's ears and were even playing footsie under the table.

'They looked like they were really into it,' said one guest at Sashiko. 'They kept giggling and looking like they were the only people in the restaurant.'

Rumours from the set of *Wonderwick Woods: The Far Shores* suggest Darcy got off to a rocky start with her co-stars, though all of that seemed to be very much behind them as she cosied up to Josh Sacco. Cast and crew complained of diva-like behaviour and sources close to the film said she was threatened with being replaced.

Representatives for both stars declined to comment.

Chapter Twenty-Two

The press were eating it up, but unfortunately so was I. Even though I knew something like that was on the horizon *and* I knew it was all a publicity set-up, I still felt an uncomfortable prickling when I read the article.

Josh and I were standing side by side, watching on the monitor as Darcy and Max filmed a scene where Loreia Buckthorn held Alder hostage. Seeing her in costume and full hair and makeup was always fun: regular Darcy turned even more spiky and sharp. I had to admit after all my initial misgivings, she was actually the perfect choice for Loreia and scenes like this where she could go full high camp villain were her forte.

'You're quiet today,' Josh observed, tearing a curving section off his usual pain au raisin.

'No, I'm not!' I said, too defensively.

'Whatever you say . . .' His tone was infuriatingly light, but I wouldn't have believed me either.

We stood in silence a moment longer, watching Darcy stuff a rag into Max's mouth, something that would surely spark a thousand memes made by fans begging Darcy to do that to them.

He kept his eyes on the monitor. 'Wouldn't have anything to do with me going for dinner with Darcy last night, would it?'

'No!'

'Because it would be OK if it did.'

I exhaled loudly. 'If it did, then it's not for the reasons you're thinking.'

'What reasons would they be?'

'That I'm, you know, *jealous* or something silly like that.'

'And what would the correct reasons be?'

I thought for a moment, trying to think how to express it. I wasn't lying (well, only a little bit), there was more to it than just a faint, disgusting jealous feeling. 'I just think it makes you look like a player and me and Darcy look like we're fighting over you, that's all.'

He chewed his pastry thoughtfully. 'That makes sense.'

I mean, maybe I was a little bit jealous, but I was also right about the dynamics of the thing.

I eyed him with suspicion. 'So you're not going to tell me I'm being crazy and overreacting? You're not going to roll your eyes at me?'

Josh shook his head. 'Nah. You've got a point. Would have been much more progressive if we'd had me and you fighting over Darcy or some other permutation.

The way we've got it set up is actually the least interesting way, right?'

I laughed. 'Right! Unfortunately I am, very boringly, one hundred per cent straight.'

'Do you wish it had been the other way around?'

'How do you mean?'

'Like I'd stepped out with Darcy first, then you. So it looks like you're the alpha dog, or whatever?'

'Don't be ridiculous,' I said, rolling my eyes even though he was a bit right. It was annoying when Josh was right, and he was right more than usual these days. It was starting to feel like he actually might understand what went on in my brain for the first time ever. I didn't really like it.

'Well,' he said, still not taking his eyes off the monitor, 'you're the one that gets the kiss.'

I gulped down a sensation of rising fear. I hated being reminded of that. Why couldn't it have been right at the beginning of the shoot to get it out of the way, rather than right at the end so it was always looming over the horizon. 'You say that like it's some big prize.'

He clutched at his chest, fake-wounded. 'You mean it's not?' His infuriating lopsided grin was wider than ever.

'Shut up.' I couldn't help rolling my eyes.

'But for real, you feeling OK about the whole thing? I feel kinda bad now for pushing the . . . uh, spiciness, of the scene.'

'Did you just do it because you knew I'd hate it?' I asked, flatly.

'Uh, yeah, a little bit. I thought it would be funny, given we had to do the kiss either way because it's in the book.' Josh raised his arm and tossed the last bite of his pastry into his mouth.

'And now here we are,' I said, because I didn't know what else to say. As Josh's arm fell to his side again, I felt it faintly brush against mine, the backs of our hands grazing each other just for a moment. My stomach lurched.

'Here we are,' Josh repeated, but now he sounded . . . serious? Apprehensive? As if reality had set in for him, too.

Chapter Twenty-Three

Shoots always seemed to pass in the blink of an eye but this Wonderwick had gone by especially fast. It felt like one minute we were doing final fittings for costumes, and the next we were barrelling towards my last scene before I headed off to Ireland to film *Orientations*. And of course the last scene we were shooting was The Kiss. The dreaded kiss. The anticipated kiss. Whichever way you looked at it, it was a kiss. Between me and Josh.

The big moment came one Thursday morning when outside the studio it was pouring with rain but on the sound stage, the fake sun was filtering through to a tree-top in Wonderwick Woods. But first, Chloe had news. *Big* news: Tom Dwyer who had originally been cast in *Orientations* had dropped out and been replaced at the last minute with none other than Ben Sage-Whittle. *How's THAT for strategic?! Obviously no pressure if you've changed your mind since coffee, but!!! Auspicious!* Chloe had emailed enthusiastically. That was something to look forward to, a much-needed diversion from . . . whatever it was I was feeling about Josh.

I waved at Martin going into his trailer from across the car park and he beckoned me over. 'Ems, are we feeling all right? I know you were a little apprehensive about today,' Martin asked me, arms folded across his chest in a pose of concern that I could see *right* through.

'I'm feeling fine,' I reassured him, not that it would make any difference if I wasn't. 'Just ready to get on with it.'

'That's the spirit! And the little addition?' He raised his eyebrows expectantly. The 'little addition' was me pushing Josh against a tree trunk, to show this wasn't just a gentle, romantic kiss as it was written in the book, this was passionate and it was all coming from me. Or rather from Linderley.

'That's fine, too.'

'Because we can always take it out if you really don't want to?'

I shook my head. 'No, if that's what you guys think is best.'

'I promise you, Ems, I'm going to keep everything as short as possible,' he said in a tone so placating it was almost patronising. 'It'll be over as soon as you know it!'

'Great, thanks, Martin. Was there anything else?'

'No, no, you get on with things and I'll see you there.'

I took myself off to craft services for a herbal tea, knowing coffee would only make me even more jittery, plus I didn't want to have coffee breath to kiss Josh with. On the way back, I saw Josh leaning against the basketball hoop outside his trailer, phone in one hand, vape in the other.

'I thought you were committed to the real stuff?' I nodded down at his vape.

'I'm trying to quit altogether but . . . it's a hard habit to break.'

'I think you can do it. I mean, you've changed enough over the past few months, how hard can it be to give up smoking?' I said with a laugh. I was still nervous, but there was something soothing about being around Josh today. I'd often criticised his laid-back demeanour as a sign he didn't care, but today it felt like exactly what I needed.

'Well, today it's all for you, Montgomery,' he said, sliding the vape into his pocket.

'Oh?'

'I figured it would be polite.' He shrugged. 'To you, I mean. For the kiss.' He didn't meet my gaze, and I felt like I was missing out on an opportunity to look into his soft, brown eyes.

'That's . . . very considerate, Josh. I should be changing into costume so I'll see you out there?' He gave me a little salute and I disappeared into my trailer to dress.

As someone who prided myself on always feeling on top of things, it struck me that I very much did not feel on top of things right then. I liked being certain! Liked being prepared! I did not like . . . whatever this was. I was dreading the kiss but also part of me was looking forward to it. Josh had been my work nemesis for the past seven years and now not only was he being kind and professional, I was feeling . . . stirrings for him. I wanted to get out of there and head to Ireland (and Ben!) but I also didn't want this chapter of Wonderwick to end.

When Carrie knocked on my trailer door to pick me up, I jumped about a foot in the air. I'd just finished my third swirl of mouthwash that day.

'You feeling all right?' she asked me, holding my phone as Juliet did final touch-ups on my makeup before we started shooting. Butterflies zoomed around my stomach but I told her I was fine. She handed me my phone for one last check of my emails before we started filming, but on the screen was a text from my dad.

> *Hope shoot is going well, darling. OK if I move some more money around?*

I didn't have time to think too much about it so just fired off a quick reply that it was all going well and it was fine for him to do whatever he needed. I handed the phone back to Carrie and headed towards my mark on the sound stage.

George the hair stylist was shielding Josh's face with one hand as he aimed a canister of hairspray at his head with the other. Despite George's best efforts, Josh burst out into a wheezing cough and he doubled over, trying to catch his breath. He looked so vulnerable, not at all like the mischievous, destructive person I'd known for so long.

We stood on our marks. We had filmed the preceding dialogue of the scene the day before, so today was just about shooting the few lines leading up to the kiss, and the kiss itself. Quiet descended onto set and I heard Jonas call action. My stomach lurched. It was happening.

Josh had the first line: 'I can't help but feel things are different between us now. Things have changed, haven't they?'

'I think maybe they have,' I said, my mouth dry.

'So . . . what now?' Josh infused his line with such a hunger that I desperately hoped he would be able to recreate on the next take. It felt so raw, so urgent, like if Rowan and Linderley didn't resolve things *now now now* then he would lose his mind.

He was looking at me in a way that Rowan had never looked at Linderley before, and in that moment I realised that was the point. The kiss hadn't come out of nowhere, instead it had been built up to over everything the characters had gone through together, the way they had changed and grown up, the things they'd seen and done. The people they had lost and found, and the people they had become.

Finally, the last line before the kiss. I wondered if the camera could pick up the way I was shaking. 'Rowan, I want this. I want you,' I said, fixing him with a look of such intensity I felt like I could burn a hole right through him. I stepped forward and put my arms around him, our lips meeting, me pushing him up against the trunk of the tree, his tongue in my mouth, his hands around my waist, the hunger with which we were devouring each other under the studio lights, in this make-believe world. It was like we were in a bubble, where all that mattered was *this kiss*. That this kiss was the point of the whole film, maybe the point of my whole life. I felt him reach between the waistband of my skirt and the billowing linen shirt I was wearing on top and feel the skin on my back, pulling me towards him with the same force with which I was drawing him towards me. It felt like we were melting into each other, two magnets finally close enough to snap together.

I knew that on the next take I would do it with even more force, even more passion. I wanted to experience it again, except more, more, more. I wanted to do it again and again, for the lighting to be wrong, for the sound to be off, for a stray hair to have fallen across my face. I wanted to kiss Josh again and again because this was the place that I could do it, where it was safe and controlled and nothing was real, it was all just the magic of Wonderwick.

'Cut!' Jonas called, and approving chatter burst out across the set.

But Josh and I couldn't move apart. It was as if there was a spell on us and we were glued together, gazes locked on each other, his eyes scanning my face, maybe looking for a reaction, to see what I was thinking, feeling. Our breathing was heavy, both of our chests rising and falling intensely. His hands felt hot around my waist and I simultaneously craved distance from him and didn't want us to let go.

'That was . . . better than the last one, right?' I said quietly, as we finally moved away from each other.

'The last one?' Josh asked, frowning at me. I swallowed. Clearly he didn't remember, but I did. A stupid prank he had played on me at the wrap party for the second Wonderwick film, something that cemented my complete lack of trust for him.

'Nothing.' I shook my head.

'We're gonna have to do it again like eight more times, aren't we?' Josh said, apprehensively. It was funny to see him out of sorts like this, not his usual laid-back self. I thought he was well up for this and that I was the one who was nervous, but right now it seemed like he was out of his depth while I was at least pretending to keep it all together.

'Only eight if we're lucky. I bet Martin will make us do twelve takes.'

'Speak of the devil.' Josh glanced over my shoulder and I turned to see Martin striding towards us, beaming.

'That was absolute perfection, kids! And I *loved* that sneaky little hand movement, Josh, you sly dog!'

Josh reddened instantly. 'Oh, gosh, sorry about that, Emily. I got a bit carried away, didn't I?'

I shook my head. 'It was completely fine,' I said, a little too quickly.

'I won't do it again next time,' Josh assured me, which made something sink in my chest.

Martin held up a hand. 'Don't worry about a next time. I couldn't have asked for a better take myself. I mean, literally – we don't even need to do another one! I think everyone around here could do with an early finish. You're free to go.'

That was *it*? We were done? It was all over? I felt like I had crashed down to earth with a bump.

'What?' Josh gaped at him in disbelief.

'Look, I know it was a whole *thing*, all this silly hype and build-up, but it's done now! You nailed it, we got a perfect take, let's not let it get stale by repeating it over and over again. You did a great job and I'm proud of you.'

'Thanks, Martin,' I said, smiling weakly as he strode off. If I'd known it was the only take, I would have . . . what? What would I have done? I didn't know, but I knew that something felt off, incomplete, unresolved.

Josh and I stood in silence for a moment. It was as if everyone but Martin knew to leave us alone, just for a moment.

'Well.' I looked away. 'That's me done.'

'What do you mean?'

'I'm on another film, I have to go to Ireland. This was my last day on Wonderwick.'

'Oh, of course,' Josh said, a look of surprise passing across his face. 'Sure, I knew that. I guess I just forgot . . . amid all the . . . you know.'

I nodded. 'Well, this has certainly been an interesting shoot.'

'Sure has, Montgomery,' he said, fixing me with a sad smile.

I held my arms out for him, something I can't remember volunteering to do once on Wonderwicks gone by. 'This really *has* been an interesting shoot,' he said.

He pulled me tight against him and I could feel the taut muscles of his chest against mine, trying not to run my hands over his broad back.

'Thank you for . . . you know, for trying,' I said quietly into his ear.

'Thank you for believing that I could try,' he whispered back.

And then it was all over. He was being whisked off to another stage and I was left adrift. What was even the point of me now? I thought to myself as I headed back to my trailer.

Darcy was strolling towards me, dressed in her Loreia Buckthorn costume and makeup. She had her last scene today too, while Josh was staying on another few days to film bits that neither of us were in.

'One take, huh?'

'I'm as surprised as anyone!' I said as brightly as I could manage. My head was spinning, I didn't want to be feeling all of this right now.

'We were watching on the monitor.' She looked over her shoulder to where a few of the supporting cast were deep in intense conversation. 'You fucking nailed it.'

'I guess we did!'

'And it turns out Linderley was the real girl boss all along, not Loreia.'

'Ha,' I said, weakly.

She was eyeing me warily, something guarded in her expression. 'And was it, like, *real*?'

'What do you mean, real?'

'You know, like a real kiss,' she asked, expectantly.

'We just did what we had to do for the scene, that's all!'

She paused for a moment. 'I can just . . . never figure out what's going on with you two, you know?'

'Nothing's going on,' I said, which was true.

She nodded, like that was enough for her. 'So, you're off?'

'To Ireland. No rest for the wicked!'

Darcy smiled. 'Emily Montgomery, you are the least wicked person I've ever met. And I mean that as a total compliment.'

'Ha, thanks, Darcy.'
'See you on the press tour?'
'See you there.'

In the car on the way back to the house for the last time, I had the thought again: if I'd known that was the only take, I would have made it last longer.

JOSH

It was the wrap party for the second movie, *Beyond the Forest*. Back then, neither of us had to dash off to another project and could enjoy the party with the rest of the crew. Tommy and Max and I stood at the edge of the dance floor, sipping the one single illicit beer we thought we could get away with unnoticed by our chaperones. Emily was dancing unselfconsciously, limbs flailing, huge smile on her face, finally out of her shell after how nervous she'd been on the first movie. She was dancing with Carrie and Maria, the second assistant director, and she looked, somehow, just right. Not cool, not edgy, not like a new blockbuster movie star, but just herself. I knew that was something I hadn't quite mastered myself, always messing around, trying to get attention to deflect from the fact that I didn't really know what I was doing, trying to show Emily up so she wasn't always the Wonderwick golden child. But Emily knew who she was and stuck to it, and goddamn if I didn't envy her for it in ways I wasn't mature enough to articulate then.

'Right, lads, time to crack into my private reserve,' Tommy said as we tossed our cans into a nearby recycling bin. He then produced another two cans of beer from pockets on either side of his cargo pants. He waved one at me. 'All right, Hollywood boy, bet you can't chug this in ten seconds.'

'Bet I can,' I replied without a moment's thought.

'Ha, no way.' Max shook his head.

'Oh, bitch, you *know* I can,' I laughed, reaching out for the can.

Tommy yanked it back out of my reach. 'Why don't we make this more interesting?'

'Go on,' I said, cautiously as Max and Tommy looked at each other, clearly coming up with some horrible plan. They turned back to me with a huge grin on both of their dumb handsome faces.

'Whoever can chug their beer the fastest wins.'

'OK . . .' I said, waiting for the catch.

'Don't you want to know what happens to the loser?' Tommy's eyes were glinting with mischief.

Before I could answer, Max excitedly burst out, 'Loser has to kiss Emily!'

'You in?' Tommy was fizzing with merriment.

'Uh, sure . . . I mean, as long as you're OK with kissing Emily because I'm definitely not gonna lose,' I said, nonchalantly.

'Ha! Did you hear that, Max?' Tommy scoffed. 'This one thinks he can challenge *us* in a chugging contest.

Do they teach you that at Beverly Hills School for Boys?'

'It's called Beverly Hills High School, actually,' I mumbled as he handed me a can. The two of them argued amongst themselves about who would be the one to take me on, since there were only two cans, and finally it was decided I would go up against Max and Tommy would adjudicate.

The second I had that can in my hand, I knew I had made a mistake. Why had I agreed to it? I agreed to it because . . . well, who knows why. If you asked me I'd say it was because I absolutely could not turn down a dare from Max and Tommy, or because I thought it would be funny, a prank, a joke, whatever, or because I wanted to wind up Emily. But there was, I hate to admit, more to it than that. As soon as Max suggested it and Tommy sec-onded the idea, I felt this ping of curiosity, like a weird desire for something I knew I shouldn't want.

'Three . . . two . . . one . . . go!' Tommy called once we had popped the seal on our cans. Like a maniac, I threw the can back against my lips and started to inhale the beer, swallowing as often as I physically could, try-ing to resist the urge to take a breath. I couldn't lose. I didn't want to find out what would happen if I did. I was guzzling the beer down at a rate of knots, sure that I was going to beat Max, when—

'HELL YEAH!' Max roared, turning his beer can upside down to show it was empty. I knew there was still some left in mine. I had lost. Shit.

'You know what that means.' Tommy leered at me, his face the picture of absolute glee.

'Step on it, Sacco,' Max urged me. 'You've got some smooching to do.'

I glared at them as they both made kissy faces at me and pointed in the direction of Emily, who was blissfully unaware, twirling away on the dance floor.

'Don't rush me, Christ. If I have to do this, lemme do it in my own time,' I said, my head spinning. 'You don't want her to get suspicious, right?' I needed to wait for a moment when Emily was on her own.

'You can't just *say* you did it and not do it, mate,' Tommy chided me.

'I won't! I promise, I'll do it. But you can't expect me to walk up to her right there and do it, can you?'

'I mean, we'd rather you did.' Max shrugged.

'Nope, nuh-uh. Lemme handle this my own way,' I said, as sharply as I could manage as an insecure seventeen-year-old.

We stood for a moment watching the dance floor, and then Emily said something to Carrie before walking off on her own.

'Now's your chance!' Tommy elbowed me in the ribs.

I sighed, just to really underline how much I didn't want to kiss Emily, and headed off after her, catching up with her just outside the pub.

'Hey, Emily,' I said, wanting to get this over and done with as soon as humanly possible and with no witnesses.

She fiddled with the little metal bit on her dungarees. 'Hi, Josh.'

'Uh, I just wanted to, uh—' I said, before leaning forward and kissing her. She jumped a little but didn't pull away, which, frankly, surprised me. I wouldn't tell Max and Tommy that, I would report that I'd given her a quick peck on the lips and the deed was done and we would say no more about it.

But no such luck. The door burst open behind us and their hysterical cackles filled the night air. At the sound of the hyena-like laughing she jerked away from me, her face the picture of bewilderment. And then she realised. It was all a joke. The kiss was a joke. She was a joke. She was *the* joke.

She covered her mouth with her hand, eyes wide with total horror, then ran off around the back of the pub as the boys slapped me on the back and congratulated me on being true to my word. I felt sick with guilt. I'd never intended on them bursting in like that, never wanted her to find out that it was a dare. I don't know *what* I wanted her to think of it, I hadn't thought that far ahead, but I never, ever wanted to make her feel the way I knew I had made her feel.

'Don't fucking tell anyone about this, all right?' I looked between them, trying to get them to understand how deadly serious I was.

'Ha, all right, Joshy,' Tommy said, laughing.

I took a deep breath and did something I'd never done before and haven't done since. 'If you tell anyone about this, you will never work again, do you understand me?'

Tommy and Max looked genuinely scared. 'Er, yeah, sure, man.' Max forced out a laugh, clapping me on the shoulder. 'Don't worry about it. This will stay between us, yeah?' He turned to his friend who just nodded, eyes wide in fear. They didn't deserve me to go that hard, I'll admit, but having seen the look on Emily's face when she realised it was a joke I knew that it couldn't get out.

'Christ, she's not that bad,' Tommy chuckled.

'That's not what I fucking mean, you freckle-faced shithead. Don't ever tell anyone I embarrassed her like that, you hear me?'

They both nodded, and my strongly worded message must have got through to them because I never heard anyone mention it ever again after that night, no nudges or winks or gossip on the press tour. If she ever told anyone, it never got back to me. I always try to tell myself that it was no big deal for her, that she just took it as a joke and moved on, but if there's one thing I know about Emily, it's that she has many talents but 'taking it as a joke and moving on' is not one of them.

Chapter Twenty-Four

My timing couldn't have been better: I might have left Wonderwick with just a *hint* of a crush on Josh Sacco, but being thrown straight into shooting *Orientations* meant zero opportunity to nurse it.

This film was a completely different world. Written by the director himself, it was a story of a reclusive mother and daughter living in a sprawling house whose lives are disrupted by the arrival of a handsome stranger. Realities were questioned, perspectives shifted, nothing was quite as it seemed. It was all shot on location at an abbey outside Galway, and the crew kept commenting on how we shouldn't take the surprisingly good summer weather for granted. Although it had a much lower budget than what I was used to, it was still a proper, full-scale production. I didn't have an assistant, my trailer was smaller, but I didn't care because I was so excited to be trying something new. Ben Sage-Whittle was finishing up on a Beach Boys biopic in LA that had overrun, so the first few days of the *Orientations* shoot could be all business. Edgar was a much more hands-on director than Martin, keen on naturalism and getting to the emotional truth of the scene rather than pure storytelling. He would talk about Laban and Meisner and Actioning and I would dutifully read and research about acting techniques that I suppose I would have studied properly if I'd gone to drama school, rather than growing up on Wonderwick. It was challenging, but I looked at the whole experience as an exam I wanted to pass. Unlike a lot of sets, Edgar enforced that the cast and crew ate meals together rather than the cast being sequestered in their trailers. That didn't stop all the departments from naturally congregating, and I found myself sitting next to Lucy Lennon, the actress playing my mother. We'd shot a scene together that morning and I'd been excited by how rigorous she was, the questions she'd ask of Edgar, everything she would put into the scene.

'I was glad to see you signed on to this.' She was eating crisps out of a yellow bag, delicately picking them out with her elegant oval nails. 'I've always liked you in those films, it made me want to see more from you.'

'Oh, that's really nice of you.' I flushed with pride. 'I've loved watching you ever since *Take Me Home*.'

'Well, aren't we a pair of luvvies?' She laughed and offered me one of the crisps. I shook my head. 'How are you finding it? Edgar's an interesting one, isn't he?'

'It's early days yet but I'm really enjoying it. It's certainly different from what I am used to. I feel like I'm really challenging myself in lots of ways, like I have to do a lot more with a lot less. I don't have the books to draw on to know who my character is and what she wants.'

'It's a big change. A lot of actors your age wouldn't have been up for it, I can tell you that for nothing.'

I thought of my dad. I could be filming with a green screen in a studio right now if I'd taken his advice and followed the money. Instead, I was being showered with praise by an Oscar-nominated actress. I was glad I'd stuck to my guns.

'Have you worked with Ben Sage-Whittle before?' I asked, trying to sound very nonchalant.

'I have, and I like him well enough.' She flicked her eyes to my face as if she was trying to figure out what I wanted her to say. I didn't give her anything, just waited for her to continue. 'I mean, he's very good at what he does . . . you know, that British public schoolboy thing? Why?'

'Oh, no reason.'

'He's handsome, I'll give him that,' she said, raising her eyebrows at me as if it was extremely obvious why I was asking.

The day Ben Sage-Whittle arrived on set I found myself at the station next to his in hair and makeup. I would glance over at his reflection, watching him sleepily come to life over his morning coffee, his fair hair clipped back from his handsome face. He'd look up, catch me checking him out, smirk to himself while I pretended I hadn't been looking at all, just taking in the ambiance of an early-morning makeup trailer. Then it was his turn to be caught looking at me in the mirror, and back and forth we went until we were both finished.

'Nice to see you again,' Ben said, holding the door open for me as we stepped out of the trailer.

'Yes, I'd been looking forward to it since our coffee,' I said, looking up at him.

'You always seem like such a good girl, but something tells me that even without an introductory meeting you'd have been making eyes at me in hair and makeup.' He was so confident, zero need to play games. I hadn't encountered anyone quite like him before. Maybe he wasn't as awkward as his public persona would suggest.

'I've never made eyes at anyone in my life,' I said, coyly.

'I don't believe it for a second.'

'Are you usually this forward with your co-stars?'

'Oh no, only the pretty ones.'

Before I could reply, he had turned off to head for his trailer. He looked back over his shoulder and gave me a wry smile. I suppose we had to at least pretend we were hard to get.

The next day, I was reading between takes, shielded from the sun in an E-Z Up. Enter Ben. He swaggered over to the chair facing me, glanced at my book. 'My mate's just bought that.'

'Nice.' I smiled. 'I hope they enjoy it.' It was a coming-of-age story with a murder at its heart, quite literary but it was really popular with the kind of girls who followed @WhatsEmilyReading.

'No, not like that,' he laughed. 'I mean, he's a producer and he's just bought the rights.'

'Oh!' I touched my hand to my forehead. 'Of course, wow. Have you read it?'

Ben nodded. 'I thought it was quite brilliant, the writing was almost . . .' he thought for a moment '. . . luminous. And anyway, it certainly made teenage girls sound utterly frightening, which in my experience they very much are.' Josh had never talked to me about what I was reading, only stolen my books from me and hidden them around the set, so Ben certainly had *that* going for him.

'I can't imagine you having any trouble with girls,' I said, which came out a little more primly than I had intended. I was *not* a natural born flirter – maybe I needed to take lessons from Chloe.

'Oh, no, I was a late bloomer.' He crossed one leg over the other, a perfect right angle. 'I was a skinny, awkward thing until I was about eighteen, then I started working out. Fancy a turn about the grounds?' Ben asked me, like we were in a Regency novel. 'I'll hold your parasol.'

'That sounds delightful,' I said, snapping my book shut a little bit too enthusiastically. Even if I was only thinking about Josh in terms of how he *didn't* match up to Ben, I was still thinking about Josh and that needed to stop. Ben was gorgeous and I genuinely wanted to throw myself into something with him, whatever that may be.

We walked together around the grounds of the abbey. He carried himself elegantly, and I never saw him slouch or lean against anything. Every time we turned a corner out of view of the crew I couldn't help wondering if we were maybe about to kiss, and when we didn't, I was half relieved (we were at work! You didn't kiss your colleagues at work!) and half disappointed.

Chapter Twenty-Five

Filming *Orientations* was like a gorgeous dream. Every day I felt like I was pushing myself a bit further, learning more about myself as an actress outside of Wonderwick. Learning that, actually, I was pretty good at this job. Since it was being shot using natural light, we were operating on days that began and ended earlier than most of us were used to. I loved acting with Ben, too, and found the way he slid seamlessly from Ben to The Man kind of magic. I was *like* Linderley Jones, which was part of the reason I got the role in the first place, but it meant 'real acting' always impressed me. Now I had to do it myself, and found both Ben and Lucy Lennon inspiring people to be around.

'The words *feel* right but you don't quite look right . . .' Lucy said, chewing on her thumbnail as we rehearsed a scene. It was a two-hander so we could go through it on our own, and we'd found ourselves a corner of walled garden where no one would disturb us.

'What do you mean?' I asked, keen to understand. I felt like I was learning something new from Lucy every day just by being around her. On Wonderwick, there seemed to be this divide between 'the children' and 'the adults', going all the way back to the first film. We were left to our own devices and the adults clustered together in E-Z Ups without us, and certainly never socialised with us. I tried to forget those divisions and remember that Lucy almost certainly didn't see me as 'one of the children', so I didn't want to put the idea in her head. I wanted her to think of us as artistic equals, albeit two people with vastly different amounts of experience.

'I feel like there's a disconnect between what you're saying and doing, and I'm wondering if that's deliberate?' she asked. 'It's not a criticism at all, I'm just trying to explore your intention.'

No one had wanted to explore my intention with me before. That wasn't really something we *did* on Wonderwick. Lucy and I tried the scene ten different ways, seeing which felt the most natural in our bodies with all the knowledge we had about the characters, the dialogue and what Edgar seemed to want from us. It was thrilling.

I knew Josh was filming an action movie set on a submarine, and I wondered how far his acting skills were being pushed, if at all. I wanted him to know what it felt like to *work* in this way, how satisfying it was to try and fail and try again and try differently and just keep trying. I remembered what I'd said to him in my embarrassing outburst at the river. The thing I'd asked him to do was *try*. I felt like I was trying non-stop on *Orientations*.

Finally, after running the lines twenty or more times, I felt something unlock inside me. I knew I'd figured out the tone, the gestures, the eye contact. I just *knew*.

'That's the one!' Lucy grinned at me, her mass of red curls piled haphazardly on her head. 'Don't you think?'

I nodded, barely able to contain an equally manic grin myself. 'It felt right. I think we've nailed it.'

'You've nailed it,' she said, resolutely.

'I absolutely couldn't have done it without you. I love working with you,' I said, shaking my head in disbelief as we walked back towards the unit base where everyone was breaking for lunch.

I spotted Ben deep in conversation with Edgar, the two of them walking together, Ben's head bowed as he listened. Ben was often with Edgar, talking endlessly about the script and the role, trying to refine his performance with a diligence that I have to say I found very hot. When Ben looked up, spotting me, his eyes lit up and my stomach did a tiny little backflip. I tried to keep the smile off my face at the sight of his soft gold hair and sharp cheekbones in the warm midday sun.

Finally, the two of them finished their conversation and Ben strolled over towards me, his hands in the pockets of his trousers. 'Hello, you. I was wondering if you wanted to get dinner tonight?'

'Just me and you?' I asked, the thought suddenly feeling a little bit real and intimidating.

He shrugged. 'Sure, that's what I was thinking. Is that a horrible idea? I thought we were . . . mutually interested.'

'Oh, no, we totally are,' I said, although I'd started to wonder if I really wanted to see this plan through. Even though I knew things were never going to happen with Josh, it still felt oddly disloyal to him . . . but if it was all just for show, a dinner out in Galway wasn't the worst thing in the world, was it? Ben was so unlike Josh in so many ways that it probably *would* be the ideal way to get my mind off him.

'Great, we can head in after we wrap.' A satisfied smile spread across his face as he tossed his floppy hair out of his eyes.

The rest of the afternoon I put my hard work with Lucy to good use and tried not to think too much about my dinner with Ben

'Today was a lot, wasn't it?' Ben asked over dinner at an Italian restaurant that evening. We'd barely made it through a quarter of a page of dialogue in the afternoon.

'We got there in the end! And I think having to do it over and over again helped me to really understand what was happening. I don't think I'd understood when I read it on the page that she doesn't actually mean any of what she's saying in that scene. I just took for granted she thought she was telling the truth.'

'That's because you're pure of heart,' Ben said, squeezing my knee under the table. I gasped a little in surprise at how forward he was being, especially in public, but kept having to remind myself that this was kind of the whole point! To be seen! 'That was OK, right?' he murmured to me over the table.

I nodded, feeling my pulse quicken. He gazed at me, deep in thought for a moment. 'I just can't get over your eyes . . .' My heart leaped, this was surely the precursor to something extremely romantic. 'They really freak me out!'

Oh.

I blinked, wrong-footed. 'Well, that's what I'm working with.'

'I don't mean in a bad way!' he insisted. 'They're just intense, that's all.' He held up a hand to cover my right eye, the blue one, and then the other to cover my left eye, the brown one. 'I wonder what you'd look like if they were both the same colour.'

Not that I'd have known what to say to that anyway but I didn't have to answer because we noticed a couple a few tables down whispering to each other and glancing in our direction. We waved at them and they laughed, a little embarrassed about being obvious, before asking if they could take a selfie with us. Once they'd returned to their table, Ben gasped.

'I can't believe we haven't discussed the news of the day,' he said, his eyes wide with delight.

I furrowed my brow, trying to figure out what he meant. 'What's that?'

'Haven't you seen?'

'Seen what?'

'Well, you know how Evan Cole just came out?' he said, referencing a young, handsome Hollywood star that had announced his relationship with a man via Instagram the day before. I nodded. 'Howard Hunt did this deranged post about how America needs fewer boys like Evan Cole and more very fine young men like Josh Sacco,' Ben laughed and shook his head. Howard Hunt was the Republican presidential candidate and was famous for making deranged pronouncements on things that had nothing to do with either himself or the presidency. 'Being called a very fine young man! By Howard Hunt! Can you imagine anything less dignified?!' Ben was almost hooting with amusement.

'Oh God.' I grimaced. 'Poor Josh.'

'I'd be mortified if I thought I appealed to a man like him,' Ben said, knocking back the last of his wine. 'Shall we head home?'

'I think so, it's been a long old day,' I told him, as I turned over my worries about Josh's PR situation in my head.

Ben paid, and I quickly fired off a text to Josh saying I was sorry that he'd got dragged into this whole mess, but that I knew he would handle it right. As we walked back to the hotel, hands brushing against each other's, I couldn't help feeling awful for Josh. It was one thing to be in the news for things you'd done, but it was another to get unwillingly dragged into a story by some maniac with bad politics and bad intentions.

When we got back to the hotel, we paused on the landing outside our rooms. 'That was nice, thank you for suggesting it,' I said, feeling at exactly the same time a spark of attraction to the person I was staring at *and* the profound hope that he wasn't going to invite me into his room.

After a much-needed night's sleep, very much alone, I woke to a text from Courtney.

OMG! Have you seen this?! I'm kind of obsessed?

With a link to a news article. Overcoming my natural suspicion that it was some kind of spam, I clicked the link. It was a news story about Josh, responding to what Howard Hunt had said, with an embedded video.

I clicked 'play', and there was Josh, sitting lazily in a chair across from Stacey Holmes, an entertainment reporter I had met before. 'So, Josh,' she asked, 'what do you think of Howard Hunt calling you "a very fine young man"? Is he someone whose approval you seek?'

Without even pausing for breath, without even think-ing, Josh said, 'Howard Hunt is a fucking fascist and he needs to keep my name out of his mouth.' My hand flew to my mouth in delight. Not that I would expect Josh to roll over and pretend he enjoyed this endorsement by the presidential candidate, but I didn't necessarily expect him to go nuclear, either. I would expect a combination of his parents and his team would have constructed some delicate, slippery response that wouldn't ruffle anyone's feathers, let alone those of the potential future president of America.

'That's pretty strong, isn't it?' Stacey asked, fishing for more from Josh.

Josh just flashed her a smile, shrugged his shoulders and crossed his legs, sitting even further back in the chair, even more relaxed. 'Just my opinion, Stacey. Pretty sure we still have the right to free speech in this country, don't we? He can say I'm a fine young man and I can call him a fucking fascist. And I can also say that I think Evan Cole is a prince, and braver than Howard Hunt will ever be.'

'So you think Howard Hunt is a fascist?'

'If it looks like a duck, walks like a duck, quacks like a duck . . .' He threw his hands up in submission. 'It's probably a fascist fucking duck, Stacey. Anyway, I thought we were here to talk about movies, not politics. Don't be pulling the old switcheroo on me,' he said, roguish grin on his face so powerful that it clearly disarmed her. And then the clip ended.

I watched the clip again, this time with a greater sense of pleasure because I knew what was coming. I felt a swell of pride fill my chest. I knew the kind of pressure we were under to remain apolitical, and there was almost no one in the cast you would have expected this of less than Josh, someone who had shown almost no interest in anything contentious, never really expressed even the mildest political opinion, barely even did the standard celebrity 'Register to vote!'-style content. When I scrolled to the bottom of the article, the comments were predictably divisive. Some along the lines of 'he's right and he should say it', 'finally a celebrity with a backbone', 'I've always thought he seemed like a smart young man', but also more than a few suggesting he was a traitor, should be shot, was an ungrateful bastard, that he was part of the liberal Hollywood Illuminati, that his parents were trying to control the White House, that he should be shipped off to fight a foreign war to toughen him up, and on and on and on.

I replied to Courtney:

Good for him

I thought this shoot would be a Wonderwick-free zone. Or did I mean a Josh Sacco-free zone? But that was an impossible dream. Just because filming Wonderwick had ended, it didn't mean I was ever really free of it. The universe and everyone in it was just too big a cultural force. It was everywhere.

Ben and I had the same call time so shared a car to set that morning. 'Gosh.' Ben looked up from his phone when we were nearing the abbey, a bemused smile on his face. 'Your old pal Josh has really put his foot in it, hasn't he?'

I liked Ben. He was handsome, talented, fun to hang out with. I fancied him and I respected him. But there was always this sense of distance between us when it came to Wonderwick . . . or maybe just when it came to Josh.

'I feel like you're saying he didn't mean to say what he said in the interview?' I ventured, cautiously.

'And you think he did mean to?' He frowned at me as if the idea hadn't crossed his mind.

'Yes, I do, actually. I think he probably felt really embarrassed and angry when Howard Hunt said that about him, and he thought about it and he decided that was how he wanted to respond.' I had criticised Josh myself in the past for not thinking things through, but this wasn't exactly the heat of the moment.

'It's not going to do much for his career, though, is it?'

'Some things are more important than our careers,' I said, feeling irritation rise in my chest. I knew that I sounded both naive and preachy, but I meant it. To him this was evidence of Josh's immaturity and impulsivity. To me it was proof that he wasn't just a brainless Hollywood puppet, that he had a backbone and wasn't going to roll over to please the man who was likely to be the next US president. I liked Ben, but he didn't get Josh. I could talk shit about Josh Sacco, but Ben couldn't.

'You really think that?' A smile danced on his lips.

'Yes.'

'That surprises me. You've always seemed so sensible.'

I shrugged. 'I guess there's more to Emily Montgomery than sensible.' I hoped we didn't have to talk about Josh anymore. For someone that seemed to dislike him, Ben brought him up an awful lot.

Chapter Twenty-Six

The next day was Saturday, and I was reading in my hotel room, wondering what to do with a day of freedom when I heard a knock on my door. Something told me before I even opened it that it would be Ben.

'Fancy a swim?' he asked, towel thrown over his shoulder, classic tortoiseshell Ray-Ban Wayfarers perched on top of his blond head. 'I've been going most days. Would be nice to have some company for a change.'

I nodded, grinning at the suggestion. It felt spontaneous and romantic, plus I would get to see him in his swimming trunks. He knew where we were going, and we strolled the half-hour walk from the hotel to the beach as conversation flowed easily between us. Our hands kept brushing against each other's as we walked, and neither of us moved apart. It was all a foregone conclusion, I just had to give myself over to it.

We got to the beach and laid our towels down on the sand. For some reason I had been expecting pebbles, and the sight of the pale, creamy-coloured sand felt like a good omen. I kicked off my sandals, pulled my dress off over my head and underneath was a sleek, black, high-leg classic Hunza G crinkle swimsuit. I wasn't a bikini girl but as I stood there I couldn't help wondering if I should have gone for something more revealing.

'Very chic,' Ben said, eyeing me approvingly as I twisted my hair into a neat little topknot to keep it dry. He was wearing red-and-white striped trunks and I tried not to stare at his big, muscular legs. I tied my hair up and he grabbed my hand and led me towards the shore.

As soon as my feet touched the water I had to suppress a scream. It was *so* cold! It was a beautiful summer's day but the water had *not* got the memo.

'Oh my God!' I exclaimed involuntarily. 'I thought it was going to be *nice*! How have you seriously been coming every day!'

'It's still the Atlantic!' Ben said, plunging all the way in, the water darkening his fair hair. 'Besides, you get used to it after a while.' Drops of water ran off his smooth chest.

'I just didn't think it was going to be quite . . . this . . . cold!' I gasped. Why had I agreed to this! I thought it was going to be a fun, sexy time and instead I might die of hypothermia.

'Come on! It's not so bad!' He urged me, and I steeled myself and ducked under the water, up to my shoulders. It was, in fact, quite bad, but it didn't kill me. We swam breaststroke, keeping our heads out of the water. We talked about his childhood in Oxford, the expensive schools, the drama classes, his path to fame. Even though we both *seemed* like we were somehow from the same world, it was nothing like my experience of going to an open audition for Wonderwick, swallowing down the anxiety of skipping school to go, even though my mum had told me it was OK, that I wouldn't get in trouble.

The light danced on the water and there was a sense of delight in the air – children building sandcastles on the beach, mothers dangling babies' feet into the water, serious swimmers cutting through the waves.

'I'm not used to this . . . swimming with my co-stars,' I told him.

'Not too many beaches near Smithdown, I suppose.'

I shook my head, the topknot feeling a little loose. 'This is all just really different to Wonderwick.'

'Well, you're working with people who got their roles through talent rather than nepotism.'

It wasn't hard to know who he was talking about, but I played dumb.

'Oh, you mean Darcy?'

'Of course, and Josh Sacco, naturally.'

'Ah,' I said, as if the idea hadn't occurred to me. 'He's all right.'

'Really?' Ben asked with a wry smile. 'I thought you'd be far too clever to get on with him. All I ever hear is what a time-wasting brat he is. No impulse control. I heard they were talking about getting him an earwig because he wouldn't learn his lines.' This was true, and would have been a pretty devastating blow to Josh. Only the most difficult or lazy actors needed an earpiece to be fed lines through, and I felt a huge sense of relief that he'd got himself together before that had become a necessity.

'He turned things around, I think those days are over. He's pretty good once he gets his shit together . . . and I think he's grown up a lot recently.' Ben knew my feelings about Josh's response to Howard Hunt and I wasn't going to have that particular fight again.

He gave me a sceptical look as we headed back towards the shore. It was just shallow enough for me to stand, and we paused, waist deep in the water. 'Enough about him.' He pulled me towards him, my skin covered in goosebumps. 'This is fun, right?'

I couldn't help smiling at how inevitable it all felt. A strand of hair had come down from my bun. He lifted it, tucked it behind my ear. I looked up at him and nodded, everything tingling with anticipation. When finally his lips met mine, the culmination of a shoot's worth of flirting not to mention the effort on behalf of our publicists, it felt . . . good. Yes, it felt good. It made sense. Ben and I made sense.

Luck of the Irish? Emily Montgomery and Ben Sage-Whittle Find Love On Set

By Rose Bell for MailOnline

Wonderwick Woods star Emily Montgomery has found love on the set of her new film *Orientations*, with none other than indie favourite Ben Sage-Whittle. The pair have been seen in intimate embraces in various pubs and restaurants in Galway, as well as swimming together in the icy Atlantic. The couple have been posing for selfies with fans, who have reported on social media seeing them hand in hand. Although clearly not keeping the new relationship a secret, the pair remain committed to their privacy and have refused to comment personally, though publicists for the two young actors confirmed in a joint statement that Emily and Ben are 'very happy together and excited to see where things go'.

The new couple are shooting *Orientations*, the latest film by Edgar Malek, at Gorman Abbey outside of Galway. It marks Emily's first movie outside of the Wonderwick franchise, as the latest instalment has tongues wagging over a kiss between her and co-star Josh Sacco which has been called 'steamy' and 'intense'. What will Ben have to say about that?

Chapter Twenty-Seven

Galway had been good for me. I loved the scale of the city, how friendly the people were, the many delicious places to eat, even the swim in the sea. I had woken up on my last Sunday morning there with the intention of going for a long run, when a FaceTime call came through on my phone. It was only when my mum's name appeared on the screen that I realised I hadn't been doing a good job of keeping in touch with my parents since I'd been in Ireland.

'Hello, Mum!' I greeted her cheerily waiting for her face to appear on the screen. My run could wait, I wasn't in a huge rush to get out and I assumed she wanted to gush with approval about the news stories about Ben and me. But when eventually she appeared on the screen, she was sitting side by side next to my dad, and they didn't look happy. At all. 'What's up?'

The pair of them glanced at each other, waiting for the other one to speak, but neither did. 'What?' I urged them, feeling my pulse quickening. Something was wrong.

'We wanted to talk to you, sweetheart,' Mum said, finally. 'Obviously we would rather have this conversation in person but we don't think it can wait much longer.' I was coming home the following week, so whatever they had to say must have been pretty bad.

'The thing is, love, the thing is—' Dad tripped over his words. The tension was almost unbearable.

'What? Please just tell me!'

'When you get back from Ireland, we won't be living together anymore,' Dad said quickly.

I couldn't imagine a stranger way to put it. To say what he seemed to be saying.

'What? Why?'

'There are a lot of reasons,' Mum said, shaking her head, looking off to the side. I could imagine the picture she was looking at – a print of a Mark Rothko painting that hung in the living room. 'There isn't just one.'

'For God's sake, Ruth, just tell her!' Dad burst out before burying his face in his hands.

'What?'

'It's my fault,' he wailed, and I realised Mum was stony-faced.

'What have you done?' I urged him.

'I've . . . I've had a bit of a problem with . . .' He cleared his throat. 'With gambling.'

'What do you mean?! What gambling?'

'It's so stupid.' He shook his head. 'It's so bloody stupid. It's just too easy. You get into it and you think it's just a bit of fun and you'll spend what you put in and then forget about it, but you *don't*. That's how they get you! You think the bad stuff won't happen to you, that it's something that happens to *other* people, people who are less clever than you, but it's not about being clever.' He kept talking, the words flowing out of him like blood from a wound. 'So you do that classic thing of chasing your losses, convincing yourself that the next one will be different and the next one after that and the one after that, that statistically your luck *has* to change because you've been on a losing streak for so long and surely it has to end any minute. But it doesn't, and you still have nothing to show for it, and now you have even *less* than nothing. So you move money around, borrow from here and there—'

I couldn't help cutting him off at that moment. 'Is that what you were doing? When you'd ask me if you could move money around? Covering your losses from online gambling?' I asked, my mouth dry. 'Not for the business?'

'I'm sorry, Emily. I hate that I lied to you . . . to both of you.'

It was almost impossible to take in. What would he have done if he didn't have a daughter with more money than she knew what to do with? What sort of situation would he be in right now?

'And so,' I said, disbelieving. 'You're breaking up.'

'The trust, Emily,' Mum said simply. 'It's just gone. I can't be with someone who could have this kind of secret life.'

I didn't think she was wrong. I couldn't get my head around it. My parents were *separating*? After all this time? And it was because my dad had racked up God knows how much in gambling debts?

'How much?'

'What, love?'

'How much was it?'

He took a deep breath and named a number that I hadn't even imagined possible. I felt sick.

'Say something, Em.'

'I don't know what to say.' We sat in silence for a moment. 'And you can't pay it, can you?'

'Well, I mean . . .'

'I have it. I'll pay it off.' I could make more money, couldn't I?

That was when Mum lost her composure. The tears came fast, and my heart absolutely broke for her. 'For God's sake, how has it come to this? You taking money your daughter has worked hard for, just to pay off stupid gambling debts! How could you do this?' It was like she had forgotten I was there and they were just continuing an argument they'd been having without me.

'Love, I couldn't ask you to do that.'

'Why not? You've already taken enough from her as it is. Why stop now?' Mum snapped, and to be honest I thought she had a point. I just wanted to throw money at the problem and for it all to be over.

'Let me think about it,' Dad mumbled.

'So is this it?' I looked between them. 'You're break-ing up?'

'We need some time apart, that's all. I'm going to Uncle Jack's for a bit. I don't blame your mum for need-ing a bit of space.' Dad looked broken.

'A trial separation,' I offered.

'Exactly.' Mum nodded.

And that was how a normal Sunday morning went completely to hell.

With shaking hands, I put in my headphones and laced up my trainers. On my walk to the lift, I passed Ben's room. For just a moment, I considered knocking. I even made a fist, held up my hand, as if I was daring myself to knock and ask him for time and attention. As I withdrew my hand, I realised with a sinking feeling that the person I really wanted to talk to was Josh. Not the old Josh who wouldn't have been able to even *pretend* to listen to a word I was saying, but the new Josh, the kind, thoughtful Josh I'd got to know. But he had his own stuff going on, and more to the point, we didn't have that kind of relationship, did we?

I ran down to Claddagh Quay, around South Park, along Grattan Beach and back into the centre of town. I'd just turned a corner, wanting to head up towards the cathedral, when the blare of a car horn cut through the nebulous swirling thoughts that were clogging up my brain. I gasped in horror at how close I had come to get-ting run over, which would have been entirely my own fault, and doubled over on the pavement trying to catch my breath.

'Emily?' I heard someone saying my name. I really *wasn't* in the mood for a selfie with a fan, but I would do it if I had to. 'I thought that was you!' It was Lucy Lennon. I was so relieved to see her that I burst into tears on the spot. 'Hey, hey, what's going on?' She drew me into a gentle hug. I cried into her shoulder in a way I hadn't done since I was little, and certainly not on a busy street corner on a Sunday morning.

'You look like a woman in need of a coffee. And breakfast.' She looked at her watch, a sleek analogue style with a dark snakeskin strap. 'Or rather, brunch. Join me?' Before I could answer she was marching me back in the direction I'd just come from, down towards the quay. Luckily we didn't have to wait long for a table, and soon I had a steaming flat white in front of me.

'So.' Lucy fixed me with an intense gaze. 'What's going on?'

I tried to hold back tears as I told her. It wasn't even a long story – I had so few details, and all of it had been going on behind my back.

She nodded, thoughtfully, listening without interrupting or giving an opinion.

'That must be really awful to find out. I'm so sorry, Emily. And to not be able to see them right now must make it even harder.' She gave my hand a reassuring squeeze. 'Has Ben been nice about it?' I didn't blame

Lucy for assuming that Ben and I were closer than we actually were.

'I haven't told him yet. I . . .' I trailed off.

'Yes?'

'I was going to, but then I realised I just . . . didn't want to, I suppose.' I couldn't look at her when I said it.

'So are you two seeing each other, then?' she asked, casually sipping her coffee.

'It's sort of heading in that direction, I think,' I said, a little apprehensively.

She looked at me, twitched the end of her nose. 'I only ask because I know he's not popular with the crew. He can be abrupt . . . impatient, entitled, that sort of thing. Just wanted to make sure he wasn't like that with you.'

I tried to keep my face neutral and composed. 'No, of course not. Why would someone say that about him?' I asked lightly, though I knew why.

She shrugged. 'You know how these things work on set.'

I bit my lip. 'I don't know. Don't get me wrong,' I added, quickly. 'In lots of other ways he's wonderful, and I really like the idea of being with him. It's just . . . every so often I see this side of him that makes me miss—' I stopped myself. I'd said too much, and I didn't want to start talking about Josh right now, not one bit. 'That makes me wonder a bit, you know?' I regretted it as soon as I said it. It felt like the genie was out of the bottle and I wanted it to go back in. I wanted the image of Ben and me to be perfect, to be exactly what the press wanted for both of us, to be in a couple that made *sense*, two people who were compatible and boosted each other's image, reflected something good back on each other.

'I think wondering is always worthwhile, Emily. It means you're not just accepting the status quo, you're thinking about it, making sure it's all enough for you.'

I sighed and covered my face with my hands. 'He's gorgeous, he's charming, he's talented, isn't that enough? Why isn't that enough?'

Lucy sighed. 'Sometimes it just *isn't*. That's just how things work. It doesn't always make sense.'

'But I want it to make sense! I want it to work!'

She took a breath, like she was trying to psych herself up to say something she knew she shouldn't. 'And you know why else?'

'Why?'

'Because he's not kind. You need to be with someone who's kind. He can make all the sense in the world on paper but if something is holding you back,' she said, holding up a hand to stop me from protesting. 'I'm just saying, you should trust your instincts.'

'I'm not much of an instinct person, that's the problem. I absolutely *hate* doing things on impulse.' I covered my face with my hands.

She shrugged. 'I don't know if you have to be one or the other. I think we all contain both.'

I thought about how Josh had become more considered over the filming of the last Wonderwick. Maybe I needed to do the same, in the opposite direction. Maybe I needed to stop looking for sense and clarity and logic. Maybe that was true, but this didn't feel like the moment to be taking big swings. I needed stability, continuity.

I sighed, always grateful for her presence, her wisdom. 'Lucy, why aren't you . . . you know, an Oscar winner? It doesn't make sense. You should be the most famous actress in the world.'

'Whenever you wonder why an actress isn't more famous, the answer is either going to be because she's a proper nightmare to work with, or because she refused to sleep with someone important. Do I strike you as a proper nightmare?'

I shook my head.

She smiled wryly. 'That's just what happens to women who don't play the game. Who don't let the men in the room tell them how it's going to be. Who don't let them do whatever they want to her.' I blinked at her. 'You can be as talented as you want but being a woman with boundaries is one sin Hollywood can never forgive.'

I could read between the lines, and it broke my heart. 'Thank you for this, Lucy,' I said, meaning the breakfast and the chat. But I wanted to say more, to open myself up to her. I didn't want to be the restrained, embarrassed person I'd been for so long, always holding back, scared of showing affection. 'It's been amazing working with you, actually. I'd grown up in such a specific world and hadn't played anyone other than this one iconic character and you really . . . well, you showed me this whole world of possibilities. You're amazing.'

The skin around her eyes crinkled with delight. 'What a lovely thing to say! I don't know if you realise it yet but this film . . . it's going to be big for you. Not big like Wonderwick, but big in other ways. I hope you're proud of it.'

I knew *Orientations* was good, but so were a lot of films. I'd never done a non-Wonderwick film before, so I had nothing to compare it to. I hoped every actor went home after a day of filming with the sense they'd worked on something brilliant that day, so it was possible Lucy was right and I didn't quite comprehend what *Orientations was* for me.

'I am proud,' I said, trying to fight back tears. It had been a long day already and it wasn't even lunchtime. 'I miss it already.'

But there was no avoiding it: I had to go home.

Chapter Twenty-Eight

Getting back to London was like falling to earth with a crash. My summer of fun had come to an abrupt end as soon as I stepped off that Aer Lingus flight at Heathrow and reality set in. My parents were living separately for starters, I still couldn't quite get my head around that. I also couldn't unthink all the thoughts I'd started having about Ben.

Ben arrived back in London the week after me and we'd been invited (via our publicists) to a party that would cement our 'status'. Chloe was delighted that her 'strategic alliance' between Ben and me had been so successful, and I couldn't face telling her that things felt decidedly different now we were back home. I wanted to do well at this, and had been just as delighted as Chloe that we actually did want to get together. If things didn't work out with Ben, especially so soon, then it would feel like a failure.

'What's this party for again?' Ben murmured in my ear as we entered the Soho Hotel, a doorman seamlessly swinging the door back for us.

'Lulu Otani's Mulberry collab,' I told him. I would probably have been going anyway as Lulu was a friend, but it seemed like a low-maintenance public event for us to go public at.

'God, I hate this sort of thing,' he sighed, as if he was above it all. Handbags, parties, all of it silly. I had to say, Ben certainly felt a lot less shiny now we were back in London. Or maybe it was that the reality of dating him was setting in. I felt as if I'd invested a lot of mental time and energy in Ben and this was actually our first real date. If this was what our relationship was going to be like, I didn't know if I could sustain the headspace.

We were each handed a margarita as we entered the extravagantly decorated space, which was hung with riotously bright decorations in the same shades as the handbags Lulu had 'designed'. I waved across the room at Liana Blum, a model friend of mine I hadn't seen in a while. She mouthed back 'He's so cute!', pointing at Ben and I couldn't help but blush. She was right, he *was* so cute. And talented. And clever. And dedicated to his work.

'You made light work of that,' Ben said, nodding down at my empty glass.

'Guess I was thirsty,' I said lightly.

I placed it on a passing tray of used glasses as another waiter with a tray of fresh cocktails sauntered in the opposite direction like a beautiful ballet. I picked one up and took a sip. 'Are you going to keep up this pace all night?' Ben nodded in the direction of the margarita.

I shrugged. 'I'm hardly *drunk*.'

'No, but you will be.'

'And maybe it's OK if I *do* get drunk. It's not a big deal.' The party was packed and we were surrounded by people, hemmed in on all sides. It didn't matter that there were lots of other famous people there, the sight of Emily Montgomery and Ben Sage-Whittle, newly minted golden couple of the British film industry, was going to draw some attention.

'I just don't want you making a fool of yourself, that's all,' Ben said, his voice tight. It was then that I noticed a guy in a white baseball cap with his phone out, trying to be subtle but obviously photographing or filming us.

I nodded towards him. 'Don't say anything too interesting, that guy has got us under surveillance.'

'Fucksake,' Ben muttered under his breath. 'Am I ever going to be able to go anywhere with you without someone being right up my arse with a camera?'

I knew the feeling. Ben led me to a small room where they sometimes held private events. Tonight it was empty, everyone thronging the main event space.

'Is this how it's going to be?' Ben asked, arms folded across his chest. He tossed his fair hair back off his forehead and looked at me with a stern gaze. 'Now we're actually together we just bicker?'

'I just wanted a second margarita! I don't know why you're making such a big deal out of this, it's not like

I'm doing body shots or openly hoovering up a bunch of coke!'

'I don't want you embarrassing yourself, that's all!'

'When have I ever done that? I'm literally famous for not doing that, to the point of it being a bit weird given I was basically a child star and they famously love hoovering up coke and embarrassing themselves. Emily Montgomery demurely sipping a second drink while dressed in vintage Chanel is the least interesting head-line possible.'

'Well I am just so sorry I don't want to be a Holly-wood party boy like Josh Sacco!' Ben said sarcastically, throwing his hands up in defeat.

'What does Josh have to do with any of this?' My cheeks reddened at having to say his name, a little prickle of excitement dancing in my chest.

'It's obvious from the way you talk about him that you have feelings for him!'

'Ben, I'm with *you*, and I don't know why you have to bring Josh up all the time. He has nothing to do with me, we work together on one film series and that's it, we don't even hang out when we're not on Wonderwick! I haven't seen him for months!'

Ben shook his head, laughing, but he didn't say any-thing.

'What?' I urged him. I didn't want there to be things hanging in the air between us, I wanted us to be able to talk properly, like adults.

'You know the one thing you didn't say?' I raised my eyebrows, waiting for him to speak. 'You didn't tell me I was wrong. You didn't say that you don't have feelings for Josh.'

He was right. I didn't say it. And I didn't say it because I just didn't know how I felt. The idea of having these feelings for Josh was so unwelcome to me, so inconvenient, so . . . vaguely taboo that I couldn't think of a single person I could talk to about them. Saying it out loud would make it real in a way I just couldn't face. And anyway, maybe I *didn't* have feelings for Josh, maybe everything had just got all jumbled up and confused after the kiss. But the fact I couldn't talk about it with anyone meant I was never going to be able to sort those feelings out either way.

I knew I couldn't explain all that to Ben, so instead I looked him in the eye and said, 'My feelings are my own business, what I actually *do* is sometimes your business. I don't know exactly what you're accusing me of but I don't appreciate it.'

'I'm not *accusing* you of anything,' Ben said, mocking.

I couldn't help feeling I was too young to be in a relationship like this. Lucy's words in my ears.

'Yes you are! Jesus, Ben, we're not meant to be fighting like this! Not this early in . . . whatever this is meant to be! It was supposed to be fun! Something our publicists cooked up that we could maybe actually *enjoy* rather than having to fake it! But tonight isn't fun for me and I don't think it's fun for you either. So why don't we just draw a line under it and move on?'

He stared at me, blinking slowly. 'Is that what you want?'

I thought for a moment. The answer was yes and no at the same time. I wanted his protective force field around me, the permission to not deal with how I was feeling about Josh. I wanted the distraction, the good times, the fact I really did fancy him. But the rest of it? I could live without.

'Yes,' I said, quietly.

'So that's that then.' His voice was stiff. I don't think he was used to being rejected and didn't enjoy not being the one who called the shots.

'That's that.' I felt a pit open up in my stomach. I'd done it, and I couldn't take it back.

'Well then, I'll leave you to it,' he said, yanking the door open violently and storming out.

I was alone. I thought it would feel better than this.

Ben Sage-Whittle and Emily Montgomery on the Rocks – Couple in Stormy Row at Celeb Party

By Jamie Andrews for MailOnline

Partygoers at the starry launch event for model Lulu Otani's collaboration with Mulberry were stunned to see an argument break out between Wonderwick Woods lead Emily Montgomery, 21, and the rising star actor Ben Sage-Whittle, 26.

The couple, who had been pictured kissing while filming upcoming indie movie *Orientations*, were pictured arguing in full view of partygoers before Sage-Whittle led Montgomery to a private room to continue the row behind closed doors.

When asked what the argument had been about, one witness said, 'It was pretty obvious it was about drinking. I couldn't hear everything but it sounded like Ben didn't want Emily to have another cocktail. They hadn't been there long and she didn't seem drunk at all, so I'm not surprised she pushed back.'

The pair were later seen leaving the private room separately, with one photo showing Montgomery looking red-eyed and tearful before leaving in a taxi.

Although speculation has linked Emily Montgomery to her co-star Josh Sacco, she was seen engaging in a very uncharacteristic PDA with Sage-Whittle while filming in Ireland. Not known for her high-profile relationships, this is only the second time Montgomery has been seen dating someone in the public eye, after a brief fling with singer Daniel Holm two years ago. Sage-Whittle, however, has had a string of famous girlfriends, including the model Emma Colwin, *Hambledown House* co-star Vivienne Crawford and photographer Charlotte Newell.

Representatives for the pair remained tight-lipped about the future of the couple, stating: 'As far as we know Emily and Ben are very much still together, but the status of their relationship is between them.'

Good Girl Gone Bad? Emily Montgomery Goes on THREE-DAY BENDER Following Break-Up From Ben Sage-Whittle

By Jasmin Church for MailOnline

Angelic actress Emily Montgomery, 21, known for her role as Linderley Jones in the Wonderwick Woods film series, has been spotted partying in London three nights in a row, leading many to ask if she's gone off the rails since breaking up with Ben Sage-Whittle, 26, earlier this week.

Montgomery hasn't spent much time grieving their relationship and instead has been dancing her troubles away at various celebrity parties. On Friday night, she was seen sampling the wares at the launch party for fellow actor Ryan Morgan's new tequila brand, Cactus, while Saturday night was the thirtieth birthday party for the Black theatre company Diasporique, which she attended with Wonderwick co-star Courtney Williams. Sunday night's entertainment came in the form of a birthday party for model and actress Dalia Shepherd, where Emily could be seen putting on a leggy display in a barely-there miniskirt and knocking back cocktails and dancing until the small hours.

Many are wondering if Montgomery is trying to shake off her prim and proper image, with a public break-up and heavy partying all in the same week.

Chapter Twenty-Nine

'Chloe, I know it's a big job,' I took a deep breath. 'But it's what I want to do. It's what I need right now. Something big to focus on.'

'And the rights are available?'

'Miraculously, yes.' I nodded. Lying on my sofa, bored, staring at the ceiling, hungover after one too many nights out, I had asked myself a simple question: *What do you really want to do now* Orientations *is over?* And the more I thought about it, the more obvious it was that Josh was right. I should turn my passion for books and my experience of films into production. I'd been telling anyone who would listen about this book, *Easy Work* by Eleanor Blomquist, so figured that might be a decent place to start.

'And you reckon this is going to pull you out of your funk?' Chloe grimaced at me from across the table. 'Of the whole messy post-Ben thing? Not that I didn't love the wild party girl version of Emily that seemed to come out to play in recent weeks. She was an interesting plot twist.'

'Well, Emily Montgomery contains multitudes and I'm on a mission to enjoy my youth but also do something to set me up for the future.'

Chloe nodded, a wry smile on her face. 'Twenty-one years old and the wheels are in motion to set up your own production company. You are literally the only person I can imagine pulling it off.'

'Believe it, baby,' I said, raising my coffee cup to her before taking a sip.

'You know this is going to take time, right? You can't just set up a company overnight?'

'I know that. I'm serious about this! I'm not acting on some sort of whim! You know me: I'm more than willing to put in the work.'

'You never do. Hey, I heard Arthur Hemmings thinks you're cute,' she said, namedropping a handsome young British actor.

'And did you hear that from Blake? He's friends with Arthur, right?' I grin at her. She had been casually dating him ever since the party for the Wonderwick video game, which felt like a lifetime ago. They were practically married by Chloe's standards.

'Maybe I did, maybe I didn't,' she said, enigmatically.

'I think Arthur Hemmings is cute but I'm done being set up for a while. I've got other things to focus on. The press tour for Wonderwick, then *Orientations and* trying to set up my own production company. I can't be getting into something new right now.'

She sighed. 'It was worth a try. Anyway, I just need to make a quick call, be back in a second.'

While Chloe was away, I slid my phone out of my Miu Miu tote. My heart leaped at the sight of Josh's name on my screen.

Hey, how are you doing? I just wanted to check in with you since you seem to be drawing a lot more attention than usual these days! Heard on the rumour mill you'd broken up with your boy Ben? True or false? If true, I always thought he was kind of a jerk. If false, glad to hear it, great guy etc. See you in Singapore, I guess!

'What are you smiling about?' Chloe asked me, sliding back into the booth. I don't think I had been doing too much smiling recently, so it was probably a nice change for her.

'Oh, nothing,' I said, dropping my phone back into my bag and trying to wipe the grin off my face.

'Come on, spill.'

'Honestly it was nothing, just a text from Josh!'

'A text from Josh Sacco had you looking like that?' She raised her eyebrows and whistled. 'Oh, boy.'

'It's not like that,' I said, blushing furiously.

'Maybe it's time to admit it is a little bit like that?' Chloe grasped my wrists and looked me dead in the eye.

'There's nothing to admit.' I shrugged.

'You keep telling yourself that, babe.'

'I plan to.'

'Speaking of plans, even though things didn't, er, work out with you and Ben, the whole thing has been kind of great for Wonderwick hype. You having a steamy romance then a fairly public break-up has given you a certain *je ne sais quoi* . . . disrupted public perception, if you will.'

'I'm glad to hear it,' I said, dryly.

'Actually it's probably better that it all fizzled out now, might be a bit boring to have you in a serious monogamous relationship with a completely appropriate boyfriend by the time the film comes out.'

'Do I have to do any more . . . you know, publicity-baiting?' I wanted her to believe it was because I found the whole idea of it embarrassing or degrading, but I knew deep down it was because I wanted to signal to Josh that I was single.

Chloe smiled at me and shook her head. 'You've done enough. I don't think it's a natural fit for you, babe.'

'Are feeling good about Singapore? I bloody wish I was going with you!'

'I'm only going for two nights! It's hardly going to be a holiday!' I said, even though I knew I was looking forward to it, the idea of seeing Josh again looming huge in my mind. 'Anyway, you're coming to LA, right?' That was the next stop on the tour after Singapore: home turf for Josh.

'Right! And on the Legacy Pictures private jet! Thanks to you!' She reached out her hands and wiggled her fingers against my forearms in excitement, her long oval nails scratching pleasantly at my skin.

I waved her away. 'It's nothing. It'll be fun.'

'And I hear things are progressing nicely on the Vespucci deal?' She smiled conspiratorially at me. I nodded, barely containing the huge grin I felt at being signed as the new brand ambassador for a rebooted prestige Italian fashion house, complete with hot new British designer at the helm. It felt like the perfect blend of my reputation for, shall we say, 'heritage brands' with my desire to try new things and figure out my own image, on my own terms.

'I think it's all going to be wrapped up soon, should be announced at Venice.'

'Very appropriate,' she nodded, sagely. 'It's all coming up, Emily, isn't it?'

She was right. The only thing that was missing was romance.

Chapter Thirty

Singapore welcomed me with a thunderstorm. It felt like a suitably dramatic beginning to the Asia premiere of Wonderwick, a film that already was starting to feel like a dream I'd had a long time ago. One thing I knew was real was that Josh was hot on my heels, his plane from LA landing a couple of hours after mine came in from London. My stomach kept doing somersaults at the thought of seeing him again, like the idea of him had kept building up and up and up in my brain since we'd last been in the same place. I desperately hoped that when I *did* see him, it would all feel like a big disappointment and that I'd been crushing on a fantasy for all these months. Absence makes the heart grow fonder, right? That was the best possible outcome: being faintly embarrassed that I'd been thinking about him at all. I was actively seeking cringe! Craving the ick, even.

The premiere was that evening, and the publicity team had scheduled a couple of interviews with major Asian outlets at the hotel before I had to get ready to go out. By some miracle or more likely administrative oversight at Legacy, I had the next morning free before more press in the afternoon. Time off on a press tour was *not* something I would take for granted. Nor would I take for granted the beautiful, elegant suite at Raffles. I like hard work as much as the next person, but I had to fight the urge to stay in my room and take a long bath when I knew I had a press junket to attend in another part of the hotel.

Wonderwick was big in Asia, so the interviews had been divided up between the cast for maximum coverage. Josh was in the room next door, and all I could think about while I was talking to the journalists was the fact I was going to see him soon, for the first time in months.

Walking from the interview room back to my own room to meet the makeup artist, I spotted Darcy and Josh in conversation in reception. It was a bit of an anticlimax, encountering him there like this. I'd thought there would be . . . I don't know, *fireworks* or something. He was leaning against a pillar in the big atrium, while she stood in front of him. They didn't look like they were talking about anything particularly important, and Josh waved at me so I went over. I hugged them both, and Darcy seemed a little taken aback.

'Oh, yeah, it's my new thing. I'm trying out this concept called *hugging*,' I said, lightly.

'I like it!' she said, smiling. She was nowhere near as spiky and intimidating as she had once been. I guess you could say the same thing for me, too.

'I was just saying to Darcy we should have a post-premiere drink in the bar later. Can't stay at Raffles and not have a Singapore Sling, right?'

'Sounds fun, I'll see you both there,' I said. 'I've got a makeup artist waiting for me so I have to dash!'

I didn't want to rush off, but I wanted as much time as possible to get ready. My outfit for the premiere was a long-sleeve minidress, kind of sixties inspired. I was continuing my trend of trying to dress a bit more *fun* while also still dressing like myself. I could do long sleeves with a short dress or strapless with a long dress, but not both. I wanted to feel like me, and between the gorgeous hair and makeup and the perfectly cut dress, I did.

The evening itself was thick with humidity, and another dramatic storm passed just before we headed for the cars to take us to the huge cinema Legacy Studios had hired out. The green carpet was lined on either side with press and photographers, with fans crowding outside the entrance and most of them dressed up in costumes or wearing some kind of Wonderwick merch.

Courtney squeezed me tight when she saw me on the green carpet. 'You look amazing!' she said, eyeing the cream lace babydoll dress.

'So do you!' She was wearing a bias-cut satin dress in the most delicious shade of hot pink, paired with chunky orange sandals.

'And what do we think of Josh's look for the evening?' She cast an eye over Josh's outfit. 'I have to say he's really stepped into his own recently.'

He was wearing a beige linen suit with a crisp white T-shirt underneath. It had a slightly higher neck than your average T-shirt and gave a deliciously eighties effect. 'Very smart. Him and Tommy look like they're having fun.'

We watched as they performed some viral dance for an Asian entertainment network, only for Max to catch sight of them and demand they started again so he could get involved. With all the excitement of everyone being back together, I almost forgot we had a film to show. Although we would often slink off at premieres, none of us had seen the film yet so we all stayed in our seats, watching the hard work of all those months at Smithdown coming together with the magic of post-production.

And the magic of the kiss.

On screen, our chemistry sizzled in a way I didn't know possible. I had spent so long worrying about this kiss, how we could ever make it believable. Now, it was almost *too* believable. I felt my pulse quicken, my breath catch in my throat. People around me turned to look at me with knowing smirks, raised eyebrows, a sense of where-did-*that*-come-from? I didn't know where it had come from, either. All I knew was that it had shifted something in me, and seeing it again just made me want it more.

As Josh and Darcy had planned, we regrouped at the bar. Well, most of us did. Tommy and Max were out partying somewhere, but the rest of us – Josh, Darcy, Courtney and I – were back at Raffles, a round of their signature Singapore Slings in front of us.

'Are we gonna talk about it . . .' Courtney raised her eyebrows at me. 'That kiss?! Girl!'

'Don't!' I blushed, covering my smile like a giggling schoolgirl.

'That was *legit* hot. Not hot for a film, but just . . . hot!' She kept her voice down but Josh shot a glance in our direction. He caught my eye and we smiled at each other, holding the gaze a little too long.

'I know! I can't believe it!'

'So I feel like if there was something going on between you two then I would know about it, right?'

'Court, there's nothing going on between me and Josh.' I yawned widely. 'Jet lag is absolutely ruining me. And I know whatever time I go to bed I'll be wide awake at like . . . five o'clock in the morning.' I was grateful for an opportunity to change the subject.

'Whenever I go away I always get some cheeky sleeping pills,' she said, rummaging around in her bag. 'Want one?' I eyed them warily. 'Come on, they're not, like, heroin. I get them from my actual doctor.' She paused. 'In *London*,' she added for effect, to reassure me that they weren't being handed out like sweets from some private office in Hollywood.

'All right,' I said, holding out my hand.

'Oh, don't act like I'm forcing you!'

'I'm not! I want one! I need a good night's sleep, I didn't get a wink on the plane.' She handed it over. 'Thank you, Courtney, you're the best.'

'What are your plans for tomorrow morning?' Josh asked the table. 'I was thinking maybe we could all hang out? Do something together with our rare window of freedom?'

'Uh, I'm flying home?' Courtney offered. 'Aren't you?'

'No, I'm staying another day, Legacy has got us on some show tomorrow afternoon.'

'Me too,' I added.

'I should have guessed it was just the mere mortals that were flying halfway round the world for one night only,' she said with a chuckle.

'Darcy?' I offered, holding my breath with hope that she would say no. It wasn't that I didn't want to spend time with her, I just felt this huge certainty that if I spent some proper time with Josh, I would feel clearer about everything, one way or the other. 'Want to hang out with me and Josh?'

She shook her head, her sharp blonde bob slicing against her cheeks. 'I've got a meet-and-greet. I'm huge in Singapore.' She shrugged.

'Oh, that's a shame!' I said, maybe a little too quickly.

'Guess that just leaves us,' Josh said with a small smile.

'I guess it does.'

'Well, I'm going to bed. I don't want to hear about all the fun things you two are going to get up to tomorrow without us.' Courtney hugged us both in turn.

Once she'd left, Darcy sighed heavily. 'I still feel like such an idiot for how I behaved in the beginning. It's like I can't shake off this fear that everyone still hates me.'

I shook my head. 'No one hates you, honestly. You've been totally delightful ever since the . . . er . . .'

'Jonas threatened to have me recast? Yeah, remarkable the effect that can have on a person,' she said with a laugh.

'Yes, that.' I smiled back, sipping my drink and feeling a wave of affection for Darcy. She might be a nepo baby and my rival for the Wonderwick fan's affections, but she definitely hadn't had it easy.

'I can't believe I almost jeopardised everything for . . . what? A reputation for being cool? What even is that?'

'Being cool sucks, I've decided,' Josh said, smashing a peanut against the marble table under the heel of his hand before extracting it from the shell. Each table had a hemp bag full of peanuts and guests were encouraged to sweep the shells onto the floor, something Josh was clearly enjoying. 'Maybe this was the Wonderwick that killed cool once and for all.'

I shrugged. 'Maybe cool is just being yourself. Whoever that is.'

'I'll drink to that,' Josh said, clinking his glass against ours.

Darcy hoovered up the last of her cocktail and announced she was going to bed. 'Gotta be bright-eyed and bushy-tailed for the fans, even if I don't know what day it is!'

Josh and I sat, alone together for the first time in a long time. It felt slightly thrilling.

'You still think it'll be fun, just you and me?' Josh asked, finally breaking the silence. I couldn't tell if he wanted me to say yes or no. In the minutes since the idea had been suggested, I'd grown unpleasantly attached to it. I liked the thought of having one-on-one time with Josh.

'So, what's the plan?' I asked, sipping my Singapore Sling. Suddenly, I felt emboldened. Maybe it was the cocktail, maybe it was the prospect of spending time with Josh. It filled me with a confidence I hadn't felt before. I realised I wanted Josh to know how much I liked him. I wanted to flirt with him, I wanted to give it a go and see what happened.

'You've got the suite next to me, right?' I nodded. 'I can knock for you tomorrow morning after breakfast. I don't think I'm gonna make it to the buffet,' he said, stifling a yawn. 'I'll knock for you at the front door, rather than the one onto the cute little verandah. Don't want people to see me sneaking around that partition, thinking I'm a thief.'

'See you then.' I pulled the maraschino cherry off the cocktail stick and placed it on my tongue, making sure

I was making eye contact with Josh the whole time. He looked like he was about to faint, but that might have been the jet lag. It was as if I was play-acting, trying on what it would feel like to be someone more sexy and assertive than myself. I thought about what I'd said earlier, about how *cool* was being yourself, and wondered if I wasn't being a hypocrite. But it struck me that for so long I'd had a fixed idea of who I was, and thought I had to stick to that, for the fans, for the studio, for my family. It was OK for me to try things out, harmless things, not berating drivers or runners like Darcy had, but little things.

'Uh, yeah, see you then,' he mumbled before disappearing off to his suite, his jacket thrown over his shoulder.

Chapter Thirty-One

Bang! Bang! Bang! I was awoken by a sharp rap of knuckles on the door leading to my verandah. It had to be Josh. I looked at the time on my phone and gasped in horror. Courtney's sleeping pills! I'd slept so long that I'd missed breakfast, and now Josh was coming to pick me up and I was in my pyjamas! Confident, sexy Emily had been too short-lived.

I ran my fingers through my hair, checked I didn't have hideous morning breath, and went to the door.

'Woah!' Josh said, surveying me in my pyjamas – fortunately a little navy silk set with cream lace trim. 'Did you forget we had plans?'

'I'm so sorry, I didn't realise I was going to sleep so late! Just give me ten minutes? I promise I don't need much time!'

'I've heard *that* before,' he said with a smirk that was equal parts infuriating and charming.

'I'll see you in reception in fifteen minutes?'

'See! It's already got longer!'

'I'll make it twenty if you don't let me get dressed!' I warned him.

'All right, all right, though you look pretty cute in this if you want to stick with it.'

I rolled my eyes and started shutting the door in his face, not least because I was suddenly aware I was not wearing a bra and that would be pretty obvious to him.

'See you there,' he said, winking as he strolled away nonchalantly.

I showered and braided my hair so I didn't have to wash it, knowing the humidity would wreak absolute havoc on it even if I did. I did a quick light face of makeup and chose a simple navy linen shift dress and Dior l'Amazone gladiator sandals, with a cream cotton shirt rolled up neatly in my bag if I needed it, along with an essential umbrella. I wasn't going to get caught out now I'd seen not one but two thunderstorms in the space of twelve hours. The dress was shorter than I would usually wear, but I'd been consciously trying to wear more things that were slightly out of my comfort zone, just to see what it was like. I checked the time on my phone as I headed out the door and over to reception. Conscious of the need to make the most of my time with Josh, I'd done it in thirteen minutes.

Josh was slouching in a dark wooden rattan chair in the vast vaulted atrium, but leaped to his feet at the sight of me. 'I'm impressed! I thought you'd keep me waiting!'

He was wearing a 'don't look at me' famous person base-ball cap, which felt to me like a total waste of his dark curls and often had the opposite effect anyway, causing people to look at you even more.

'So, what's the plan?' Both of us were carrying a nerv-ous energy, like we both sensed time was slipping away and we would have to be at the TV studio for our inter-view before we knew it.

'I figured we could walk around, see some cool shit, eat something delicious . . . whatever we have time for before this filming later. Or do you need a more, uh, structured plan than that?' he asked, eyeing me hopefully.

I shook my head. 'It sounds perfect.'

Our first stop was the botanic gardens. The air was heavy with humidity which made the earthy fragrance of the soil and the occasional scent of the flowers feel even more alive, even closer. We walked together, side by side, as we made our way slowly and without pur-pose through the gardens, ducking under huge leaves, strolling through arches festooned with vines and flow-ers, along paths dappled with sunlight. It was all a bit Wonderwick Woods, actually. The gardens were busy with tourists like us, but a sense of peace had settled over us as soon as we arrived, an unspoken agreement that we didn't need to be *on*, didn't need to be coming up with endless conversation. That it was OK for us to just *be*. The orchids were a particular delight for the senses, their scent cut through everything with their heavy sweetness, and I had to resist the urge to reach out and touch each of them, the colours almost too good to be true. I paused in front of one, Singapore's national flower. Josh stopped next to me and read the label.

'National flower, huh? Kinda makes me want to pick it . . . take it home,' he said with a smile.

'Josh.' I gave him a 'don't even think about it' look.

'Come on! I'm kidding.' He laughed.

'Old habits die hard! I wouldn't put it past you! Now you're making me wonder if you went out and picked all those flowers yourself.' Josh pushing me in the river felt like ancient history, but strangely walking into my trailer filled with flowers seemed like only yesterday. As if time had passed too quickly in the new era of us.

He frowned at me. 'What flow—' Then he remembered, his cheeks flushing pink. 'Oh, that. I think I made some local florist's day with that order. They probably didn't need to open again all week.' He took off his cap and ran his hands over his hair, his fingers creating a channel through the waves.

I cleared my throat a little awkwardly. 'It was very kind of you.'

'The least I could do, obviously. And I'm not gonna pick the Singapore orchid. Can you imagine what the sidebar of shame would do with that, it'd be JOSH SACCO INSULTS ENTIRE COUNTRY.'

We kept walking, pausing every so often to look at something – a cool insect, a butterfly with colours we'd never seen before, a bird with unbelievable plumage. Sometimes we'd break into brief conversation, but mostly we walked in companionable silence. Josh agreed that the tropical botanic landscape was very Wonderwick, all massive tree trunks and spreading canopies. 'It's like we can't escape it,' he said.

'Do you want to escape it?'

'Escape is a strong word but . . .'

I didn't say anything, just waited for him to speak.

'I'm just at a point where I'm wondering if there's more to life than Wonderwick, you know?'

'Of course I know,' I said, gently. But the difference was, I really *did* know. I'd filmed *Orientations*. I'd taken on a character that wasn't Linderley Jones, worked with people that weren't the same old cast and crew, had to dig deep to find the emotional truth of the scene, as Edgar would put it. 'It's just a question of what you think you want to do next.'

'Ah, I'll figure it out. I've got options. I'm having meetings . . . talking to people . . . I know Lisa has me in mind for something.'

'Lisa Halley?'

'The very same.' That would probably be another big budget Legacy Pictures film. I wondered how different to Wonderwick that would actually be for Josh. 'There's this new superhero thing they're casting for . . . it's called *Eagle Heart*. Very all-American. I think she thinks it'll help, uh, *realign my image* after the Howard Hunt thing.'

It sounded like propaganda to me, which doesn't often make for good cinema. I didn't want to be a downer, so I kept my thoughts to myself.

'You all natured out? Time for some architecture?' Josh asked.

'I guess so!' I said, brightly. I wanted to show Josh that I was enjoying my time with him, whatever we were doing. That the actual location didn't really matter, that I was just happy to be spending time with him, one-on-one. It seemed ridiculous now, the idea that other people had been invited. It was so obvious that we were meant to have this time together.

He looked down at his phone for a moment and I realised I hadn't even thought about the outside world since we'd been here. His eyes were bright as he held the screen up for me to see. 'You get this?'

I took my phone out of my pocket and propped my sunglasses on my head to read. The afternoon's filming had been . . . cancelled!

'A fire at the TV studio! Can you believe that?! I mean, it says no one was hurt so I don't feel so bad,' Josh said with a grin.

It was as if the universe was conspiring to prolong our hangout. When else would Josh and I get to spend a whole day together in a foreign country?

'What should we do now?' I asked, feeling slightly high on the freedom and the extra time with Josh.

'There's somewhere I would like to go, if you don't mind me being the boss for a while? Or maybe not boss but . . . tour guide?' he said, tentatively.

'I'm in.'

We left the gardens and hailed a taxi, Josh giving the driver the next location which meant nothing to me as I didn't know Singapore. Neither did Josh, I thought, but he seemed to have done his research. When we emerged from the taxi into what seemed to me a perfectly pleasant but normal street, Josh was already beaming. He paid the taxi driver and stood with his hands on his hips, looking up at the building in front of us. 'Streamline Moderne,' he sighed, his eyes almost misting over.

'What's that?' I asked, unable to suppress a smile at his obvious passion for . . . something, even if I didn't know what it was.

'It's a late art deco period. These are from the late thirties, pre-war, and they incorporate all these elements of modernity and travel – elements that look like airplane wings, details that evoke a steam train, that sort of thing. It's all about aerodynamics and speed and powering into the future, while still keeping the basics of the art deco aesthetic. Singapore has some amazing examples, as you can see.' He gestured to the building in front of us. When I looked again with this new knowledge, I realised he was right: they weren't just beautiful, they spoke of the future, a building on the move.

'You're into architecture?' I asked, blinking at him. Obviously, I found this delightful, but it was the first I'd heard him mention it, ever, in the seven years we'd known each other by this point.

'Why, is that such a surprise?' he asked, sounding a little wounded.

'No, not at all! Just not something we've really talked about before,' I said lightly.

'It's one of the best things about LA, if you ask me. Other than the ocean, the weather and the Mexican food. We have these unbelievable buildings all over town, beautiful, streamlined designs with insane details inside and out, the mosaics, the gold, the geometry . . . show me a vertical window and I'll be a happy guy. There's this one, the Eastern Columbia Building, it's in downtown and it's fucking *stunning*, I can't even tell you. It's a 1930 Claud Beelman building, all turquoise terracotta, this gorgeous sunburst design, ugh!' He shook his head with unbridled enthusiasm. 'I keep thinking about buying a loft there but haven't pulled the trigger. Life is long.' He shrugged.

I couldn't help staring at him, I felt so overwhelmed by this side of him I'd never seen before. Josh Sacco, architecture nerd?

'What?' he asked.

'I'm just surprised, that's all. I never knew this about you,' I said gently.

Josh looked at me, his eyes soft. 'You've gotta realise by now that there's a lot you don't know about me.'

'I . . .' I began, not knowing what to say. He was right: our relationship until the latest film was mostly based on me ostentatiously ignoring him and him winding me up. 'Of course, I know that. I guess the first few films weren't really conducive to getting to know each other.'

He shook his head. 'I just want you to know there's more to me than meets the eye. Promise.'

There was something in that vulnerability, that desire to impress me, that made me fancy him more than any gym workout ever could.

'I know that. Promise,' I said back.

We walked the streets of Tiong Bahru, every so often turning down paths leading us past residential blocks of flats, Josh pausing to admire every facade, to point out details to me, to explain what made it special, different, the way they existed in three dimensions, the curves, the long vertical lines, the decoration. I tried not to look at his face too much as he spoke, because his enthusiasm, his knowledge, his warmth had such a transformative quality on him that it made me absolutely melt, and he could *not* see that. I wanted to keep my cards close to my chest, see how things played out. I was cautious, rightly, and this version of Josh was testing my limits in ways I didn't know possible.

'They don't make 'em like that anymore,' he sighed, sadly.

I had truly never seen this side of him before. I felt almost ashamed. I'd shown even less interest in Josh than he'd ever shown in me. Of course he was the 'aggressor' in a sense, always winding me up, picking on me, trying to embarrass me. But I'd barely made an effort with him.

As I watched him photograph the art deco frontage of the market, its red lettering gleaming in the late afternoon sunlight, I realised exactly what the problem was. When you've known someone for years, since you were a child really, how do you even *start* going about things differently? How do you interrupt the pattern of how it's always been? Not warring with him on set was a big enough change, but going from even *that* to . . . something more? I didn't know if it could even be done.

'I'm starving, you want something?' He nodded at the market. The unbelievable smell of the place hit me like a truck, along with the realisation that since I'd missed breakfast, I hadn't eaten all day.

'Sure,' I said, as if it didn't matter to me either way. That was what girls were meant to do, wasn't it? We weren't allowed to be hungry, weren't allowed to want things.

Josh furrowed his brow. 'Wait, have you eaten at all today?'

I shook my head, knowing I couldn't make up a lie since he'd been with me the whole time. 'But I'm fine! Let's go in?' I was starting to feel a bit light-headed.

'You take a seat, I'll go foraging. I'm an absolute fiend for char kway teow and I never met a roti I didn't like. You ever had shui kueh? I'll get us some,' he murmured, his eyes scanning the market, taking in all the many and varied thrilling options.

I slid onto a shiny black bench in front of a Formica table and watched as Josh buzzed from one stand to another, surveying their offerings. Finally, he returned, his arms laden with various plates heaped with food.

'Hope you're hungry. Well, I know you're hungry, so I went a little overboard,' he said, setting the various options down in front of us.

The smell of the noodles made my mouth water instantly, as if I could already feel the flat rice noodles against my tongue. Hungrily, I set upon them with chopsticks, taking in the rich, deep flavours, the juiciness of the prawns under my teeth, the fibrousness of the spring onions, the uneven texture of the little pieces of scrambled egg.

I paused for breath, closed my eyes and said, 'Josh, this is the most delicious thing I've ever eaten in my life.'

He beamed, proud that he'd made a good choice. 'Wait till you try the roti. I got it with dhal for variety but I can always go back for the chicken,' he offered.

We grazed on the food he'd chosen, chatting about what made it all so delicious, how lucky we were to get to be here, how we should never take it for granted.

'I feel actively sad that the roti is gone. I think it might have changed my life,' I sighed.

'You want another? I can get us some chicken and roti?'

I nodded. 'That sounds good.'

He bounded off, full of the joy of a day of no responsibilities, eating delicious food in a foreign country. As I waited for him to come back, I realised there was something I wanted to ask him about that we'd never discussed. He'd brought it up earlier, so I knew it wasn't off limits.

'Can I ask about the whole Howard Hunt thing?' I asked, gently, tearing off a piece of roti.

Josh looked surprised. 'What do you want to know?'

'I don't know exactly. I guess I want to know if your response was something you came up with as a team or if it was just you.'

'Ah.' His face clouded with something like sadness. 'You think it seemed kinda . . . impulsive?'

'No,' I said, quickly and firmly. 'No, absolutely not. I don't want you to think that for a second. I thought it was unbelievably brave. And cool.'

'Wow . . . that means a lot coming from you.' He shifted in his seat. 'You were kind of on my mind that day, in a weird sort of way. The whole pushing-you-in-the-river episode is a bit of a blur, as is almost everything you said to me afterwards, although I *absolutely* understood the general vibe of what you were saying. But the one thing that really got to me was the word "integrity". I'd never really thought about it before, but I can, like, still *hear* you saying that: "you have absolutely no integrity".'

I wanted the ground to swallow me up. I couldn't believe I had spoken to him like that.

'And I thought, you know, this is a good opportunity to prove that I have integrity. That I'm not just going to benefit from Evan Cole being thrown under the bus like that, just accept this deranged praise from a—'

'Fucking fascist?' I supplied.

'Emily Montgomery, I have *never* heard you curse before.'

'It doesn't count. I was quoting.' I felt a little overwhelmed at the idea that anything I'd said had affected Josh that much, for better or for worse.

'So, yeah, I guess in a weird sort of way it was down to you.'

'That's . . .' I swallowed, not knowing what to say. So I went for something simple. 'I'm proud of you.'

'There was a time when hearing *that* would have been even more shocking to me than hearing you curse.'

'Well, I hope those days are behind us.'

'Me too.'

We held each other's gaze, back to the comfortable silence of the botanic gardens. But this time it felt heavier. Not so comfortable, as if there were things deliberately being unsaid. It felt like too much to hope for, the idea of *something happening* with Josh. What did I even mean?

What did I even want to happen? I had no idea, since I'd barely let myself consider it a possibility.

We had been out of the market for maybe a minute tops, when the heavens opened. I gasped at how instantly and violently the rain hit us, my eyes wide with both horror and amusement. We just looked at each other in disbelief for a moment, everyone scrambling for cover or opening umbrellas, which reminded me I had actually brought one with me. I quickly produced it from my bag and opened it, holding it above our heads. We could have run back to the market for cover, but for some reason we just . . . didn't. It was as if we liked being in our own little world like this. We stood there, blinking at each other, smiles creeping across our faces at the situation we'd found ourselves in. With the rush of people going on around us, it felt like we were in a bubble, protected from the outside world by a shared fiction that we didn't have to go anywhere, nothing was happening, we weren't being soaked to the skin. As the rain pounded down on the umbrella, the little veil of privacy, I knew that this was when the *something* was going to happen.

Josh looked down at me, tiny drops of rain clinging to his eyelashes. Finally, after what felt like an unbearable wait, he pulled me towards him, one strong arm around my waist and whispered, 'Emily, do you want this?'

I nodded. And then he kissed me, our mouths finding each other, my free hand cupping his sharp jaw, the other clinging on to the umbrella for dear life, his tongue pushing against mine, our teeth meeting in the feverish, clumsy frenzy. Imagine the Rowan/Linderley kiss moment and multiply it by a thousand. A million. That was what it felt like to kiss Josh *for real*. The screen kiss was intense but controlled. This was pure desire, no restraint. It was almost too much to believe. I felt as if my whole body was on fire, every inch of my skin prickling with desire, wanting to kiss him so hard I melted into him.

We pulled apart, but Josh didn't release his hand from my waist. He blinked at me, wiped the raindrops off his lashes. 'That was good, right?' He sounded just as surprised by the whole thing as I was, but he couldn't keep the smile off his face.

I nodded, my heart racing. 'That was good.'

He swallowed, staring me in the eye as if he thought I might disappear at any moment. 'It's crazy how . . . different it felt from . . . you know . . .' He seemed almost embarrassed, as if it was childish of him to have thought of our Wonderwick kiss as real.

'And I thought *that* was good,' I said, reassuring him I felt the same, my entire body fizzing, my thoughts in chaos, wanting him to do it again.

'Oh, that was good,' Josh said, a little more confidently. 'But this was something else.'

And that was when the rain stopped. It was as if it had appeared by magic, done what it needed to do, and moved on. I collapsed the umbrella, shook it off and slipped it back into its cover. When I looked back at Josh, he was smiling, a slightly bashful, irrepressible grin that he couldn't have hid even if he tried. Just like the rainstorm, it was as if the pressure had been lifted off us and we could spend the rest of the day together, secure in the knowledge that it had happened, and that the world hadn't ended. In fact, it had been incredible. There was a sense of calm around us now, the security that it *would* happen again and we didn't need to rush anything. It would all take care of itself.

We took the train a couple of stops to Chinatown so we could see it at night, and walk the rest of the way back to the hotel. On the train, we held on to the overhead rail and just looked at each other. Every so often one of us would break the spell, look off to the side, before reconnecting, knowing the other would still be there. I realised my heart was beating hard, but not fast. Everything was just right.

As we walked the busy streets zigzagged with red and yellow lanterns, I felt Josh's arm slink around my waist. 'Is this OK?' he murmured into my ear.

'It's . . . very OK,' I reassured him. I felt silly, like I wanted to play it cool but didn't know how, and I knew deep down that I didn't *have* to play it cool anymore. We were way, way past that.

We had no purpose, nowhere to be, just wanted to be out on the streets like normal people. Our strolling took us to a rooftop bar, where we had a drink and surveyed the city. Josh laid his hand on my thigh under the table and I felt my whole body relax, rather than tense up.

'It feels kinda like everything conspired to make it happen today,' he said as we sipped the last of our cocktails.

I laughed and shook my head. 'I still can't believe we tried to get other people to join us!'

'Yeah, that would have been kinda buzzkill energy.'

'Speaking of buzzkill, do you think we should go back to the hotel?'

He sighed. 'I guess so. It's been a fun day, though, right?'

'Right.'

On the walk back to Raffles, I felt sick with nerves, both at the idea that we were definitely going to have sex tonight, and the idea that we definitely weren't. I didn't know which scared me more. I couldn't tell what he was thinking or what he thought I was thinking. He'd been the one to instigate the kiss, so would he be the one to instigate sex, or would that have to be up to me? And if so, *how* would I do it?

Back at the hotel, we walked silently towards our rooms, arriving at his first. 'Well, this is me,' he said, but he didn't immediately turn to touch his keycard against the door. I couldn't tell if he was waiting for me to suggest that I came in, or if he wanted me to give him space.

'Thanks for a fun day,' I said, deciding not to roll the dice right then, but I *did* step forward and kiss him gently on the mouth. I felt him melt against me, his arms wrapping around my body, the kiss getting deeper and less gentle as he pressed me to him.

'*Fun* is one word for it,' he said, releasing his hold on me.

I turned towards my room, looked over my shoulder and said *very* casually, 'See you at the next junket.'

When the door closed behind me, I had to face facts: my feelings were anything but casual. I was completely obsessed with Josh Sacco.

JOSH

I have kissed Emily Montgomery three times in my life. First as a teenage jackass messing around with my buddies. Next as a character from a multimillion-selling book series. And finally, today, I got to kiss her as me. And it felt fucking fantastic.

I've dated models, actresses, singers, random girls who slid into my DMs. None of them have made me feel like Emily does, and it drives me fucking crazy. Why her? It makes not one iota of sense to me. Of all the girls in the world, why does it have to be her? Because if it's her, then I have to confront the fact that I've wasted time, that I've been a goddamn jerk, that I want to be with someone who probably only looks at me as a fling, a stupid Hollywood nepo baby, not someone good and serious and talented like her. No wonder she went for Ben Sage-Whittle. That's a pairing that makes sense, even if I do think he's an asshole, and believe me, I *very* much do.

But it *is* her. I know it's her, and now I know she feels the same about me. I can't keep telling myself it's impossible, because now I've had proof it's possible. It's just fucking terrifying, that's the thing. We have at least one more Wonderwick to film together, if not two since the studio's developed this cute little habit of splitting up the final instalment of their projects into two parts. So let's say two more movies. If I go rushing into this and I fuck it up . . . it doesn't bear thinking about.

I want to storm out of my room, pound on her door and find out what happens next. Every fibre of my being wants me to leap into action, to *do something*, to push this moment into the future. We know where my tendency towards impulsivity has got me before. So I don't go out there. I force myself to lie on the bed, not moving. If I'm completely still then there's less chance of me jumping to my feet and running to her. I stare at the dark wood fan over the four-poster, watching its blades go round and round and round, willing it to hypnotise me. If I just keep staring at it until I fall asleep then I can't get to my feet and let them carry me to my door, and out my door and to Emily's room. She's probably asleep already. It's past her bedtime.

So who's knocking on my door?

Chapter Thirty-Two

I knew he wanted it too, but I knew it had to come from me. The second I stepped into his room, it was like a switch had been flipped and it was *on*. My hands were in his hair, his arms were around my waist, I was pushed up against the door feeling my whole body screaming out for his touch. So far he had only kissed me, but I wanted more. No, I *needed* more. Something in his eyes told me he wasn't sure how to proceed, that he was holding back, as if I might change my mind at any moment. But I was all in.

'Touch me,' I whispered in his ear.

He swallowed, his breath catching as he moved his hands up my sides, gathering the fabric of my dress and pulling it over my head. A gasp escaped his lips as he took me in, his thumb lightly grazing my nipple through the sheer gauze of my bra, and even that felt like an earthquake. He unhooked my bra before getting to his knees, tracing a line of hungry kisses down my stomach to . . .

But before he got there he leaped to his feet, wrapped his arm around my waist and picked me up in one swift movement. 'That's it, we're going to bed,' he said, carrying me to the huge white expanse that seemed just *made* for this moment. He threw me down, a playful smile dancing on his lips, and then he was on top of me, his mouth moving down and down again and then finally . . . oh my *God* finally, the heat, the pressure, the sparks of his tongue against my clit, his fingers pushing inside me, then his hands on my hips pulling me towards him. I arched my back, wanting to be closer to him, somehow even more under his touch than just lying on the bed, like I couldn't bear to be away from his hands, his mouth, all of him and as I felt him moan into me, I felt this intense rush and I couldn't stop myself saying his name as I sank my hands into his hair, my fingers tangling in his curls.

Whenever I'd had sex before, it was as if I was trying to push myself to come quickly so they could stop, like I was inconveniencing them and wanted to let them get on with something more important, but this time it was more elemental than that: I *needed* to come, needed to experience the release of everything that had built up inside me. I couldn't stop saying his name over and over as his tongue swirled into me and just as I edged towards my orgasm, he murmured my name back and it pushed me right over the edge. The release was like nothing I'd ever felt before, radiating waves covering my whole body, leaving me panting, desperate to feel it again and again.

'Fuck . . .' Josh propped himself up on an elbow and looked at me, the aftershocks still pulsing through my body. 'Is it always like that?' He looked starry-eyed, almost disbelieving.

I felt my cheeks flush, shook my head.

'Just for me, huh?' He didn't sound arrogant, or even the slightest bit cocky. Just overwhelmed with the moment.

'This is starting to feel a little . . . uneven,' I said, pulling at his T-shirt. 'It doesn't seem fair for you to keep your clothes on.'

He grinned at me and rolled over to the edge of the bed, standing to yank his top off over his head, letting his shorts drop to the floor. All that was left were his tight grey jersey trunks, which left absolutely *nothing* to the imagination. I could feel myself getting wetter at the sight of him, everything in me desperate to feel him inside me. 'You can do the rest.' He moved back towards me, planting a hand on either side of my shoulder and holding himself up as I completed the task. 'Now we're even.'

Gazing up at him as he reached for a condom, I could barely believe this was all happening. Rolling it on with one hand, he pushed my leg aside with the other so he could tease me slowly before he sank himself into me, the force of it so exactly what I needed that it made my head spin. I could hear myself letting out sounds that I didn't even know I knew how to make, burying my face in his broad shoulder so I didn't feel self-conscious about how intensely I was feeling *everything*. But Josh wanted to see it all, leaning back so he could take in the look on my face, feel it all with me. He watched my expression as he sped up to a more intense pace, holding my hips as he pushed deep inside me, harder, deeper, and all I could do was run my hands over the muscles of his chest, his shoulders, his back, now slick with sweat. He looked down at me like I was the most miraculous thing in the world and as I rolled my hips I watched his jaw go slack, his eyes flickering with intense pleasure, and I felt my eyes roll back as I came again. In that moment, I realised I didn't care how I looked, only cared how I felt, how we both felt.

He closed his eyes, lost in intense concentration, clearly trying to hold back, but it was no use. 'Shit,' he said, panting heavily, as exerted from the orgasm as if he'd run a hundred-metre sprint. 'You're just too . . .' He looked at me dreamily, cupping my face in hand. 'Hot.'

Josh settled himself on the pillow next to me, his breathing steadying.

'I don't think anyone's ever called me *hot* before,' I said, rolling over to look at him.

'Well, they're idiots.'

'Clearly you know something they don't,' I said, with a shrug.

'And now I *really* know it,' he said as he ran a hand up my thigh.

Falling asleep in Josh's arms was not something I had ever expected to happen, but as I drifted off, my body exhausted but my mind at peace, I realised it was everything I wanted.

Chapter Thirty-Three

Ever since Singapore I'd felt like I was walking around with a stupid smile on my face. A stupid smile that might as well be a sign saying I Had Actual Sex With Actual Josh Sacco. Not even just once! Singapore was the first stop on the press tour, and since then we'd done sneaking around in Sydney, sneaking around in London, culminating in the last stop of the press tour: LA.

I'd wangled it so Chloe was on the plane with us. If the studio was going to cater to my whims once in a while, I might as well use it for my friend to fly on a private jet.

There were four seats on the plane: one for me, one for Josh, one for Chloe and one for Lisa from the studio, who spent a lot of time with her glasses on and noise-cancelling headphones in, replying to emails. Chloe sat opposite her, in the seat adjacent to mine across the aisle, while Josh was opposite me facing backwards. The three of us chatted amongst ourselves while Lisa worked, before she decamped to the sofa behind the seats when our chatting got too animated even for her noise-cancelling headphones. I felt his foot come to rest against mine, a smile instantly creeping across my face. In response, I moved my foot slowly backwards and forwards so he knew I knew his was there. He deliberately avoided eye contact with me, smiling as he stared out of the window at the endless blue, and wispy white clouds.

With a lurch of my stomach, I noticed Chloe watching us and felt hot all over, like I'd just been caught stealing sweets (who am I kidding, I've never done that). It wasn't like me to be careless, but I hadn't even been thinking for a *second* about the fact that other people were around. When were we going to go public? Were we going to go public? And if so, with what? What were we? Was Josh my boyfriend? Could Josh be my boyfriend? Was Josh the kind of person that could be someone's boyfriend?

While Josh was looking out the window, Chloe raised her eyebrows at me and mouthed, *What the fuck?* I just smiled and shrugged, like it was no big deal. It felt funny, after all this time, to surprise Chloe like this. She'd seen, there was no point hiding it from her anymore and I might as well not feel guilty about it.

'Can I interest you two in a drink?' Josh asked, a knowing smile on his face. 'Champagne?'

'I think that would be delicious, thank you, Josh!' Chloe said. While he was bending to extract the bottle from the fridge and fill three glasses, she leaned forward. 'Since when has he been polite and helpful? And what's more, what the—' she started, but Josh was back.

The three of us resumed our chat, slightly giddy with the champagne and the fun of the barely kept secret, until Lisa, glasses pushed on top of her head, leaned across the back of the seat and said, 'Hey, Josh, would you have a minute to chat?' I wondered if this was the project he'd mentioned to me in Singapore. The one with the stupid patriotic name. *Rock, Flag and Eagle* or whatever it was called. Knowing how profoundly *Orientations* had changed the direction of my career, and knowing that Josh was at least slightly curious about trying something different made me worry about him jumping into another big-budget franchise. But it was Josh's choice, not mine.

'What's up, Lisa,' Josh said enthusiastically, following her back to the section behind.

Chloe looked at me, her mouth open in disbelief. 'What the hell was all that?!' she whispered. 'Playing footsie with Josh Sacco! What is the meaning of this?' She was absolutely vibrating with excitement.

I couldn't stop myself from smiling, covering my face with my hands and looking at her through my fingers. 'Look, it's not that I'm keeping things from you,' I said, finally dropping my hands.

'Really?' she asked, arching her eyebrows so high they almost disappeared into her hair. 'Sure looks like it!'

'No, I promise. I just barely know what's going on with it all myself. It's a whole new thing. Very undefined. I'm approaching with caution.'

'That sounds more like the Emily Montgomery I know. But that is by *no* means enough details for me.'

'It's sort of been developing since this film . . . the shoot didn't start well but things sort of changed halfway through and the more I got to know him, and got a sense that maybe he was capable of being different to the person I'd decided he was. I don't know, I just found myself *wondering* about him.'

'Well I never,' Chloe said incredulously, shaking her head.

'Please don't say anything to anyone,' I begged her.

'I won't, I promise. Even though I'm *dying* to obviously,' she said, clinking her glass of champagne against mine.

I sighed, happily. 'I guess so.'

We touched down at Van Nuys, the private airport that served LA, and when we were shepherded towards separate cars, I was overwhelmed with the urge to kiss Josh goodbye. I didn't, I couldn't, it was too soon, too public, we hadn't talked about it and I didn't want to go rushing into something like that the way the Old Josh would. Instead I hugged him and said I'd see him for the press events the next day, leading to the premiere. Even a goodbye hug was more than I'd have done on previous films. I couldn't quite believe how much things had changed over the course of one movie after all this time.

The sun was setting as we drove to the Beverly Hills Hotel, traffic backed up on the I-405 and we idled alongside the scrubby hillside of the canyons. British actors often hated on LA, called it soulless, but I loved the trips I took there. I mean, I probably wouldn't want to *live* there but you couldn't deny there was something magic about it. This part of the journey wasn't necessarily magic, but once you got into the city, the palm trees lining wide city streets never failed to make me feel like I was somewhere special. I mean, palm trees! Real palm trees! It seemed too good to be true, too designed to make everyday life feel like a holiday. But they were real. Maybe Josh was like LA. Often dismissed as shallow and vapid, of low cultural nutritional value . . . and yet. A person that could make everyday life feel like a holiday.

Chapter Thirty-Four

Being in LA meant full-on, entire days of US press. That could mean anything from interviews with the biggest fan sites to photo shoots for magazines to filming content for social channels to in-person events. Darcy was hosting a meet-and-greet at the flagship store of the cosmetics brand with which she was launching a Wonderwick-themed palette. Courtney was filming Instagram content where she would go up to random people on the street and test their Wonderwick knowledge, and if they got all the questions right she would invite them to the premiere.

Max and Tommy, always a popular double act, even went on Getting Spicy, an insanely popular YouTube channel featuring celebrities eating chilli dogs made with increasingly spicy chillis. Half eating competition, half physical endurance test. Due to the fact they are insanely competitive, Max ended up eating the final chilli dog made with a ghost pepper because Tommy had tapped out at the previous level, before announcing he was back in the game when he saw Max do it and survive. Rather them than me and Josh . . .

We had instead been enlisted to do a video for the YouTube channel of FunZone, the biggest entertainment website in the world to establish how well we knew each other . . .

TRANSCRIPTION OF JOSH SACCO AND EMILY MONTGOMERY'S APPEARANCE ON FUNZONE BFF TEST

Josh Sacco: Oh we're absolutely going to nail it, we're going to knock all the other co-stars out of the park, no doubt.

Emily Montgomery: What is this 'we'? I'm going to nail it.

JS: Fighting talk!

EM: It's basically an exam! You know I'm going to nail it!

JS: All right . . . [throws his hands up]

EM: You're confident now but once we get started it's going to be like you've never met me before.

JS: Can you quit it with the trash talk?!

TITLE CARD: FUNZONE BFF TEST

[CARD: QUESTION 1 – When did you first meet?]

EM: A nice easy one to start with! At least we can agree on this, right?

JS: Uh, yeah, we can agree that I was kind of a dick!

EM: So it was the first day on the set of Wonderwick Woods, the first one—

JS: You're not gonna tell the whole story are you?

EM: Not if you don't want me to!

JS: We were introduced in this green room, yada yada yada. Emily could tell I hadn't learned my lines and so to deflect attention from my own, uh, shortcomings, I said something hella shady about what she was wearing.

EM: You did! Horrible little boy.

[CARD: QUESTION 2 – What were your first impressions of each other?]

EM: Josh, you obviously thought I was such a little nerd, didn't you?

JS: Absolutely. And you thought I was the laziest guy alive?

EM: I certainly did!

[They both laugh]

JS: So yeah I'd say we know each other pretty well?

[CARD: QUESTION 3 – What's their biggest pet peeve?]

JS: Oh that's so easy, when people aren't prepared or they're like slacking or whatever. You're a hard taskmaster!

EM: It's true!

JS: What's mine?

[Giggling] EM: When you're not getting enough attention?

JS: Damn, girl, my answer would be bad driving! Why did you come for me like that!

EM: I'm sorry! It's not my fault I know you better than you know yourself!

[CARD: QUESTION 4 – What was their favourite moment from filming *Wonderwick Woods: The Far Shores?*]

JS: You want us to say the kiss, right? We'll say the kiss if that's what you want!

EM: Even though it's obviously not true. Josh, if you knew me at all you'd know it was the scene where I have to look through all the books in the archive to find the one with the spell that can stop Loreia Buckthorn.

[Leans back in his chair] JS: Well, mine was the kiss so . . .

EM: Oh I bet it was. Next question!

[CARD: QUESTION 5 – What's their idea of a perfect day?]

EM: This is more like it! Probably playing basketball and looking at cool buildings then eating noodles?

JS: OK now you're talking, that actually sounds like a pretty sweet day. I'll give you that. And yours? Hmmm . . . does it sound like too much of a burn if I say it's being left alone while you read? Because I totally do not mean it as a burn!

EM: Consider me burnt but you're not wrong.

[Pumps fist] JS: Hell yeah! You got any more questions for us? This is fun.

EM: You're having a grand old time, aren't you?

JS: Just really enjoying an opportunity to impress you, that's all.

EM: Josh!

[Smiling, looking into the camera] JS: What?

Chapter Thirty-Five

'I just mean that it wasn't very stealthy!'

'Come on, it was just for the cameras!' he protested. 'FunZone seemed happy with the video!'

'I bet they did! I thought we were going to try to play it cool for a bit!'

'You make it hard to play it cool! You're just so damn cute!'

I'd turned down a car service so Josh could drive me back to the hotel. He'd taken us via the brilliantly ridiculous LA food shop Erewhon and we were now sipping on smoothies that had set us back more than $40. It was unexpectedly hot to watch him drive, one hand on the wheel, the other draped casually over my seat.

'It's not like I *want* to keep it a secret, it just feels like a good idea for now?'

'Oh, no totally. You know me, I'm as impulsive as they come, but I still think it's worth waiting.'

I squeezed his thigh as we turned into the valet parking for the Beverly Hills Hotel.

'Just checking my co-star gets to her room safely,' Josh said with a wink, tossing his keys to the valet.

'Again, not very stealthy!' I whispered to him, but he was whistling nonchalantly as we made our way to my room. 'You know, if you wanted to stay in a pool house my parents have one you could use,' Josh said, appraising my lodgings.

'This isn't a pool house! It's a presidential bungalow!' I protested. Not that there was any way I was going to stay with him at his family home anyway. That would be *way* too much, too soon.

'Presidential pool house,' he said, teasing. 'So, you want me to go?'

I shrugged, as if I didn't mind either way. He sat on the edge of the bed. 'I suppose I've got some time before I need to start being beautified for the premiere.'

'You could go just the way you are and you'd still look perfect.'

'You have to say that,' I said, rolling my eyes.

'You know that I absolutely do not. Come here,' he said, and I straddled him on the bed. He drew me towards him, our lips meeting in a deep kiss.

'Do we really have to go to the premiere? Can't we just stay here?' I asked him.

'I never thought I'd see the day that Emily Montgomery would be trying to skip out on work responsibilities to hang out with *me*,' he said, gazing into my eyes like he really couldn't believe it.

'You've been a bad influence on me.'

'Debatable. I think I've been a *good* influence on you, if anything.'

'Are you going to fuck me or not?' I said, hitting him with one of the absurdly fluffy pillows adorning my bed, laughing at the mock shock on his face.

The answer was, of course, yes. He reached up between my legs and pushed my underwear aside, using his thumb to move in rhythmic circles against my clit that emptied my head of thoughts and instead filled it with stars. It was like Josh always knew exactly the right thing to do, exactly the right way to touch me in that moment. He unzipped his fly and pulled his trousers off, and I lowered myself onto him, pushing him deep inside me. Sex with Josh always felt like an out-of-body experience to me, as if I became someone else. Or maybe it wasn't that at all, it was that I was *in my body* more than ever, was that I was actually becoming *myself*, and that Emily wanted to dig her nails into his back, let her hot mouth find his neck, watch his teeth bite down on his bottom lip, feel our bodies move against each other with the only purpose being pure pleasure. No scenes to film, no deals to strike, no selfies to take. Nothing mattered outside of this room. My hips ground down against him, hungry and desperate for him to fill as much of me as humanly possible, to feel every inch of him, the mouthwatering border between pleasure and pain.

'Fuck . . . Emily . . .' he panted, his eyes dreamy and bewildered, as if he still couldn't quite believe we were doing this. I moved my hands to his shoulders, feeling the muscles and the sinews under the skin, watching his muscular chest rise and fall with every breath until the wave hit, and I collapsed on top of him, both of us delirious.

And then he really did have to leave, and I really did have to get ready for the evening ahead, holding the secret between us like a precious thing.

If I'd found the Singapore premiere intense, it was nothing compared to the reception we got in LA. The premiere was held at the TCL Chinese Theatre, probably the most iconic cinema in the world. The crowds were *huge* and intense: I'd almost managed to forget about about the Wonderwick fervour while I'd been working on other things, but these fans were here to remind me that it was not going *anywhere*.

Chloe shuffled me along the line of reporters and I tried with every fibre of my being not to keep looking over my shoulder for Josh. I was being interviewed by a *Deadline Hollywood* reporter on the red carpet when wild screams filled the air at the appearance of Darcy in an absurdly short, tight, white minidress, a gloriously excessive version of her character's iconic white costume. She posed, icy and angular, her hair looking even sharper than usual. I couldn't help but smile. This was what I'd been afraid of? It felt amazing to see everyone so excited about her. And now, I really meant it. I wasn't just telling myself that, reciting lines off a press release. Darcy's popularity meant absolutely nothing to me, other than that it brought even *more* hype to our films.

Finally, I made it down the line and found myself in front of the press photographers at the exact same moment as none other than Josh Sacco. He had never looked more handsome. Funny how a black suit didn't look so boring when it was as well cut as this, utterly fitted to the body. His hair was pushed back from his face, giving him the look of an old Hollywood star. I had to fight the urge to run up to him, wrap my arms around him and kiss him, but this was *not* the moment. Instead, I posed demurely for photos next to him, allowed him to slip his hand around my waist.

I felt Josh withdraw his hand, say, 'I think we've done enough here, let's go,' and turn towards the entrance. I turned on my heel to follow him when—

Oh. Oh no. The first thing I felt was my spiky heel snagging on the red carpet, next the ripple effect up to my ankle, finally the unstoppable sideways movement as my leg buckled under me. Surely one of the worst feelings in the world is the heart-in-mouth moment when you realise you're falling and there's absolutely nothing you can do to prevent it from happening and, oh my God, no, not here in front of all these people, all these cameras, my co-stars, not me, not now . . .

But I never hit the ground.

'I got you.' Josh smiled down at me. I wasn't on the floor. I was in his arms, looking up at him. I was like a ballroom dancer in the arms of my partner, an elegantly choreographed ending to a dance. I blinked at him, heart thudding away at my ribcage, unable to believe my luck, for what felt like minutes but was actually just seconds. 'You all right?' The gasp of the crowd echoed in my ears, only rivalled by the sound of a million flashbulbs capturing the moment. Thank God for Josh.

I nodded at him, adrenaline pumping through my body. In one elegant move, he lifted me back onto my feet. He held my hand overhead, and murmured, 'Give them a twirl, show them you're in control.'

Carefully but confidently, my hand in his, I twirled on the spot like a ballerina, letting my dress swish around my thighs, laughing with the relief of someone who had basically just cheated social death. I came to a stop as one photographer shouted, 'Was that planned, Josh?'

He shook his head, a roguish grin on his face. 'No way, man. I just love supporting my co-star,' he said with a wink.

Chloe intercepted me as Josh strode on ahead, giving me a backwards look and a smile before turning to his own publicist. 'Oh my God, Emily, are you OK?!' Chloe panted at me, eyes wide.

'I'm fine!'

'OK good because that was *amazing*.'

I felt a smile creep across my face. 'And we didn't even plan it.'

'Who needs planning when fate takes care of everything! So, are you going to go public soon?'

'I don't know.' I twitched my nose in thought. 'I want to but I just don't want to push things too far too fast.'

She sighed. 'Very wise, although I'm living for the reveal.'

'You'll be the first to know when we do.'

'I'd bloody better be, it's going to be a lot of work to roll out something this epic,' she said as we congregated backstage to be paraded on before the film started.

'You're already big news, classic Sacco stealing the show.' Max bounded up to me, his bow tie lopsided. He held up his phone and showed me a photo on the E! Instagram account. It was a *great* photo, completely straight on with Josh in the middle, his arms under my back, my body in a strangely elegant backbend with my long, straight hair cascading down, grazing the red carpet. I swiped to the next photo, and saw it was me, laughing, one hand covering my mouth but my eyes full of joy, and the other hand in Josh's, held overhead. Not only had he saved me when I needed him to, he'd played the whole thing perfectly. What could have been a complete disaster, the kind of thing that could have made it into a listicle titled 'Ten Red Carpet Nightmare Moments', was now immortalised forever as something cute, playful, even . . . romantic.

Finally, when the audience were all seated, we filed onto the stage to rapturous applause.

'Thank you for joining us for what I truly believe is the most exciting instalment yet. Not to mention the most romantic!' Martin said to a chorus of 'oooh-s' from the audience. 'I'm lucky to get to work with such an incredible team on these movies, some of whom you see here on the stage, but most of whom you don't. But we're lucky to have a few of the stars with us tonight, and I'm going to hand the microphone over to our two leads – Emily Montgomery who you know and love as Linderley Jones, and Josh Sacco, your very own Rowan Clearwater!'

'Uh, thanks, Martin,' Josh said, a little caught off guard. 'I don't have much to add to what you've already said much better than I could, so I'll leave the rest to Emily!'

'Thanks, Josh, and thanks, Martin. It's always such a pleasure to share with you the product of all of our hard work. It's such a team project and Wonderwick is very special in that way. We're a tight little family, and I know that can be a scary place to walk into, so I just wanted to properly welcome Darcy,' I said, holding my arm out towards her. Her eyes met mine and I wondered how different this would feel if I was still afraid of her, still threatened by her. As it was, we could enjoy the moment together. The audience cheered even louder, and I knew they were in for an amazing night. 'I really hope you enjoy what we've made for you! Wonderwick forever!'

We took our seats, strategically positioned so we could sneak out part-way through. I was proud of the film but didn't necessarily need to see it again. Instead we had dinner together before the official after-party. I was seated next to Darcy, who laid a hand on mine and said, 'It was so kind of you to say that before the movie.'

I shook my head. 'Oh it was nothing!'

'I mean it, I'm glad I'm working with you. You're a good example.'

'Well, thank you, I suppose,' I said, blushing furiously.

'So, is it true about you and Josh?'

'Who told you?'

'Oh so it is true! No one had told me, I was just picking up on a vibe.'

Damn! I'd walked right into that one. What an idiot. 'Please don't tell anyone.'

'I won't, I promise,' Darcy said, eyeing Josh across the table. 'He's a funny one, isn't he? You think he's going to be all macho bullshit but he's really quite sweet. He used to date my friend, nothing serious, but he's one of those guys where no one who's dated him has a bad thing to say about him.'

I felt flushed with something like pride. 'That's good to hear.' I paused. 'So you're not . . . you know . . .'

'Jealous?' She laughed. 'I mean, I guess I got a little swept up in his hype.

Just then, Josh looked up from his conversation with Martin. He met my eyes and smiled at me, and for a moment, everyone else melted away.

I was falling *hard* for Josh, both literally and metaphorically.

@EnchantedLucy This is the cutest thing I've ever seen in my LIFE

@WonderwickHollow54 Screaming crying throwing up I never knew how badly I needed this

@HighT0wer This feels so huge lol I never thought this day would come

@Buckthornite You're fckn deluded if you think that was real

@TreetopGrrrl You're fckn deluded if you think that was fake! She obviously twisted her ankle?

@Buckthornite I have it on GOOD AUTHORITY from a SOURCE that it was staged

@TreetopGrrrl Because Josh is actually in love with Darcy Jackson, right? [eyeroll emoji]

@Buckthornite Exactly

@RowansBabe Well you would say that wouldn't you

@EnchantedLucy Did you guys not see their co-star test video??? The chemistry! That CANNOT be faked.

@WWForever OMFG CAN YOU SHUT UP AND STOP ARGUING AND JUST ENJOY LINDERLEY AND ROWAN SHARING A MOMENT

@EnchantedLucy Yes sorry you've lost your god-damn mind, conspiracy theory brain rot freak

Chapter Thirty-Six

'Oh, Emily, this is so glamorous! Why haven't you brought me here before?!'

'I haven't *been* here before, Mum! Wonderwick isn't the kind of thing they show at the Venice Film Festival!' I said gently, as we cruised from Venice airport to our hotel. We were staying in the city, but the festival itself took place on the Lido where there were fewer luxury hotels. I had huge cat-eye sunglasses and a headscarf on and I felt *exactly* like a movie star.

'If I'd known you doing independent films would mean I got to take a speedboat across the Venice lagoon, I'd have told you to start doing them sooner,' she said, squeezing my hand.

It was so humid that it felt like being in Singapore again, but I was so excited to be there that I didn't care. My mum was my official date to the world premiere of *Orientations*, while Josh was on a boys' holiday in Ibiza with Max and Tommy and some of their friends. Not that he'd have been my date at the festival: we hadn't even talked about him coming with me. It felt safer to take it slow. If I had my way, I'd be shouting it from the rooftops. I knew I shouldn't obviously, but I was just so fizzy with feelings for Josh and I hated having to keep a lid on them. *Wonderwick Woods: The Far Shores* had exceeded the studio's expectations breaking all previous records for the franchise, in large part thanks to the kiss which was now surely the most re-blogged GIF in Tumblr's history. Now it was time to turn my attention to publicising *Orientations*.

We checked into the hotel – the Gritti Palace – and I made sure to accompany Mum to her room just to see her reaction. She'd stayed in nice hotels when chaperoning me before, but this was something else completely. The opulence of the room was breathtaking and it was worth every penny to watch her face beam with delight at the sight of it.

'Isn't it wonderful?' She looked around, taking in the chandelier, the hand-painted wallpaper, the huge gilt-framed mirror, all of the authentic antique furniture in curving polished wood and button-backed upholstery, the herringbone wooden floor covered with immaculate rugs. It was totally gorgeous, and that was before she walked over to the window for the view of the canal.

'It's incredible, Mum. I'm so happy you're here. Thank you for coming with me.' I knew she'd been having a hard time with the trial separation, the fallout from the gambling debts, and that I hadn't been there enough. I'd thrown money at the problem because that was what I *could* do, but I wanted to show that just because she wasn't my chaperone anymore that didn't mean she wasn't part of my life and my work. Being able to do this for her, including her in this life, made me feel like the luckiest person in the world.

I joined her at the window and opened it so we could survey the Grand Canal like it was ours. Boats cut through the water, leaving satisfying trails of white in their wake. Happy tourists, commuting Venetians, people who had come to town for the festival, all of human life was down there. Including . . . No! God, why! Of course Ben was here, of *course* I knew he would be here intellectually, knew that we would have to do press junkets and red carpets together, but I hadn't actually *properly* thought through what it would be like to be forced back together with him. Horrible.

I got a text saying the Italian glam squad had arrived, courtesy of Vespucci, so I kissed Mum goodbye and headed back to my room. We'd meet again later to travel by boat to the Lido, where the Palazzo del Cinema would host the world-first screening of *Orientations*. I had someone painting my nails while someone else blow-dried my hair while someone else did my makeup. I almost felt like I was in a car wash, being buffed and polished from all angles. But it was worth it. By the end of the afternoon, I felt incredible.

Obviously Lucy and my mum hyped me up, Edgar gave me an inscrutable compliment and Ben ignored me, but it was only when I stepped off the water taxi that I understood what a *moment* this look was for me. The press release announcing my status as Vespucci's spokesmodel was going to all major world press as I stood there.

'What are you wearing?' asked an Italian *Vogue* journalist.

'Vespucci couture,' I told her, looking down at the magnificent dress I'd been fitted for over several sessions back in London. It was a strapless dress with a corset bodice that came to two sharp points on either side of my chest (*very bitchy*, as Chloe had put it), in the deepest petrol blue-green silk printed with huge warped flowers. It was nothing like anything I'd worn before, a mix of sleek old Emily and the experimental new era I was in. My hair was scraped back into the slickest bun you've ever seen, showing off a huge gothic floral cuff snaking its way up my right ear. For someone known as a 'natural beauty' for so long, I really leaned into the drama of the look and took the Vespucci makeup artist's suggestion of going for a blood-red lip. But *real* blood, the way it darkens as soon as it meets the air. It was a striking contrast against the pared-back approach he had taken to the rest of my face, and I absolutely loved it.

When we all had to line up on the steps of the Palazzo del Cinema for the photo call, I made sure I was at one end of the line, with Lucy and Edgar providing a buffer between Ben and me. It's not like I was *trying* to make it an awkward vibe, I just wanted him to understand that we were absolutely not friends. I'd already had to fend off questions about him from entertainment journalists on the red carpet, politely wheeling out stock phrases like, 'No, sadly that relationship didn't quite work out for us but he's a very talented actor,' and 'As you'll see in the film, we worked very well together as colleagues.' Fortunately, I couldn't answer questions all night: we had a film to screen.

Because I'd been so busy with Wonderwick promo, I hadn't been able to watch *Orientations* yet myself. It wasn't until the lights went down that the nerves hit me: I'd been too distracted with everything else to actually wonder if the film was any good. I knew it probably was, and knew I didn't have anything to worry about, but what if Edgar had gone mad in the edit? What if it turned out completely differently to the film we thought we were making? As the opening credits rolled, it really hit me how much the film meant to me. I desperately wanted it to work.

And work it did.

I couldn't help looking around at people's reactions as *Orientations* played on the screen in front of us, the film illuminating their faces. Maybe I was being completely deluded, but I had a sense that the whole Palazzo del Cinema was spellbound. God, I hoped I had got this one right, that this gamble had paid off. I couldn't imagine a room full of people watching *Dinky Daffy and the Detective Squad* like this, anyway.

While the closing credits rolled, we were extracted from our seats and led up to the stage again. The response was deafening. We just stood there, beaming, as the audience applauded. I waited for them to stop, desperate to be able to debrief with someone, excitedly rehash the whole experience with my mum. But they didn't stop. It just went on, and on, and on, and on.

'What do we do?' I whispered to Lucy.

'Stand here and look pretty until they stop,' she said.

I'd heard of these mad standing ovations at the end of films at festivals, but this felt completely ridiculous, and utterly wonderful. Looking out at this sea of faces, I didn't have to wonder anymore if they liked it. I knew they did. I knew they loved it. I had to fight back tears as I realised Lucy had been right that morning in the café: this was going to be big for me. I didn't know exactly what that meant, but I knew I liked it.

Finally, the applause petered out and we were allowed to leave the stage, allowed to head back to the hotel and try to sleep. I was overflowing with joy and excitement, and wished Josh was here to share it with me. I understood why he wasn't, that it was too soon and we weren't ready to go public yet, but that didn't stop me missing him. As I was getting ready for bed, a text came through from him.

That's my girl! So, so proud of you.

I fell asleep feeling like I couldn't really ask for anything more.

Over an early breakfast the next morning, I addressed the elephant in the room with Mum. I had a full day of press, interviews with journalists from around the world about *Orientations* now it had screened, but I wanted to carve out this time just for us. 'How's the, you know, the trial separation going?'

She shrugged, threw her hands up in defeat. 'Honestly, I don't know. I didn't want it in the first place but it felt like a way to draw a line under the whole thing. I couldn't just let everything carry on as normal, I needed him to really think about what he had done.'

I nodded. It made sense, not being able to just move on from something like that. 'And now?'

'We're talking more, so that's something,' she said. 'And—'

But before she could finish her sentence, a figure loomed over our table.

'*Buongiorno*, Emily. Just thought it would be polite to say hello rather than studiously avoid you,' Ben said.

He held out his hand gallantly. 'Lovely to meet you, Mrs Montgomery.'

I waited for her to gently encourage him to call her Ruth, but she didn't.

'Nice to meet you, too,' she said tightly. I couldn't believe they hadn't met before, but equally the whole summer felt like a fever dream to me now so if you'd said I'd spent it filming a *Space Jam* sequel on Mars I'd probably have agreed with you.

He looked down at me, arms folded, probably judging the fact I had two types of pastry on my plate. 'It's silly, all of this avoiding each other, don't you think? We have a film to promote after all.'

I shrugged. 'I'm not avoiding you, I just don't have anything to say to you.'

He smiled, a cruel little twist of his mouth. 'If you insist. Well, I'll leave you to it,' he said, striding off to his own table.

'Ugh, he is so awful, I don't know what I ever saw in him!'

'He's quite handsome but there's more to life than that, isn't there?'

'I'm realising that.' I checked the time. 'I have to go and get ready for the press junket, I'm sorry, Mum.'

'You're beautiful just the way you are!'

'Well, now I'm the Vespucci spokesmodel, I can't be seen with a hair out of place, and if they're happy to pay for it, I'm happy to sit there and have someone do the hard work for me.'

'Will I see you again, darling?'

I thought about it for a moment. 'Maybe not, you might be gone by the time I'm done.'

'Well, in that case,' she said, getting to her feet and drawing me into a tight hug, 'I'm beyond proud of you.

I know Dad is, too. This is more than we could have ever dreamed of for you, darling.' The mention of my dad made me want to cry. In the midst of all this success and happiness and fulfilment, it felt wrong that this was so off-kilter. I tried not to think about it too much, but whenever I had to confront it the whole thing hit me again like a tidal wave.

The publicity work for *Orientations* had been orchestrated – thanks to the hard work of Chloe – like an elegant dance that meant Ben and I never had to speak to each other. Instead, I had to spend the day speaking endlessly to everyone *but* Ben. The festival had been subject to some scrutiny the previous year for giving almost no press access to 'A-list talent', so in response we had been scheduled for a gruelling day of publicity. It reminded me of when we were on the press tour for the first Wonderwick film, delirious with fatigue and brain-addled with jet lag, and one of my more experienced adult co-stars had once drily observed to me that A-list actors didn't get paid to act in the film, they got paid to publicise it. I had quickly discovered he was right.

We did hours of round-tables, followed by some one-on-one interviews with the biggest news outlets in the world. At first I had been nervous, a little unsure how to talk about the film, about my role and the work that had gone into it, but I soon found my own words, my own account of making the movie that was now the talk of the festival.

'Well, Emily is very special. I think it's easy to underestimate her because of her relatively limited experience, but I could see something in her. I knew there was potential there if she was given the right material,' Edgar said to a French film journalist who was nodding sagely as his dictaphone took in our conversation. I'd heard Edgar say a version of this several times already and it never got any less exciting to me. The fact I was someone that people could *see* the potential, the talent, the untapped reserves of *something*. That meant so much to me.

The evening wrapped up and we were transported back to the Gritti Palace, the night air thick and full of drama. Venice was such a magical place, and I couldn't believe I was the surprise star of the festival.

When I put my keycard to the reader on the door, I almost didn't want the night to be over. I thought about going to Lucy's room and asking if she wanted to get a drink in the bar. But best not, since I had an early meeting with Vespucci about a big photo shoot I had booked in Milan in a few weeks. Grudgingly, I figured I should probably get my beauty sleep. Pushing open the door, I was hit first with the knowledge that the lights were on, followed by the stomach-dropping realisation that there was someone in my room.

'What the fuck?' I gasped, wondering if those were the last words I'd ever speak in my short life. At least I'd be going out on a high.

'There's my girl!' beamed none other than Josh Sacco. He was lying on the bed in a white T-shirt and grey jersey shorts, his arms stretched out towards me. It was the best thing I'd ever seen in my life.

'I thought you were a murderer-stalker!' I said because the alternative was bursting into tears, a mixture of relief and unadulterated joy at the sight of him.

'I'm sorry, I'm sorry! I thought it would be romantic! Your mom helped, got the hotel to issue another room key!' So she was in on it too?! This meant she *certainly* approved more of Josh than she did of Ben.

'What are you even doing here?!' I asked, delight washing over me like slipping into a warm, deep bath.

'I couldn't stay away.' He shrugged. 'Don't ever look up how much it costs to fly from Ibiza to Venice in September. Promise me.'

'Josh!' I ran into his outstretched arms and just lay on top of him for a moment, breathing in his scent. All deep and earthy, smoke and wood. 'You're too much.'

'You deserve the world. Your movie is gonna win the Golden Lion, I just know it.'

A day ago I'd have rolled my eyes at him and told him to shut up, that there was no way we'd win the biggest award at the festival. But now? It was starting to feel deliciously possible. 'Don't say it! Don't jinx it!' I had the absolutely crazy idea of taking Josh with me to the ceremony. Wouldn't that be something?

'Fine, how about no more talking?' he said, his hand against the back of my neck, pulling me towards him, unzipping my dress so I could wriggle out of it and throwing it to the floor next to the bed. Undressing Josh was like unwrapping a Christmas present, his body just the right side of ludicrously ripped to still be fun. I ran my hands over his chest, his shoulders, just delighting in the feeling of him *being there*. It was incredible how quickly I'd been able to shift from seeing him as this person I'd known since I was thirteen to a completely different kind of person, like he'd been playing a role before and now he was fully himself. I felt as if I was fully myself, too, in a way I hadn't known was possible.

We lay together in the bed, feeling almost drunk on the pure pleasure of being back together. 'Want to get room service?' I asked him.

'Sure do, you've worn me out,' he said, sitting up against the button-back headboard.

When the hotel staff arrived with a tray full of various pastas under a huge silver cloche, Josh's eyes shifted nervously around the room, as if he was trying to blend in with his surroundings and make himself invisible.

'Should I have hidden in the bathroom?' he asked as the door closed behind them, a healthy tip in hand.

'It's fine, they're sworn to secrecy.' I shrugged. 'Official Hotel Secrets Act or something. Why, are you embarrassed about going out with me?' I asked, playfully.

'Christ no,' he said, twirling some spaghetti around his fork. 'I just want us to take things at a pace that's right for us.'

'Me too.' I settled onto the bed next to him. 'Eating room service on the bed always makes me feel like I'm a kid again. Not a kid, I mean, but early Wonderwick. It felt so decadent! It's not like my parents were short of money but if we stayed in a hotel we would *never* order room service. So it's something that always reminds me of when that changed. And because I was a kid I would *always* eat it on the bed, just because I could. It felt so rebellious!'

'That's a very Emily Montgomery kind of rebellion,' he says, leaning forward and planting a kiss on my cheek.

Josh ate his outrageously expensive room service and we watched Italian TV, which Josh only sporadically understood. 'It's good for the brain. I'm sure I'm taking it in by osmosis?' he said, when I questioned why we were watching it. I just rolled my eyes and kissed him, because truthfully I felt happier in that moment than I had in a long time. The success of *Orientations*, being able to share the moment with my mum after everything she'd gone through, feeling so beautiful in my dress, the announcement of the Vespucci deal, and to top it all off, Josh being here? It was better than I could have thought possible.

Ben Sage-Whittle and Emily Montgomery Create Frosty Atmosphere on Venice Red Carpet

By Jamie Andrews for MailOnline

Former lovers Ben Sage-Whittle and Emily Montgomery were unable to avoid each other following their very public spat as their film, *Orientations*, had its premiere in competition at the Venice Film Festival last night.

The pair, who met on the set of the movie, were seen strategically positioning themselves to avoid having to speak to each other or be photographed next to each other on the red carpet and at the press junket today.

The actress, twenty-one, has entered the awards race conversation for her role in Edgar Malek's *Orientations* as the plethora of glowing reviews repeatedly highlighted her performance as Annie, a young woman in a difficult relationship with her mother which is disturbed by the appearance of a handsome stranger. Montgomery stars alongside Sage-Whittle and Lucy Lennon.

At the official festival press junket for *Orientations*, the pair were asked how their relationship affected the shoot, with Sage-Whittle tersely replying, 'It didn't. Next question.'

Rumours have deepened about a potential romance between Montgomery and her Wonderwick

Woods co-star Josh Sacco, following yet another intimate moment on the red carpet. Their easy rapport at the US premiere for *Wonderwick Woods: The Far Shores* was in stark contrast to Emily and Ben's awkward body language at the Venice Film Festival. The pair have not confirmed their couple status but industry sources say it is an open secret.

Chapter Thirty-Seven

The next morning, I awoke to the faint sound of Josh in conversation on the little standing balcony. I could see him from my bed, watched him speak into the phone as he slouched back against the railing. I knew I wouldn't be able to keep all of this a secret much longer. Finally he hung up and came back to bed. I had a meeting with Vespucci in the morning so we wouldn't be able to linger too long.

'Sorry, did I wake you? I tried to keep it down.'

'It's OK. Who was it?' I propped myself up on my elbow and looked down at him, his dark eyelashes even longer and thicker from this angle, a cross-hatch of inky darkness.

'Just Lex, my agent,' he said, but there was tension in his voice.

'Oh? All good?'

'Yeah, just in final negotiations on my contract for *Eagle Heart*.'

'Is that the superhero thing Lisa wanted you for?' I knew it was, but I didn't want him to know I'd been thinking about it.

He nodded, his eyes flicking over my face trying to gauge my reaction.

'That's great!' I said, maybe a little too enthusiastically. I didn't really think it was great.

'Really?'

I frowned at him. 'Of course!'

'You really think that?'

'Why wouldn't I?'

'Because you're . . . you know . . . you're on this different path now, everyone is raving about your new movie, you're the hot new serious actress,' he said. 'I guess I thought maybe you'd think less of me for doing it.'

To me, the fact *Orientations* was going down well was irrelevant. What mattered was the fact I'd given it a go in the first place. Even if it had flopped, I would still have been glad to try material that stretched me, exposed me to different ways of working, even that *paid* me vastly less, just so I understood what it was like to exist outside of Wonderwick.

'I don't think less of you at all, I just . . .'

'What?'

'I would just love to see you really flourish as an actor, rather than just a star. Do you know what I mean?' I said, tentatively.

'We *are* actors.'

'Of course we are, I know that, it's just a really specific world that we've been operating in. I'd *only* done

Wonderwick, at least you've been in other things, even if they were blockbusters.'

'Wonderwick is what made you, too! It's not like you're better than blockbusters!'

'It's not about being *better*, it's about wanting more. It's about *and* not *or*. I believe you can do more, can do something different, if you let yourself try. I just don't want you getting trapped in these huge machines, doing franchises and spin-offs of franchises forever and never finding out if you're *more* than that.'

'So you think I'm making a mistake?'

'I'm not here to tell you what to do.'

'No, you just judge me for the decisions I make instead, right? It's the same old thing we've been dealing with for years. You're smart, sensible, hard-working Emily and I'm lazy, stupid Josh who just wants to make dumb shit while you're doing the *real* work, right? I remember your reaction when I said I wanted to work with Edgar Malek!' he said, something I had completely forgotten about, that conversation in the alley at the Wonderwick video-game party where they sprung Darcy on me. 'You were completely baffled by the implication that I might aspire to something like that! And now you're judging me for, what, knowing my place?'

I didn't even know where to begin, didn't know how to explain that I was mortified I'd made him feel like that, and how getting to know him over the past year had completely changed the way I thought about him.

That I'd been wrong, and that I believed in him, truly. I wasn't judging him. Tears stung my eyes. All I could manage was, 'Why are you pushing me away?'

'Why are you pushing *me* away?'

'I don't even understand what we're arguing about! It feels like this has come out of nowhere!' I was starting to panic, like this was all spiralling out of control and I desperately wanted to reel it in.

Josh shook his head. 'I shouldn't have come. This was your time, you didn't need me around to drag you down. You're a shiny balloon and I'm a dead fucking weight. You and Ben? That made sense. You and me? I don't know, Emily.'

'Josh.' I held my arms out to him but he was already packing, throwing his things into his suitcase like it was a bin.

And then he left.

I did the Vespucci meeting in a haze of disbelief, barely listening to a word anyone was saying, nodding and smiling politely, knowing that there were people there whose job it was to be paying attention. Two nights later *Orientations* won the Golden Lion. Oh, and I won the Marcello Mastroianni Award for Young Actor or Actress. The first award I'd ever won for acting.

It was the most exciting moment of my career and it still felt like a loss.

JOSH

Why the hell did I do it? Why did I pick a fight with her like that? And why did I have to bring up her goddamn stupid ex who didn't know how to treat her? Christ, I'm no better than him, am I?

During that whole fight with Emily, I wanted to scream, shout, break things, to get her to understand that I was just being a fucking asshole because I was scared and insecure. What was I scared of? Oh, everything. Or more specifically, the fact that she was right, that I was going to waste my life doing superhero movies which were more a testament to my workout regime than they were to my acting skills. I wondered if deep down she knew the reason that I would never sign on to a movie like *Orientations* was that I was too scared to try, too scared to throw my hat in the ring to try something more serious because if I failed then I would *know* I was a good-looking but mediocre actor with Hollywood producer parents, his most marketable asset his abs. If I never tried, I could always preserve the belief that I had it in me, it was just untested.

Emily isn't like that. Emily's brave, as well as talented. She's riding high, she's the It Girl, she's signing deals and starting companies and winning awards and what am I doing? Just fucking floundering, doing the same old shit I've always done. Except now it's worse because as well as doing that, I'm pushing away the girl I love and that I want to be with. I'm crazy about her. After all this time, I know I'm crazy about Emily. And maybe being with Emily is just like all the supposed untapped potential inside me: maybe it's better not to try at all than to try and to find out that it fails.

Oh, I'm a coward? Fuck yeah I'm a coward. Always have been. A brave person wouldn't have been intimidated by a nerdy and well-prepared thirteen-year-old girl and proceeded to borderline torment her for years! That's coward shit! A brave person would have kissed Emily at that wrap party and fucking *owned it* rather than playing it as a joke, embarrassing her in front of our friends. A brave person would take risks with their career, try to break out of the image they've fallen into. Not me! I'm a coward! Emily deserves better than that.

She deserves better than me.

Chapter Thirty-Eight

Everything after Venice felt grey. It didn't help that I came back to a gloomy London, the city beneath a dense grey sky, always under threat of rain, but not in an exciting way like Singapore, just . . . predictable. I should have been riding high, but instead I felt totally adrift. I had this sense that *everything was wrong*, even though everything was right, except for my parents, and me and Josh. I was finally the woman of the hour, sleek and glamorous and taken seriously, after being a strange little child actress for so many years. So why wasn't I enjoying it?

Whatever the problem was, the solution, as always, was to work. Take meetings, go to Milan for a two-day photo shoot for Vespucci's new signature handbag, talk to Glen and various lawyers about buying the rights to Eleanor Blomquist's book for adaptation while we were in the process of setting up the company, doing press for *Orientations*. Anything I could to keep myself busy. I checked Josh's Instagram every day. I couldn't help it, I needed to see where he was, who he was with, if he was being photographed with another girl. If so, he was completely within his rights but it would have devastated me. I had no interest in meeting someone else. I'd flick through magazine features on 'hot young British actors' and feel nothing, no flicker of interest or even curiosity. I hoped this wasn't me done forever, just pining after Josh for years while he moved on. So, I did what I do best, and I worked.

When I wasn't working I was working out, and my star had risen so much in the past year that runs through Regent's Park had become impossible. I'd traded them in for running on a treadmill and taking classes at a gym in Marylebone where I (yes, even Emily Montgomery!) had to linger on a waiting list for a month before they deigned to give me membership. I was walking home across Regent's Park, my muscles aching after a particularly spicy Reformer Pilates class, when my podcast was interrupted by an incoming call. It was Glen.

'Emily!' he boomed in my ear.

'Hi, Glen!' I said, and I forced myself to do it cheerily. I'd slipped into this way of thinking recently where I was just *poised* for bad news. It didn't matter that things were going well, anything could be taken away from you at any minute. I was convinced every call from Glen was news of my cancellation, something bad about a project I was being considered for, that Legacy Studios had folded overnight. I didn't used to be like this, but I couldn't help looking at everything through . . . whatever the opposite of rose-tinted glasses was.

'Just a sec! I'm going to add Chloe into the mix!'

Intriguing.

'Oh, Emily!' Chloe sounded like she was spilling over with excitement and her tone of voice made my pulse speed up a little bit. Whatever this was, it was . . . *good*?

'We wanted to both be on the call when I told you the good news!'

'Yes?' I urged him, nearly dying of curiosity and impatience.

'You've been nominated for a Best Supporting Actress BAFTA! Isn't that incredible?!'

I felt the hot prick of tears in my eyes. My heart leaped, my stomach did somersaults, everything felt tingly and warm. 'I have?' I choked out. I mean, I knew it was kind of *possible*, but I didn't in a million, billion years think it would actually happen. To me? The girl from Wonderwick?

I sat down on a park bench, watching people go about their day. They had no idea what was happening to me. I didn't matter to them. I was insignificant. But I was having one of the most incredible moments of my life! Right here on a gloomy afternoon!

'You have, babe! Are you happy?'

'I'm so happy!' I said, even though 'happy' felt completely inadequate for what I was feeling right then. 'This is huge!' I'd been aware that nominations were coming out this week but I honestly hadn't thought of myself as a serious contender.

'Vespucci will be delighted, they really took you on at the right time!' Glen said, his voice glowing with pride at the hard work of his colleagues in commercial part-nerships.

'I guess I'm going to need a dress!' I said, breathlessly.

'Hell yes you will!'

'And it's being announced to the public tomorrow, right?'

'Uh-huh,' Glen confirmed. 'But I know you are the epitome of discretion! You too, Chloe. I can trust you to keep a secret?'

'My lips are sealed!' she assured him.

I let their words wash over me as they chatted amongst themselves, offering the odd 'mmmm' or 'yes' or 'no', but I couldn't focus on anything other than the fact I had been nominated for a BAFTA! Me! I couldn't believe it. Literally couldn't believe it, like it was all a joke. But it wasn't. It was real!

I walked back to my flat as if I was floating. I waved at babies in prams, said hello to every dog, admired every tree, smiled at every tourist. I resisted the urge to run up to every person and shout, *Did you know I have been nominated for a BAFTA?* Everything looked that little bit brighter to me, the sun fighting to come out from behind the clouds.

Sitting on my cream bouclé sofa with a cup of coffee, I had to fight the urge to call my parents and tell them. I was seeing them together later in the evening for the first time since their big announcement. I'd seen them separately, of course, but this was the first tentative push towards unity they'd attempted with me and I *really* didn't want to get my hopes up.

I'd let things get a bit messy (by my standards, anyway) so I spent the afternoon tidying the flat. Funny how even these boring tasks felt more bearable when you were floating with good news. Of course, I wasn't going to *win* but that didn't matter. Just to be nominated at this point in my career felt . . . huge. Unthinkable! Wonderful beyond words!

My parents arrived, bottle of wine in hand even though I'd told them not to bring anything. It was funny how the sight of them together felt strange even though it was normal, as if I'd been carrying around the weight of their separation in my mind even when I couldn't see it.

'The place is looking really lovely, Ems,' Dad said, running his hands over the pale blue paint in the living room.

'Thanks, I've tried to make it feel homely.'

'You've got your mother's eye for design.'

'Oh, shush, you!' Mum said, nudging him but smiling. Was this their version of flirting? Given the circumstances I had to admit this was better than I could have expected.

'Shall we have a drink before dinner?' I asked, getting some wine glasses out of the cupboard.

'Oh, go on,' Dad said, gamely.

Even if they weren't *together* together, they at least seemed to have reached a kind of peace. I wondered if I told them about the BAFTA nomination, that might sort of help seal the deal somehow. I knew that it was a silly thought, that it didn't work like that, but part of me thought maybe I could tip the scales in their favour by sharing my good news. I poured some wine and looked at them both, my eyes flicking from one to the other. 'Can you keep a secret?'

'What is it?!' Mum asked.

'Well, don't leave us hanging!' Dad chorused.

'I'm not meant to tell anyone, so you *have* to promise to keep it to yourselves. It's only until tomorrow lunchtime, though, and then everyone else will know. OK? Can you definitely promise to keep this secret for . . . oh, fourteen hours?'

'Promise,' Mum said, exasperated.

'Dad?'

'Of bloody course! Who am I going to tell?'

I took a deep breath. 'OK, so, the news is . . .' I paused for suspense.

'Come on!' Mum urged me.

'I can't believe it but I've been nominated for a BAFTA,' I said, the words hanging in the air for just a second before they were really understood.

Mum instantly screamed, which prompted Dad to whack her with the back of his hand. 'Ruth! You nearly gave me a heart attack!'

'Oh, Ems, that's the most wonderful thing I've ever heard!' She leaped to her feet and drew me into a hug.

'I don't know why you're so surprised,' Dad said, wrapping his arms around both of us at the same time. 'It's what you bloody deserve. What a film!'

'We're so proud of you, love!' Mum's eyes filled with tears.

'I couldn't have done it without you two,' I said, feeling overwhelmed with the emotion of the moment.

'Nonsense,' Dad said, sniffling a little bit.

'No, I . . . I really mean it. You both did so much for me. Mum especially, giving up work to chaperone me. I don't know how to express how much I appreciate it.'

Dad's lip quivered. I'd never seen him cry! 'We're so proud of you. Really.'

We all resumed our positions on the sofa, but instead of making everything feel lighter, that brief outpouring of emotion had left something hanging in the air. I knew we had to talk about The Situation.

'So,' I said, clearing my throat. 'What's going on with . . . you know?'

Mum and Dad looked at each other out of the corner of their eyes, each waiting for the other to speak. 'Well,' Dad began. 'It's been hard. I betrayed you and your mum's trust. And I'm not proud of it. At all.' His tone was stiff, clipped. 'And I honestly don't blame her for reacting the way she did. It was what I deserved.'

'But we've tried it, love, and the whole trial separation thing . . .' I held my breath. 'Well, a trial was good but it's not really us. Your dad got mixed up in something he shouldn't have, and he knows it.'

'I bloody do know it,' he said, resolutely. 'I can't ask your forgiveness enough. All I can do is prove to you I mean it when I say sorry.'

'So you're . . . ?' I asked, tentatively.

'Back together.' Mum nodded. The relief was instant and glorious.

'And I'll pay you back.' He sounded utterly firm but the money wasn't what mattered to me.

I shook my head. 'It's OK, Dad. You don't have to. That's not important to me. What's important to me is you never getting into this situation again.'

There were tears in his eyes. 'I promise, darling. I promise. I'm . . . well, I've been getting treatment. It's an addiction and I know I can't just get past it without sorting my head out.'

I pressed the heels of my hands into my eyes, the pressure of everything finally feeling like it was lifting. 'So when you leave here you'll go back to the house? Together?'

They nodded. 'That's the plan,' said Mum. She sounded tentative but hopeful. Hope was all they needed, really. A belief that it could work. 'It's been going well for the past few days . . .' She shrugged. The knowledge they were already back living together was more than I could have hoped for from this evening.

'Well, now that's settled,' I said, getting to my feet, feeling lighter than I had in a long time. 'Let's eat!'

As I busied myself in the kitchen, I couldn't help wondering that if it could work out for my parents was there a world where it could work out for me and Josh, too? But between the BAFTA nomination and my parents being back together, it felt like *way* too much to ask of the universe.

Chapter Thirty-Nine

'Here she is . . .' Lauren, the representative that Vespucci had entrusted my dress to, unzipped the garment bag. I held my breath. I'd seen it in various stages of its life, across three fittings at their London studio, but not the finished product. Until now.

'No spoilers!' Chloe covered her eyes and Lauren instantly stopped unzipping. Chloe peeked through her fingers. 'I want to see it for the first time on Emily!'

'It's not my wedding dress!' I protested, but secretly I liked her insistence on ceremony. This was the BAFTAs after all – not just my first as a guest, but my first as a nominee!

'*Some* may say it's more important than that!'

'Thank you so much for bringing the dress,' I told Lauren, who had hung it in its protective garment bag in the wardrobe of the suite at Claridge's which was my base for the afternoon. 'I'm just so in love with it,' I said with a sigh.

'I'm so glad,' she said, graciously. 'And Arianne Sharp will be arriving any min—'

Speak of the devil! 'Darlings!' The celebrity makeup artist swished into the room, accompanied by two assistants. 'Mwah, mwah,' she said aloud, swooping her mouth down towards my cheeks but managing to stay about a foot away from me. 'Lauren, looking gorgeous as always. And you are?' she asked Chloe.

'I'm Chloe, Emily's publicist,' Chloe said, blinking at her, star-struck in a way I seldom saw Chloe. The assistants unpacked Arianne's extensive kit, laying it out on the table in neat rows as she sipped from a takeaway coffee cup.

'Absolutely gorgeous to meet you, darling,' she said, holding out the coffee cup so she could shrug off her fur coat, which I am 99.9 per cent sure was real, to reveal what seemed to be some kind of silk dressing gown-robe dress straight out of Moulin Rouge. Fur coat removed, she held it up with one hand, clearing her throat. Were we meant to take it? No, an assistant rushed to her and took the coat, hanging it on a coat hanger on the back of the door. 'Now, Emily, please take a seat. I have the brief from Vespucci, assuming nothing has changed, Lauren?' Arianne tossed her signature jet-black hair and fixed Lauren with an intense gaze.

'No, you know what you're doing!' Lauren said, quickly, as if she didn't want to linger too long now Arianne had swept in. 'I'll be on hand for dressing once Emily's good to go.'

Arianne clapped in the air. 'Right then! Take a seat.' She pulled out the stool in front of the table by the window in my suite, and straightaway, without saying a word, one assistant was on either side of me, clipping my hair back from my face with protective tissues to stop foundation from smudging into my dark hair. She got to work, massaging creams and potions into my skin to make sure it was completely optimised to receive the makeup she was about to bestow on it. Her assistants – still unnamed, not introduced to us – would wordlessly hand her pots and bottles, as if they knew her needs so well they didn't require further instruction. 'You,' she said, dabbing some thick, luxurious balm onto my lips that was heavy with the scent of honey, 'have *beautiful* lips.'

'Thank you!'

'So many girls your age are already getting fillers but you have such a wonderful, natural look. And those eyes! Exquisite. Fascinating, even. Everyone tonight will know you have an Arianne Eye, they will be jealous, nobody but you will have this!' A memory came back to me of Ben holding his hand over each of my eyes to see what I'd look like if I was 'normal'. God, I may be going to the BAFTAs without a hot date but I'd rather that than still being with *him*.

I realised Chloe was standing and staring at the whirlwind taking place in front of her, bewildered by the sheer presence of Arianne Sharp. It took a lot to impress Chloe but Arianne was clearly enough. Although we were joined by a manicurist and a hair stylist, Arianne was always the one running the show, everyone else manoeuvring elegantly around her like an elaborate dance. She would click her fingers and an assistant would hand her a brush, or a palette, or some tweezers, or some eyelash glue. The command she had over the situation was sort of magic. The manicurist worked away on my nails, buffing and pushing back cuticles and filing to a pretty, delicate oval, while the hair stylist sprayed and blow-dried each lock of hair before braiding it into a loose fishtail, strands set free around my face. I would periodically glance over at Chloe, who alternated between tapping away on her phone, a little smile creeping across her face, and staring at Arianne as she worked her magic. Every time I opened my mouth to ask Chloe what she was smiling at, Arianne would start doing *something* to my face that meant I felt like I couldn't disrupt her flow by talking.

Finally, Arianne stood back and admired her handiwork. 'Darling, you look simply marvellous. You have the Arianne look but you make it your own.'

I turned around to face the mirror, the tabletop looking like a bomb had gone off in a makeup factory though the two assistants were hurriedly tidying up and packing away already.

She was right: I did look 'simply marvellous'. The most subtle smoky eye, elegantly contoured cheeks, the perfect nude lip, utterly classy and luxurious but still kind of . . . sexy? Not just polished and pretty but grown-up, sort of steamy, definitely a new feeling for me.

Finally, it was time to step into my dress. Lauren from Vespucci was on hand to 'dress' me, a task I used to think I was capable of doing myself until I entered the wild world of couture, all elaborate fastenings and hidden layers. We disappeared behind the stylish folding screen that had been erected in the hotel room.

'Oh, I can't wait to see!' Chloe called excitedly from the other side of the screen.

'Ready for the zip?' Lauren asked, and I nodded. As she drew the zip up my back, it didn't matter there was no mirror back here. I could *feel* the way it fitted me like a glove.

It was time to step out. Lauren helped me slip my feet into my shoes – a pair of delicate-heeled sandals with criss-crossing silk straps encasing my foot – and turned the handle on the bathroom door.

Chloe's gasp, her hand flying to her mouth, told me everything I needed to know. 'Babe!' She looked like she was about to cry. 'I mean I've seen you look amazing before but . . . this is something else!'

'You like it?' I asked, hopefully.

'I love it,' she said, sounding like her heart was melting.

I stood in front of the full-length mirror standing in the corner and looked at myself.

The colour hit me like a punch in the face. A vibrant cornflower blue so luminous it was almost neon. I had no idea how Vespucci had achieved it, but it took your breath away. At least, it took mine. It was strapless and figure-hugging, and snaking from the left-hand side of the straight neckline was a delicate row of silk flowers in the same blue as the dress. They wound their way over to the opposite shoulder and down the back. It was truly the most beautiful dress I had ever worn.

Yes, I thought, gazing at my reflection. *This is it.*

'I really want to hug you but I don't want to mess up your hair!' Chloe wailed.

'Oh, you can hug me! We can just be careful,' I said, holding my arms out to her. 'Thank you so much for everything you've done for me.'

'We're just getting started,' she said into my ear. 'Are you ready to head down? They've sent a fancy car!'

I held her by both hands. 'I cannot believe I get to ride to the BAFTAs in a fancy car with you.'

She glanced sideways, as if she wanted to look out of the window at the waiting car. 'I'll . . . I'll actually be following in a different car. I think. Depending.'

'What? Why?' I asked, a sudden sense of unease settling on me. Something was up. 'Depending on what?'

'You'll see,' she said, shrugging.

'All right . . .' I was wary and she knew it.

'It's . . . it's nothing bad!' Her tone was upbeat but there was a little catch in her voice, something holding her back slightly, and she was still typing away furiously.

I picked up my butter-soft gold leather clutch bag. 'You're being really weird.'

She looked up from her phone. 'I'm just excited for you, that's all! Shall we head downstairs?'

I nodded, took one last look at myself in the mirror, and headed out of the door. As we stood in the lift, I was so deep in my thoughts about the evening ahead that it took me a moment to realise we weren't talking. We were both distracted, full of nerves.

When we emerged into the lobby, I passed two American teenagers giggling to each other.

'I swear! He looked right at me! God, he is so gorgeous!' one said to the other, and I couldn't help smiling. I wondered if I would feel like that again, all fizzy with excitement over a cute guy. I wanted it so badly.

Just before we got to the side entrance on Brook Street where the car would be waiting for us, Chloe stopped short. 'Uh, you go ahead, I'll see you out there in a second, OK?'

'Are you sure?' I looked at her, confused.

'Yeah, you go!'

I wondered what the hell she was up to. Surely even *she* couldn't be arranging some kind of . . . romantic assignation *here* and *now*?! 'Promise, I'll be there in one minute!'

Before I could ask her where she was going and why I was meant to be loitering in the street without her, she was gone. Half of me wanted to just stand there and wait for her to reappear but I knew we needed to start heading out, so I did what I was told. I strode out onto the street, one foot confidently in front of the other, my high heels making a pleasing click-click-click on the ground. I looked down at them, admiring the crafts-manship, marvelling at how comfortable they were, and when I looked up—

Josh.

Josh Sacco.

Josh Sacco leaning against a gleaming black town car.

Josh Sacco leaning against a gleaming black town car dressed in a black suit and white shirt, a little pocket square in exactly the same shade of blue as my dress. I actually gasped. The sight of him actually, literally, took my breath away.

He beamed at me like he'd never been so happy in his life. 'Shit, Montgomery . . . I knew you were going to look good but I wasn't expecting *this*.'

'Josh,' I whispered. 'What are you doing here?'

'Well, for some reason I've been invited to the BAFTAs and I was desperately hoping that you could find it in your heart to let me be your date? I want to be holding your hand when you win.'

The adrenaline rush, the pure flood of happiness felt like it could knock me backwards like a wave in the ocean. I was so happy to see him but I was so scared of feeling the way I felt in Venice again. The high being fol-lowed by a crushing low. 'Josh, I can't do the same thing all over again! Please, if you're not really, really serious about . . . whatever we are?' I wanted him so badly but

I couldn't take it if his heart wasn't in it. 'You have to mean it this time?'

'I've thought about it *a lot*.' Josh swallowed, looking down at the ground. The blustering confidence had quietened, like a cloud passing across the sun. 'Like, a *lot* a lot, and I realised, yeah, you do deserve better, but I can *be* better. That's what I want. I want to be better for you and for myself. Or I at least want to try, not just run away and never find out what could happen between us.'

'Trying is all I've ever asked for,' I said, my heart racing.

He reached out and took my hands in his, looking deep into my eyes. 'I was a fucking insecure, immature idiot. You called it! You always knew! And you were right! I was scared of finding out I was a talentless hack at the exact moment you were finding out you're what, one of the finest actors of your generation? And I pushed you away because I knew you could see me clearly when I didn't *want* to be seen. But I don't want to live like that, Emily. I want to have a life with you, I want to build my career with you, whatever that looks like, even if it looks like you being the finest actor of your generation, and me being a talentless hack! At least I'd be a hack who gets to love the most brilliant woman. Let me try, for you, for me, for us? I won't let you down.'

I heard the click of cameras before I even knew I was kissing him. But I was kissing him. It was the only response I could think of. Actions speak louder than words, and that was the only thing I wanted to say, really. What else was there? I didn't care about the paparazzi, I didn't care about the people filming us, photographing us on their phones, the tourists, the gawkers. We couldn't keep it to ourselves any longer, and it felt *good* to share it.

For a moment, I stared at him, my arms draped around his neck, our faces millimetres apart. 'I can't believe you're here. I can't believe this is real.' I stood back so I could really take a good look at him. That lock of dark hair flopping over his forehead. His gleaming smile. The twinkle of pure delight in his eye.

'Believe it, baby.'

'ExcUSE me, young lady!' I heard a strident, foghorn-like voice which jolted me out of my beautiful oxytocin haze. I whipped around to see Arianne, half in and half out of a black cab across the road, before moving towards me at the speed of light, brandishing a lipstick. 'My handiwork means nothing to you?' she said, pressing it into my lips before I could object. 'No more kissing until the red carpet photographers have got the shot! Don't show me up or you'll never work in this town again! The Arianne lip *must* be preserved!'

Josh was shaking his head and chuckling as I stood, frozen and bewildered by . . . everything happening all at the same time.

'What are you guys still doing here?! Arianne, leave her alone!' Chloe had finally emerged and was maybe the only person who was temperamentally a match for

Arianne Sharp. 'Go! Get in the bloody car!' she urged us. 'You've got an award to win!'

Josh gallantly held the door open and I stepped in, carefully manoeuvring my dress, bowing my head so I didn't mess up my hair. But none of it really mattered anymore anyway. I didn't need to win. I didn't need to look perfect. I didn't need anything much anymore.

As we held hands in the back seat of the car on a journey I didn't want to end, I knew that whichever way the evening went, I had already won.

Emily Montgomery Grows Up

Inside the surprising new chapter of a star forging her own path

By Julia Carr

Photos by Matteo Verrini // Styled by: Ghada Khan

When Emily Montgomery glides into the buzzy brunch spot we've chosen for our meeting, I'm surprised to see she's alone. No entourage, no assistant, no publicist. Her mirror-shiny deep brown hair contrasts against the luxurious white cashmere coat that I instantly recognise as new season Vespucci. What else would you expect from the brand's latest spokesmodel? She is quietly self-possessed, a presence of maturity that goes beyond her years, and seems to carry with her an inner glow that makes her at once magnetic and a little intimidating.

I ask her about the whirlwind of the recent months, the release of the latest instalment of the Wonderwick Woods film, followed by the rapturous reception of *Orientations* at the Venice Film Festival, the announcement of her spokesmodel status and the reveal of her relationship with co-star Josh Sacco at the BAFTA awards, where she took home Best Supporting Actress.

She sighs, tucking her hair behind her ear and looking at me from behind a huge cup of blueberry matcha. 'I feel as if I've done more in the past year than I have in all the previous twenty years combined,' she laughs, her accent clipped but her tone warm and melodic. There's even something a little weary about her, or rather something decidedly grown-up: no longer is Emily Montgomery the delicate little flower that first delighted audiences in *The Legend of Wonderwick Woods*, aged thirteen. Until she took the role in Edgar Malek's surprise hit *Orientations*, she had only ever played Linderley Jones, the sharp, daring heroine of Sylvara Runequill's iconic fantasy series. As Linderley, she captured the hearts of teen girls everywhere, sparking a fandom that has seen her turned into stuffed toys, dolls, tattoos, even a robot at the Legacy Studios theme park in Japan.

'I never wanted to be an actress, I just wanted to be Linderley Jones. Everything else has been a happy accident, a way of me finding my path in life,' she says, taking a moment to pause, her beguiling eyes – famously one blue, one brown – deep in thought. 'It's strange growing up in the public eye. Everybody has such a fixed idea of who you are and what you can offer the world, or what you should want for yourself and your career, but it's been important to me to find out for myself.'

With the exposure of a mega-franchise like Wonderwick, the world has always been Emily's oyster, yet she approached with caution. While her colleagues took roles in other films, from indie movies to blockbusters, or roles in the West End or on Broadway between instalments of Wonderwick, Emily took on no other roles. Until now, she was just Linderley Jones.

On this process, she took a typically mature approach: 'Of course, there were offers, but I was always conscious of either getting typecast into another Linderley-like role, or infantilised, always tied to a vision people had of me from when I was a teenager. I knew I had time and space to decide.'

The decision she made was to sign on to Edgar Malek's *Orientations*, his second film in the English language after last year's under-the-radar hit *Two-Tone*. In *Orientations*, Emily's physical presence is a revelation, as well as the way she navigates the slippery, ambiguous dialogue in a deeply layered tale of a fraught mother–daughter relationship that's further fractured when a man knocks on the door of their isolated mansion. The all-consuming performance is a far cry from the Emily Montgomery that audiences had come to know as Linderley Jones, and reviews highlighted her performance in a film that's not short of serious actors, including Lucy Lennon and Ben Sage-Whittle.

'Wonderwick has its own big challenges: it's very physical, a lot of running around, the occasional sword fight, having to pretend I'm up against a monster I can't see which will be added in post-production, so *Orientations* was scary in its own special way. I didn't have a whole infrastructure to hide behind. In lots of ways, it was just about me, and that was very confronting but exhilarating.'

To speak of *Orientations* is inevitably to speak of her romantic life. '*Orientations* was a strange time. I'm not surprised I fell into something on the set,' is all she will say of her brief, tumultuous relationship with Sage-Whittle, now engaged to model and chef Nathalie Delacourt. Her face clouds when asked about their fling, but she staunchly refuses to be drawn. All that changes when I bring up Josh Sacco, her current love. It's like the clouds parting and sunlight shining brightly.

'I thought I would be more reluctant to talk about Josh but I can't help it, I'm just so happy with him.' She beams, before covering her mouth with her hands. The moment catches me off-guard: I've quickly become used to a certain level of reservation, a caution in how she speaks and what she will speak about. 'It was a real surprise for me. For both of us, I think. I certainly had to grapple with the idea that people could change, that feelings could change, that people continually show you who they are. I liked the person Josh showed me he is. Loved it, in fact.' She blushes deeply, and I'm struck by how young she still is, how much of her life and career are still ahead of her.

So, what's next for the newly minted indie darling? It's apt for such a reserved, cautious actress that her next project is both still untitled and shrouded in secrecy. All Emily will reveal is that it is the first film on the slate for her new production company, Wildflower, and that she's collaborating closely with the much-hyped author Eleanor Blomquist. 'I was absolutely obsessed with her novel, *Easy Work*, and I'm thrilled to be developing something new with her. It's the darkest and most challenging thing I've ever worked on, and I couldn't be more excited.'

And what's next for her and Josh Sacco? 'We're figuring it out. I thought he was a Hollywood boy through and through but I got that wrong. He's just moved into my flat in London with me. It's funny to see all his clothes hanging in my wardrobe but it makes me smile every time. I feel like I'm dreaming.'

As our time together draws to a close, I ask if she's going to miss Wonderwick when the series comes to an end after the two-parter making up the final instalment. 'It's given me everything, and now it's my turn to figure out what to do with it. So yes, I'll miss it terribly, but Linderley will always be a part of me.'

And with that she disappears into the dappled sunshine, her sleek white coat giving her an other-worldly quality. But this is a young woman who is firmly rooted in the real world, and ready to take it on. On her terms.

Acknowledgements

Thank you immeasurably to Melissa Cox for presenting me with such an amazing opportunity to use my brain in a completely different way, not to mention for being so clever and perceptive. Thank you to Claudia Kalindjian and Jayne Trotman for your wisdom and your time, and I must add that any liberties I've taken with your descriptions of film sets are completely my own. Thank you to the Royal Literary Fund: I wrote this novel during my first term as a RLF fellow. The stability and structure that the RLF fellowship gave me allowed me to get the work done, often between students. Thank you to my family, especially my dad, for giving me a love of films that made this book feel particularly exciting to me. Thank you to Rachel Mann and Daisy Arendell for making it happen. Thank you to my husband for keeping the faith at all times.